All Men Fear Me

Books by Donis Casey

The Alafair Tucker Mysteries
The Old Buzzard Had It Coming
Hornswoggled
The Drop Edge of Yonder
The Sky Took Him
Crying Blood
The Wrong Hill to Die On
Hell With The Lid Blown Off
All Men Fear Me

All Men Fear Me

An Alafair Tucker Mystery

Donis Casey

Poisoned Pen Press

Copyright © 2015 by Donis Casey

First Edition 2015

10 9 8 7 6 5 4 3 2 1

Library of Congress Catalog Card Number: 2015932052

ISBN: 9781464204685   Hardcover
      9781464204708   Trade Paperback

Poisoned Pen Press
6962 E. First Ave., Ste. 103
Scottsdale, AZ 85251
www.poisonedpenpress.com
info@poisonedpenpress.com

Printed in the United States of America

For Don

The Main Characters

The Family
Alafair Tucker, a worried mother of ten
Shaw Tucker, her husband, just as worried, but determined not
to show it

Their children
Martha, age 25
       Streeter McCoy, her husband
Mary, age 24
       Kurt Lukenbach, her husband
       Judy, age 18 months, their daughter
Alice, age 23
       Walter Kelley, her husband
       Linda, age 1, their daughter
Phoebe, age 23 (Alice's twin)
       John Lee Day, her husband
       Zeltha, age 2½, their daughter
       Tucker, age 1, their son
Gee Dub, age 20, a college student
Ruth, age 18, a music teacher
Charlie, age 16, looking for action
Blanche, age 12, a beauty
Sophronia, age 11, a tomboy
Grace, age 4, a handful

The Relations

Chase Kemp, age 7, Alafair's nephew, whom she took to raise
Rob Gunn, Alalfair's brother, a union organizer, whom she aims
    to fatten up
Sally McBride, Alafair's mother-in-law, whose opinion matters
Scott Tucker, the town sheriff and Alafair's cousin-by-marriage
Trenton Calder, Scott's deputy, whom Alafair is planning to
    add to the family

The Brick Workers

Henry Blackwood, Charlie's friend and protector
Eric Bent, Henry's uncle
Win Avey, a hothead
Billy Claude Walker, also a hothead
Dutch Leonard, a hothead of a different kind

The Townspeople

Emmanuel Clover, a scared patriot
Jehu H. Ogle, the mayor
Aram Khouri, a shopkeeper
Grandfather Khouri, a man with an unhappy past
Rose Lovelock, a woman of easy virtue
Nick, a man in a bowler hat

The Critters

Charlie Dog, an elderly shepherd dog
Bacon, a young mutt
Tornado/Hercules/Six-Shooter/Devil Dancer/Lightning Bolt/
Hero/Sweet Honey Baby, a handsome horse with a nervous
condition

July 1917

Somebody Is Going to Get Killed

Chapter One

"The world must be made safe for democracy."
—President Woodrow Wilson, April 2, 1917

Old Nick had been following the traveler ever since he left the detention camp back in New Mexico. It wasn't that the traveler made a particularly appealing target himself, but everywhere this fellow went, trouble followed in his wake. And trouble was Nick's food and drink.

The minute President Wilson had asked Congress to get the country involved in the endless blood-soaked war going on in Europe, Nick had smelled the ugly stench of hysteria and reached for his tool kit. His blades were sharp and his armaments were oiled and ready. Discord had been sown far and wide, and Nick had had plenty of work to keep him happy.

The miners' strike down in Arizona had drawn old Nick like a fly to manure, and he had been so busy maintaining disorder that at first he hadn't noticed the slender man in the thick of it all. The traveler was of middle height, and lightly built, his appearance unremarkable, except for a russet beard liberally streaked with gray, and sharp dark eyes.

On a morning in early July, Nick joined the armed posse that roused the striking miners from their beds, and helped cram them into twenty-three sweltering cattle cars to deport the troublemakers out of Arizona. Nick enthusiastically arrested anyone who looked like a miner and a couple of men who didn't, and helped himself to some of their property along the way. He volunteered to man the machine gun guarding the deportees and spent the entire trip to New Mexico basking in the miners' fear and fury as they were carried to their unknown fate. By the time they reached the barbed wire camps in New Mexico, the ardor of most of the detainees had flickered and waned. But the bearded traveler's fire of determination burned bright as ever. This one would go his own way until the end, and Nick knew that whenever a man's beliefs rubbed against the grain, sparks were bound to fly.

A few days later, as soon as his union lawyer got him sprung from internment, the traveler had headed straight for the train station at Hermanas and bought a ticket for Muskogee, Oklahoma. The strike was broken, and most of the strikers were broken as well. Nick knew there was little work left for him in the camp. So he scratched the little white scar beside his eye, set his bowler hat upon his head, and boarded the train behind the traveler. He knew the traveler wasn't going to notice him. No one ever noticed old Nick. Especially not a man whose eyes were blinded by the fire of true belief.

Chapter Two

*"If there should be disloyalty,
it will be dealt with a firm hand of repression."*
—President Woodrow Wilson, April 2, 1917

The traveler stood at the head of the alley and watched the ruckus for a long time, trying to decide whether or not to get involved. He thought not. He had just been passing by on his way from the hotel to the Muskogee train station when he heard the commotion and stopped to take a look. He wished he hadn't.

It was barely light and the sun not even up and he wasn't in the mood for a fight. He didn't much like the idea of two ganging up against one, but the blond-haired youngster seemed to be holding his own all right. Besides, it wasn't any of his business.

He had had enough strife to last him a while, and he expected he'd soon have a passel more before much longer, so he didn't see any reason to borrow trouble if he didn't have to. He had a train to catch. He was just about to move on when the fat brawler got the young man down on the bricks and started pummeling him around the head.

"Damn Red!" the fat man hollered. His skinny companion grabbed up a length of board from the end of the alley and headed over to finish the job.

The traveler sighed. He unslung his rucksack from his shoulder, pulled his little blackjack out of his back pocket, and waded in.

It didn't take much to break it up. One good slap with the cosh on the fat man's shoulder and that was that. That was generally the way with bullies. They didn't pause to figure out who had decided to even the odds, or why. One good howl from the fat one and the skinny one dropped his board and was gone before the traveler even got a good look at him. It took a little longer for the fat man to haul himself up and skedaddle. Still, he moved pretty well for a fellow of his size.

The blond youth lay where his attacker left him, facedown on the bricks with his hands clasped over his head. The traveler nudged him in the side with his toe.

"They're gone, hotshot. You can get up now." The traveler's voice bubbled with humor. Or maybe it was relief. It was not often that he managed to get out of a shindy without so much as a bruise.

The kid's head turned just enough to enable him to peer at his rescuer out of one rapidly swelling blue eye.

"Get up, boy," the traveler repeated. "Let's have a look at you."

The young man pulled one leg up, then the other, and raised himself onto his hands and knees. He grabbed the traveler's proffered hand and stood. The traveler sucked air through his teeth. The youngster was much the worse for wear.

"Your face looks like you got yourself caught in a meat grinder, kiddo. It's lucky I come along when I did. You expect you've got any broken bones or busted insides that will require the services of a doctor?"

The young man patted himself down and took stock of his wounds before answering. He was a little hard to understand because of the split lip. "I reckon I got a bruised rib, here, and my eye hurts, but I don't think anything is broke."

"Looks like them fellows had quite a bone to pick with you. What did you do to rile them up so?"

"They took issue with something I said."

One reddish eyebrow lifted. "I reckon. Did you disrespect the fat feller's mama?"

The youth studied the older man out his rapidly purpling eyes, reluctant to answer.

The traveler slipped the blackjack back into his pocket and crossed his arms. "Don't worry, towhead. I got no quarrel with a man's politics or his ancestry neither. You say something against the war? Or do you just have a German name?"

An ironic smile attempted to form on the bloodied lips. "Neither. I'm just plain Henry Blackwood. I met them two at the diner yonder while I was having a bite before my train come. When we left, we were walking the same direction, toward the station, just having a chat about this and that when I said that I kind of wish this war would get over quick because I didn't think the Germans are our natural enemies and I'm sorry we've got into a scrape with them. They took exception and thought to correct my faulty reasoning with their knuckles."

The traveler did not look amused. He fished a white handkerchief out of his vest pocket and handed it to his companion. "That kind of talk can get you killed these days, boyo, or at the least, thrown in jail. Unless you're willing to die for a currently unpopular principle, I'd advise that for the duration you keep your opinions to yourself."

Henry dabbed at the worst of the cuts on his face. "Yessir, I expect I've learned my lesson."

"You look pretty well grown. How old are you? Twenty-three, twenty-four? How come you ain't in the Army? You waiting to see if your number comes up in the draft next week?"

"I tried to join up back in April. They wouldn't let me. I got the asthma. I went ahead and registered last month, though. If I get rejected again, I may try the Navy come spring. I have no desire to get killed in a war, but better to do my duty than to go to prison for draft-dodging. Especially if them two represent present public opinion." He handed the bloody handkerchief back to the man. "Thank you for saving me. I reckon if I hustle I can still make my train."

"Well, you'd better make a detour to the station washroom and clean yourself up before you present yourself to the stationmaster. They're like to not let you on the train looking like you just got trampled by an elephant." The traveler picked up his backpack and the two men headed back out to the street. Henry limped for half a block, but his gait had straightened out by the time they approached the railway station.

"I appreciate your help, Mister, but you don't need to walk me all the way in."

"I ain't, sport. I'm heading out on the six a.m. eastbound myself. Where are you off to?"

"I'm just going up the way a bit. I came up from Texas yesterday. I'm going to live with my uncle for a spell. He's got me a job at the brick plant in Boynton."

This time both the man's russet eyebrows shot upward. "Well, I'll be go to hell. Boynton is my destination as well."

Chapter Three

"Oh, once upon a time in Arkansas
An old man sat in his little cabin door
And fiddled a tune that I like to hear
A jolly old tune that he played by ear"
—"The Arkansas Traveler" an American folk tune

Henry and the traveler didn't have a lot of time to chat once the train pulled out of the Muskogee station. Boynton was only fifteen miles down the track, and the stop at Wainright was so brief that the train barely slowed down long enough for the stationmaster to fling a bag of mail into the open door of the postal boxcar.

Henry did most of the talking. He wasn't usually such a chatty fellow, but the traveler kept asking him questions, and in such a solicitous manner that Henry found himself relating as much of his life story as he could cram into the half-hour trip.

Yes, he had just come up from Brownsville, Texas. Oh, yes, there was a lot of trouble going on down there. The border clashes hadn't slowed down because of the war. In fact, they were getting worse. That's why he was coming up to Boynton. His mother had convinced his father that it was safer up here.

The traveler and Henry got off the train at Boynton just as the sun cleared the horizon. Neither noticed the nondescript man in the bowler hat who disembarked behind them and moved into the overhanging shadow of the station roof.

The traveler hoisted his backpack and shook the young man's hand. "I wish you luck, slick. And by luck I mean I hope your number don't come up."

Henry smiled at that. He took a furtive glance around the platform for eavesdroppers before he replied. "I admit I don't want to go to war, Mister, but I expect it's my duty to give it a try. There's a lot I could do for my country if I was in the Army."

"Sorry to hear that. Good luck just the same, whether you get in or not. I reckon we'll see each other around."

"I hope so. Thanks again for keeping me from getting my head stove in. Which way you headed?"

"West of town."

"My uncle's place is to the east, just yonder, so I'll take my leave."

The man in the bowler hat watched the two men part and tapped his lip with his finger while he figured out his next move. The traveler was sure trouble, but something was not right with the blond-haired youth. He sensed it, and his senses were never wrong. He picked up his kit and took a leisurely stroll down the street that led east.

It didn't take the traveler long to walk the three blocks from the Boynton train station, through the still-shuttered downtown, and turn onto the dirt road that led out into the country.

The summer morning was already warm, and promised to be uncomfortable once the sun was high. It made for a beautiful sunrise, though, the dusty sky tinted faintly pink by the light of dawn. There was no wind to stir the leaves on the few scrubby trees that grew between the road and the endless miles of barbed-wire fence enclosing the checkerboard of pasture and cropland. The traveler had noted that the leaves of the trees had turned bottom-side-up. It was going to rain soon. Judging by the state of the crops, he figured that a shower would be most welcome around here.

He had a spry, almost jaunty gait. The big rucksack he had slung over his right shoulder didn't slow him down any. He was dressed for travel in a waistcoat and trousers, a collarless white shirt, faded red bandanna around his neck, leggings, and sturdy walking shoes. A utility knife in its sheath was suspended from his belt. His hair hung almost to his collar—not gray like his beard, or as red either, but the dark reddish brown of a chestnut horse. The wide-brimmed U.S. Army hat on his head, creased front and back in the old Rough Rider style, had seen better days.

It felt good to walk. After the prison camp, the traveler was enjoying the fresh air and the stretch of his limbs as he strode down the rutted road. His practiced eye assessed the crops in the fields as he passed. A lot of cotton had been planted. Not surprising, considering that the price per bale had shot up in the spring, when the country joined the European war.

The traveler heaved a sigh, as he did whenever he thought of the war, and firmly directed his mind to other topics. The countryside looked different from the last time he had come this way, ten years earlier. The land was more settled and cultivated, and there were many more farmhouses than there had been in 1907, just before Oklahoma had joined the Union.

He waved greetings to the farmworkers heading out to the fields as the sun rose, and began to whistle "The Arkansas Traveler" as he rounded the bend of the road at the section line.

On his right, in the distance, a young man was sitting on the top rail of a long wooden gate in the barbed-wire fence that stretched endlessly along the road. A large yellow dog lolled in the dirt at the youngster's feet, which gave the traveler a moment's pause. The dog perked up when he noticed the stranger, mildly interested rather than aggressive, and the traveler relaxed. The young man's head turned, but he didn't move from his place as the walker approached. The youth shifted his seat on the top rail of the gate, hooked the heels of his boots over the second rail, and set himself to study the approaching stranger.

The traveler guessed that the big youth was in his early twenties, maybe, until he grew near enough to get a good look at him. The boy's hands were spread out on either side of himself along the top of the rail, the sleeves of his tan shirt rolled up above his elbows. His cowboy hat was pushed back on his head, revealing a flop of straight fair hair on his forehead, and curious, lively, blue eyes. He was long of limb, but as yet unused to his considerable length, judging by the awkward way his knees and elbows stuck out all over the place as he perched on the gate.

The youngster kept his peace until the traveler stopped five feet from the fence, shrugged the rucksack off his shoulder and lowered it into the dust at his feet. For a moment, the two eyed each other, taking friendly stock. The dog finally stood up and wagged his tail lazily, nosing the stranger's thigh in hopes of an ear rub. The man complied.

The traveler reached into the breast pocket of his jacket and withdrew a tobacco pouch and a pack of cigarette papers. He looked back up at the boy, startled to see that he was even younger than the traveler had reckoned. Those still-rounded cheeks had not yet had use for a razor.

The man looped the drawstring of his tobacco pouch over his index finger and let it dangle as he slid a cigarette paper out of the package. "Howdy, sport. What d'you got to say for yourself?"

The boy flashed him a strong white grin and slid off the fence. He topped the stranger's height by half a head. "Not much, Mister."

The man creased his cigarette paper and tamped a line of tobacco out of the bag and down the center. He pulled the draw-string closed with his teeth before he ran the tip of his tongue down the edge of the paper, deftly rolled it into a tight little cylinder with one hand, and twisted the ends, neat as you please.

"Mind if I bum one of them off you?"

The traveler cocked an eyebrow, pulled a box of matches out of his pocket, fired up his cigarette and handed it to his companion.

"Thanks, Mister." The youngster took a drag and let the smoke dribble out between his teeth as he watched the stranger roll a second for himself.

"Where you bound, Mister? We don't see too many passers-by out here. This road ain't hardly on the way to anywhere."

The man drew a contented lungful of smoke before he answered. "I expect I'm headed right here, slick, if my memory holds true and this is the Tucker farm."

"It sure is!" The boy straightened and the blue eyes widened in surprise. "I'm Charlie Tucker, and this is my daddy's farm. You looking to buy mules?"

The man's eyes widened in turn. "Charlie! Well, knock me down and stomp all over me! How'd you come to be all growed up? You and me are kin, though it's no wonder you don't remember me. Last I saw you, you were just a little shaver. I'm your uncle Rob Gunn, boy, your mama's brother."

A momentary blank look on Charlie's face was quickly replaced with an expression of delight. "Uncle Robin?"

The man grinned. "That's right. Now I know you're kin to me, since none of my folks ever called me anything but Robin in all my born days."

"Well, I'll be jiggered! I thought you were in jail!"

Rob sputtered a laugh at this unstudied outburst. "Sometimes I am, Charlie Boy, and sometimes I ain't, which I ain't right now. I'm between jobs and I had a yen to stop and see my kinfolks while I was at it. You expect you could see me up to the house?"

Chapter Four

"Keep the Home Fires Burning"
—patriotic song lyric by Lena Gilbert Ford, 1914

With his old yellow shepherd at his heels, Charlie led his uncle through the gate and up the long approach to the house. The house looked the same as it had the last time Rob had visited, white, with a long porch, surrounded by a white picket fence and sitting on a slight rise. A capped well sat in front, and herbs and flowers lined the stone walk that led to the front porch steps. In the yard, a redbud sapling stood by at the side of the house. A breeze had picked up with the sunrise, and was worrying the bushes and little sapling. Rob could just see the top of a lightning-blasted hackberry tree at the back corner of the house. A slender woman was sitting in a chair on the front porch, but Rob could tell by her coloring that she was not his dark-haired sister. Surely she was one of his nieces, for even from a distance, she reminded him of his grandmother. Her hair and complexion were rather like his own, and it occurred to him with a pang that this girl could be his daughter.

She stood up and strolled down the porch steps to meet them. Her expression was mildly curious, but she smiled as they approached the gate. Her hair was rolled into a neat twist, but several auburn curls had already made a break for it and had arranged themselves across her brow and cheeks and down the nape of a graceful white neck. Her almond-shaped eyes were precisely the same golden-brown color as the shawl draped over her shoulders.

Charlie's face was wreathed in a big white grin. "Ruthie, guess who this is."

She reached out and took his hand over the low fence. She was only a little above average height, but stood so straight that she seemed taller than she was. "I hardly recognize you with that beard, but I do believe you're my Uncle Robin come to visit us at long last." Her voice was low and melodious, as though song were more natural to her than speech.

Rob shook his head. "Ruth, honey, I can't believe you knew me after all this time. You're sure not the same long-legged elf I taught to make a cat's cradle when last I saw you."

She laughed. "You remember that! Well, it's no surprise that I've changed. That must have been ten years ago! You haven't changed a bit, though, but for all that gray." She opened the gate and stood aside for them to enter. "Mama will be so glad to see you. Charlie, Mama's back in the woods. Give her a holler and I'll take Uncle Robin into the kitchen and see if I can roust up some breakfast for him."

Chapter Five

"Destroy This Mad Brute"
—U.S. Army enlistment poster

In the woods behind the Tucker farmhouse, the buffalo currants and blackberry bushes were heavy with fruit. The deep shade was occasionally punctuated with color that flared when a breeze stirred the leaves and allowed a shaft of early sunlight to illuminate a scattering of purple henbit. Every morning of the world, Alafair Tucker made her way out to the woods after breakfast was cleared away to snatch a moment of solitude, commune with nature and the Deity, and feed stale breadcrumbs to the wild turkeys who made their home here.

Her companion this morning was her two-and-a-half year old granddaughter, Zeltha Day, child of her fourth daughter, Phoebe. Zeltha was only a bit more than two years younger than Alafair's youngest child, Grace, who was far too energetic and chatty for her mother's one quiet morning ritual. But Zeltha was a peaceful, dreamy little girl, with mild, round, hazel eyes, and thick black hair that liked to stick straight up.

Phoebe had worried that Zeltha still did not talk much, but Alafair was inclined to think that the girl simply kept her own counsel. Animals adored her. Even when she was an infant, the farm dogs and cats, Phoebe's little milk goat, even wild birds, would come close when her mother took her outside.

At the moment, Zeltha was hunkered down beside Alafair's knee, doling out the breadcrumbs clutched in her fist. She had nothing to say, but the soft chortling sound she was making was so like the turkeys' that it took Alafair a moment to realize it was her.

Alafair looked after Zeltha quite a lot these days, now that Phoebe was busy tending to her husband, her house and garden, and her active one-year-old, Tuck. Truth be told, Alafair sometimes volunteered to keep Zeltha without being asked. Zeltha was such a soothing presence. Which her own lively children were not.

Alafair was not a fearful woman, but never before in her life had there been so much to dread. For a woman whose entire experience of the world extended from the western side of the Ozark Mountains of Arkansas to the middle of the Southwestern desert, Europe was so far away that she had never imagined that the fire that was raging there could ever burn her.

And it hasn't, yet, she kept reminding herself, as she scattered crumbs. Yet the United States was in it, now. She didn't have the slightest idea what that would mean. Would they come here, the Germans, so far away? Would Hindenburg send brutal men in his submarines and battleships to march across this wide country burning and killing and raping, spearing children on their bayonets? Had such a thing really happened in Belgium? The papers had said so, and even though she wasn't quite sure where Belgium was, she certainly didn't wish such a thing on the poor natives. She was quite aware that human beings were capable of unspeakable acts, yet she was always skeptical of such stories, since it was hard for her to believe that so many people could be so evil all at once.

Whether or not the tales of German atrocities were true, she had a very bad feeling about the hysteria that seemed to have gripped the country. The worst thing, though, was the horror in the back of her mind that she refused to allow the full light of consciousness. She had eight daughters, two sons, and four sons-in-law. One of her boys was sixteen. But the other would be twenty-one in a month. Barely too young for the draft lottery that would be held within a week, but not too young to volunteer. And there was talk of a second draft later in the year....

She knew it was no help to worry about something that hadn't happened yet. Sufficient unto the day is the evil thereof.

But all the common sense and biblical philosophy in the world couldn't keep thoughts of war and death out of her mind for long. Something evil was about to happen, she could feel it. She closed her eyes and purposefully narrowed her thoughts, banishing past and future together, as she concentrated on the slight rustle of the leaves in the breeze. One of the birds brushed her ankle, his feathers a warm tickle.

She was so engrossed in the smell of the earth and the turkeys' chortling contentment as they fed that it took a few seconds for her to realize that her boy Charlie was calling her. She straightened and cocked her head toward the sound, not entirely sure she had really heard him, but his voice pierced the morning again, a long call riding the breeze.

"Maaaa. We've got companeeeee...."

Alafair smiled. He sounded excited. As usual, Charlie was bringing home some action, something to set things aroil.

She tossed the rest of the breadcrumbs out of the pan onto the ground, hoisted Zeltha onto her hip, and headed out of the copse toward the house.

She cleared the tree line and stepped into the open space behind the house, then stood still for a moment with Zeltha in one arm and the old beat-up cornbread pan dangling from her hand at her side. She had emerged from the woods at enough of an angle that she could see around the house and onto the long drive that led from the front gate. Charlie and her middle daughter Ruth were walking toward the house with a slight, gray-bearded man with a rucksack. Alafair shook her head. It was just like the boy to invite a passing hobo to have a meal with the family.

But there was something familiar about the way the stranger carried himself, a jaunty, swinging stride that caused her heart to pick up the beat. She started toward the road, and then she was trotting before she even realized it. "I declare!" she said aloud. "I declare!"

Chapter Six

"Altogether Boynton is one of the most progressive cities
in the state, and its future is full of brilliant promise."
—*Directory of Boynton, Oklahoma*, 1916

Henry Blackwood unfolded a piece of paper that had been residing in his shirt pocket ever since he boarded the train in Brownsville. His father had penciled in a map with directions from the Boynton station to his uncle Eric Bent's house at the end of Kenetick Street.

He set off down the dirt street toward the dirt lane that the agent had pointed out, taking in the scenery and trying to assess the nature of the town he was about to call his new home. He was three or four blocks from the business district, so he couldn't tell much about that, but there did seem to be quite a number of people on the back streets and residential areas, all going about their day. He passed several people who nodded a greeting or wished him a good day. It was a friendly enough place, then.

The only thing he knew about Boynton, Oklahoma, was that his uncle lived here, along with maybe fourteen or fifteen hundred other souls. There was a large brick-plant that had a war contract and needed workers, a small oil refinery, and lots of surrounding farms.

He turned west on Kenetick Street. His uncle had written that he lived at the far end of the street, and it really was far. Henry trudged what seemed to him to be miles, checking the little name signs that residents had put on their fences. The houses grew farther apart as he neared the edge of town, each sitting on one-acre and half-acre plots with large gardens, chickens, and goats, and the occasional cow or horse.

He finally reached the end of Kenetick. The street turned sharply north, and according to a hand-painted street sign set high on a wooden pole at the turn, changed names. Henry looked to his left at a quiet, two-story, white-painted house sitting in the middle of a bare dirt lot. A dark-haired woman in a dressing gown was sitting in a parlor chair on the wide front porch, her legs crossed, holding a mug between her two hands. She gave him a cheeky smile when he looked in her direction.

"Good morning, honey," she called. "What happened to your face?"

"Good morning, ma'am. Oh, me and a couple fellows just had a little difference of opinion," he replied, and she laughed.

"Oh, it's 'ma'am,' is it? You looking for something, honey?"

Henry blinked at her. "Yes, ma'am. I'm looking for my uncle's house. He's supposed to live on this street, but I figure I must have passed him up."

Every word he spoke seemed to cause her great amusement. "Is that so? And what is this uncle's name, pray tell?"

Something about the woman's tone made Henry tug at his collar and gulp. "Eric Bent. He's expecting me."

The woman grinned, well aware of his discomfort. "You've reached your destination, sugar. Turn around and look to the other side of the street and you'll see a tired hovel. Your uncle lives therein."

"Thank you, ma'am," Henry said, and took himself across the lane as fast as was seemly. The house on the shady lot was hardly a hovel, freshly painted as it was and surrounded by marigolds, though it was small. Henry swung open the iron gate and started up the flagstone path when a bald, brawny man with a big mustache threw open the front door and strode out to meet him.

"I got your wire!" The man pumped Henry's hand and pounded him on the back at the same time. "Glad you're here, boy. Good God! What happened to you? You come on inside and I'll fix you up some vittles and get you a piece of meat for that eye."

Henry was propelled into the cozy little cottage and seated at the kitchen table, where his uncle handed him a small piece of chuck steak to hold to his eye. Uncle Eric placed bread, sausages, boiled eggs, jams, piccalilli, and mustard on the crisp white tablecloth. He finished by pouring Henry a mug of very black coffee and watched with satisfaction as the young man tore into the makeshift meal.

As he stuffed himself, Henry told his uncle about the long trip from Brownsville and his altercation and rescue that morning. But while he ate he did consider the fact that his uncle had changed. The mustache was familiar, as well as the burly build, but the thatch of light brown hair that Henry remembered was long gone. Well, Henry had changed, too.

Eric crossed his arms and sighed. "I'm glad you're here, Henry," he repeated. "It's been lonely since Gert died. I haven't seen you since you were…what? Fifteen, sixteen? You've filled out. You look like my sister, what with that yellow hair. Anyway, like I said in my letter, I told my boss about you and you can start your job at the brick plant whenever you want. They're desperate for hands since they got that war contract for bricks to build training centers and send to France. There's a lot of work that can be done there. You think you're up for it?"

Henry swallowed a bite of jam-smeared bread and nodded. "I am, Eric. I wish I could go to New York or Washington, though, get close to the action, since I doubt if they'll let me join the Army even if my number comes up. Did Mama write you about that?"

"Yes, she did, but don't you worry. Boynton may not be the most important hub of U.S. war industry, but these bricks are meant to build vital installations. So we'll be doing important work for our country."

"Thank you for the opportunity, Eric." Henry took a thoughtful sip. "For a while I didn't think I was going to find your house. You sure live on the edge of town. By the way, who is that woman who lives across the lane?"

"That's Rose. She and her girls have lived over there for a couple of years."

"She seems friendly."

The comment caused Eric to laugh. "She is that. I'd venture to guess that them girls have made friends with most of the male population of town and the surrounding countryside."

Henry laid his fork down on the table and looked his uncle in the eye. "Eric, are you telling me that you live across the road from a house of ill repute?"

Eric chuckled. Henry Blackwood was neither as young nor as innocent as he looked. "Yes, yes I do. And if you wish to maintain your Christian virtue, young man, you'll keep your distance. Though I have to say Rose runs a disciplined house and aside from the occasional fistfight or drunken brawl, they've been good neighbors. When your aunt was sick, Rose sent her simple-minded little housekeeper over here with good cooked meals right along. Once or twice some of the girls even came over here to sit with her. Gert was a fine Christian woman, but she didn't seem to mind being kept company by those girls of easy virtue."

"You ever go over there yourself?" Henry's question was simple curiosity and posed without judgment.

Eric shrugged. "Maybe I've been over there once or twice since Gert died, for female company more than anything else. It's a clean place, and the girls seem happy. Rose charges a hefty fare, which keeps out some of the riffraff, I expect."

"If I was to pay them a visit, I hope I could count on you to keep that information from reaching my mother."

Eric was unsure how to react. "I don't judge a man for his lapses, Henry. Just you don't go wasting your time and your wages by becoming a regular patron. Remember, you're here because you have important work to do."

"Don't worry," Henry responded with a smile, "I promise I'm a temperate man by nature. And I don't aim to let anything interfere with my war work."

Old Nick leaned back against the trunk of the big American elm that hung over the lane directly across from Eric Bent's cottage. The blond-haired youth hadn't noticed that he was being followed, and the uncle had been so engaged with his long-missed relative that he hadn't noticed the figure watching them from a distance.

Nick adjusted his bowler hat and crossed his arms, making himself comfortable in the shade while he pondered his next move.

He felt something hot on his shoulder. Perhaps a ray of sun had pierced the leaf canopy above him. He cast a glance behind him and saw the woman in the dressing gown staring at him from her porch. She stood up.

They locked eyes for some seconds. It was her gaze, Nick realized, that had burned his shoulder. He grinned and tipped his hat. The woman gave him a look that stabbed him like a knife before she went into the house.

Nick pushed himself off the tree and dusted off the tail of his suit coat, feeling satisfied. A lot was about to happen here in Boynton, Oklahoma. He had come to the right place.

Chapter Seven

"The county council of defense is the organization
of the hour in Oklahoma."
—August Aydelotte, Director
Oklahoma Council of Defense, 1917

Rob Gunn sat down in one of the armchairs, feeling contented, warm, and safe for the first time in weeks. The old yellow shepherd, Charlie Dog, had accompanied him into the parlor and flopped down on the rag rug next to the chair. Rob's eyelids felt heavy, and for a moment he drifted, the homely clatter coming from the kitchen transporting him back in time to his mother's house, and the sounds of his mother and sisters laughing as they prepared dinner.

Alafair had not changed. After a decade apart, they had fallen back into their childhood way of relating the instant they had set eyes on one another. She was still trying to tell him what was good for him, and he was still sidestepping her attempts with exasperated good humor. It was funny how comfortable that made him feel.

He could hear her in the kitchen, laughing and joking with her children while directing the action as imperiously as a queen. She was a queen, Alafair, he thought, totally in charge of her realm. He had never known anyone else with as much talent for bossing people around in such a way that they actually liked it.

Maybe she tried too hard to take care of you, but it was obvious that she only did it because she loved you so much she couldn't help herself.

A movement caught his attention and he reluctantly came back to the present. One of his many nieces had come into the parlor and sat down in the chair opposite him. She was gazing at him with mild interest, her arms stretched out along the arms of the chair. When his eyes opened, she smiled.

He blinked, trying to clear the cobwebs out of his head before he sat up straight. This was Blanche. Yes, even when this one was a toddler, she stood out in her crowd of siblings for the waves of sable hair that cascaded down her back, reflecting light like a dark mirror. Her complexion was as white as her name would indicate, though her Cherokee ancestry had given her bold cheekbones and an intriguing almond shape to the green eyes rimmed with a fan of black lashes.

Rob felt a sudden tug of protectiveness. If he figured right, the child was only twelve or thirteen years old, and couldn't possibly realize the effect her beauty might have on the wrong people. He wondered if her parents were aware of what was happening to their little girl, and if he should mention to his brother-in-law Shaw that she bore watching.

Probably not. He had no desire for a punch in the face.

She smiled at him just as Alafair came in from the kitchen, carrying Zeltha and trailing two more of his nieces with her. They all piled onto the settee next to Blanche's chair. Rob felt strangely relieved.

"Well, now, Alafair, you'd better tell me how all the kids are. Last I heard, Martha was getting married to some fellow from Ohio."

"Streeter McCoy. Yes, they got married last fall. He's our town treasurer now. He owns a pretty big land and title company with offices all over the state, and she's his partner. You'd think they would be rich as Croesus, but they put near to every penny they earn back into the business. They live in an apartment over their office. All four of my older girls are married now, Robin. Alice and Walter live in town, too. Mary and her husband Kurt, and Phoebe and her John Lee both have farms not a half-mile walk from here, one that way, and the other across the road. One or the other of them walks over here most every day, and often both. We've been looking after Elizabeth's boy Chase for a while, too. We're beginning to build up a collection of grandchildren, too. Three girls and a boy, up to now."

She nodded toward the kitchen, where Ruth was clearing away the dishes from his makeshift breakfast. "Even Ruth don't really live at home any more. Last year she went away to Muskogee while she studied piano with Miz Jesse Duke at the Duke-Richardson School of Music and Expression. Since she got back she's taken over her old music teacher's piano students. It's way easier for her to rent a room in Miz Beckie's big old house in town and give her piano lessons there." She lowered her voice. "That's what she says, anyway, though me and Shaw think it has more to do with her wanting to be closer to Trent Calder, the deputy sheriff in Boynton. We're expecting he'll be coming around asking for her hand any day now. "

"Oh, Mama!" Blanche's voice was heavy with disdain. "Ruth's grown up now. No matter what her reason is, she ought not to live at home!"

Alafair patted Blanche's knee, unperturbed. "Anyway, Robin, she is eighteen and didn't ask my opinion on the matter." She sat back and made a sweeping gesture. "The rest you see here before you, gaping like a bunch of monkeys and hanging on to every word."

"I swear, Alafair, I can't hardly believe how everybody's grown up," Rob said. "Why, I've never even clapped eyes on yon young lady Grace, and here she is almost old enough to start school."

Black-eyed, black-haired Grace, standing at quivering attention next to her mother's elbow, grinned a pearly grin. "I'm four years old. I'll be five in October."

Rob eyed the lanky child. "Is that so? Why, you're so tall I expected you were nigh on to six, at least. What about you girls? Fronie, you were just a little baby when last I saw you."

Sophronia was curled up on the settee. "I just had my birthday, Uncle Robin. I'm eleven now."

Rob was surprised. Charlie, Blanche, and Grace looked older than they were, but Sophronia was a fey little creature who seemed younger than eleven. Like her sister Ruth, she had a reddish complexion, with long pigtails hanging down her back, and a winsome dimple that appeared in her freckled cheek whenever she smiled. She was dressed in a calico shirt and a pair of overalls, like a boy. A tomboy, Rob thought, a natural reaction to her near-age sister's extraordinary femininity.

"Shaw or one of the boys will be taking Ruth back into town directly," Alafair said, bringing him back to the present. "They'll have a dusty trip, as I'm sure you noticed when you walked out here. Last year was so wet you could drown if you looked upwards, but this year has been dry as a bone, which Shaw's mother predicted it would be. 'Skimpy tails on the squirrels, dry summer,' she told us. And she was right, too. She usually is."

"How is Miz Sally these days?" Rob said. "She was always my favorite of all the in-laws."

"She's still blowing and going like always, her and Peter. She liked you, too, when you were a lad and liked to hang around her kitchen. She has always had a soft spot for a scamp."

"Well, now, Sis, I'm wounded! I've always been right serious and thoughtful. Besides, I had to have somewhere to hide whenever Dad threatened to skin me alive."

Grace had sidled over and was now leaning over the arm of his chair. He picked her up and set her on his knee. "Who's joined up with the Council of Defense around here, do you know?"

There was an instant of silence before Alafair answered. "The main CD office is in Oklahoma City. I know they're called 'Secret Service,' but there are a couple of fellows in Boynton, who don't make it any secret that they've joined up."

"Anyone you know?"

Alafair shrugged. "Some. One of them is Win Avey, who I never did think much of. Win's a bit of a hothead, if you ask me. Scott's always got him in jail for some deviltry. He makes a point of watching out for unpatriotic behavior way more than he ought. He works over at the brick plant. He's deaf in one ear, so he can't go into the Army. The other one is a widower with a little daughter. His name is Emmanuel Clover. When Miz Clover died, seems like her husband never did get over it. He dotes on his little girl like she was made of gold and sugar. I figure that he joined up with the CD because he's trying to keep his mind occupied."

Rob's leg began bouncing nervously, which Grace seemed to enjoy. "Watch out for that Avey fellow. That's the kind of fellow that likes to get into an outfit like the Council of Defense or the American Protective League. These Secret Service men can get you into a lot of trouble before you even know what's happened. How are y'all doing, Alafair, what with these new war rules and all?"

She shrugged. "All right. Better than most, I reckon. We raise most of what we eat, so we haven't been much bothered by the food restrictions. Worst thing is trying to eat one wheatless meal a day. I didn't realize how many things I make with wheat flour, and we do love our bread and biscuits and gravy. I haven't made so much hot-water cornbread since I was a girl." She smiled at the collective groan from her children. "The children don't cotton to it much anymore. It's hard to cut back on sugar, too, though we've got syrup and honey and sorghum. I been saving fat for bullets and we've been collecting peach pits for the gas masks. Shaw was thinking of buying a gasoline tractor before the war started, but as hard as it is to get gasoline now, it's just as well he didn't. My son-in-law Kurt has started his own butchering business, but we keep meatless Tuesday, anyway, like Mr. Hoover asked. Don't want anybody to think we're not behind the war effort."

A shadow passed over Rob's face. "Don't want that." His tone was dark, and perhaps a touch sarcastic. "Has anybody been giving Mary and her German husband a hard time, Sis?"

All the girls started to talk at once, but Alafair shushed them and answered herself. "Depends on what you mean by 'hard time,' Robin. Kurt never says anything, but Mary thinks that folks have begun looking at them sidelong."

"But nothing has happened?"

Alafair's forehead wrinkled at his tone. "Happened? What do you mean?"

"Has something been happening to Germans, Uncle Robin?" Rob twisted in his chair to see Ruth leaning on the kitchen door frame, wiping her hands on a dishtowel. She continued. "You travel around a lot more than the rest of us. Are you seeing things in other parts of the country that we should know about?"

"There have been some ugly incidents back on the West Coast, folks harassing those with German names, Jews, foreigners. Union men, too. I was just wondering if it's the same out here."

Alafair grinned. "Mercy, there's so many types of folks here in Oklahoma that if you only stuck to people just like you, you'd spend all your time talking to yourself." She was confident that her neighbors judged a tree by its fruit and a person by his actions. She couldn't speak for Easterners or Californians and their strange ways.

Charlie Dog lifted his head and perked his ears toward the kitchen, his tail giving the floor two or three thumps as the back door creaked and slammed.

"We're back, Mama!" Charlie called out. He came into the parlor, followed by his father, Shaw, and a leggy, yellow, flop-eared mutt who leaped at the children with wild exuberance.

Charlie laughed as the dog pawed his way up onto the settee between the girls, but Alafair was not amused. "Bacon. Get down. Charlie, get that feisty hound out of the house."

Charlie dragged the reluctant pup out the front door by the collar, then flung himself on the floor beside Rob's chair. Shaw paused in the kitchen door to remove his hat and comb his black hair with his fingers. "Well, I'll be! Look what the cat dragged in! I couldn't hardly believe my ears when Charlie told me that Robin Gunn was here." He plucked Zeltha out of Alafair's lap. She responded by throwing her arms around her grandfather's neck.

Rob stood up with Grace in his arms and shook his brother-in-law's hand warmly. Shaw was a tall, dark man with frank, hazel eyes, and a floppy black mustache that twitched with amusement when he gazed at the visitor. "So what in the pig-snorts brings you out here after all this time? Come to unionize my young'uns? They'd more than likely appreciate some bargaining power."

"Yeah, Uncle Robin," Charlie interjected. "Daddy don't want to give labor any say. Management is too tough around here."

Alafair flapped her hand at the boy. "Charlie, you've got chores to do. Blanche and Fronie, too. You can talk to your uncle at dinner. Go on, now. The cows won't feed themselves nor muck out their stalls."

The children dragged themselves from the room accompanied by a chorus of complaint. Charlie winked over his shoulder as he left. "See what I mean?"

Chapter Eight

*"The men who remain to till the soil and man
the factories are no less a part of the Army…
than the men beneath the battle flag."*
—President Woodrow Wilson

"So what are you doing here, Robin? Stirring up trouble?" Shaw
and Rob were seated at the big kitchen table, drinking mugs of
strong coffee while Alafair and Ruth stood at the cabinet and
cleaned vegetables they had just harvested from the giant garden
beside the house.

Rob laughed at Shaw's tone. "Not if I can help it."

Alafair gestured at them with a carrot. "I got a letter from
Elizabeth a while back telling me that you were in Arizona and
thought you might stop by Tempe for a visit with her and Web
after your business was done."

Rob sat back in his chair, wary. "You hear from Elizabeth a
lot?" His youngest sister Elizabeth was the smartest person Rob
knew, all intellect, sharp edges and angles.

"Oh, yes," Alafair said. "Elizabeth writes to me right along
since we took on her boy last year while she goes to law school.
She writes to Chase, too, at least a couple of times a month,
and he writes back. He's a pretty good hand with a letter, for a
little old button. He's a smart one. Just between you and me,
Elizabeth's a better mother to Chase from a distance than she

was close up. I figure once he gets of an age to have opinions about the state of the world, him and Elizabeth will be the best of friends. So have you taken a notion to pay all your sisters and your brother a visit?"

Rob relaxed. "Well, after I leave here, maybe I'll head up to Enid to see Ruth Ann. I haven't seen her since her man Lester died. Maybe her and me can finally have a chat without getting into a big fight."

Shaw gave Rob a knowing wink across the table, but Alafair was inclined to give him a scolding. "Robin, I'm surprised the union can spare you long enough to visit your folks, though. I thought the organization was unable to function without you."

Rob heaved a sigh and set down his mug. "Well, after Bisbee, I told them I aim to take off for a spell and get my breath."

Shaw frowned. "Bisbee? Bisbee, Arizona? What happened in Bisbee?"

Rob shot him an incredulous glance. "You don't know? I figured it'd be all over the newspapers."

"No, and I'm sure that if anybody around here who knows you're kin to Alafair had read your name in the papers, they'd bust a gut to get out here and tell me about it. What have you got into now?"

Alafair didn't wait for an answer. "Robin, did you do something illegal? Are you on the run?"

"No, Alafair, I did not do anything illegal and I am not on the run. I wouldn't drag you into it if I was. But considering the temper of the times, I did decide to lay low for a spell."

He looked down at his boot tips. "To tell you the truth, I've been traveling so much lately that I'm tired to my bones. I wired the I.W.W. headquarters in San Francisco and told them I had a notion to visit my sister for a while, and they said they might just barely do without me for a few weeks. I'd like to find a job of work to keep me occupied. Something where I don't have to make speeches."

"Your timing couldn't be better," Shaw said, "because I could use a good hand for a spell, and you used to know how to make yourself useful around the farm. I could give you a dollar a day plus a bonus now and then, whenever I sell a string of mules or a couple of calves. Does farm work suit your requirements, or have you organized so many unions that you've forgot how to turn your hand to the plow?"

Rob grinned and rubbed his thumb through his beard. "Not hardly! I'd be downright happy to get my hands in the dirt for awhile, and I'm your man for running stock of any ilk. I've broke my share of mules, too. If you don't mind that I'm short-term, I'd be much obliged."

"You know I'll be selling most of my mules to the Army. Fort Reno is a remount station, and they'll take as many as I can sell them."

Rob shrugged. "Me and the U.S. Army have had our differences, but I have no quarrel with how any man makes an honest living, as long as he don't take advantage of another man."

Alafair leaned across the table to refill Shaw's coffee mug. "There's an empty bed in that room out behind the toolshed where Gee Dub has been sleeping when he comes home from school. I reckon Robin could bunk with him as long as he wants and be right comfortable."

Shaw nodded. "That's settled then."

"Now I don't want to intrude on the lad's privacy," Rob objected. "I can curl up in any corner you've got."

Alafair was affronted. "You will not! Gee Dub spent twenty years of his life sleeping in this house with his brother and eight sisters. He'll be happy as a little heifer in clover to have some company."

"Well, all right, then. Sounds grand."

Alafair clapped Rob on the shoulder, clearly delighted at the prospect of having her brother around for awhile. "Good! I'll get you some quilts and a pillow for that empty bed out there. You can take meals with us or I'll fix you up a pail whenever you want."

"I feel like I've died and gone to heaven! Most of the time I'm sleeping in somebody's loft!"

Shaw was amused. "Don't the Industrial Workers of the World pay you enough to rent a room?"

"They do, but the towns I generally work in are so small that you could spit from one end to the other, and have neither hotel or boarding house."

"Maybe you'll like staying in one place so much you'll decide to settle at last, get you a home of your own."

"Maybe, Alafair," Rob agreed, but his tone made it obvious that he was just being polite. He was a man with important work to do.

Chapter Nine

"Rich Man's War, Poor Man's Fight"
— *The Worker*, national newspaper of
the Industrial Workers of the World

Shaw threw Rob a pair of leather gauntlets, brought the wagon around, and off to the fields they went. By the end of the day, the clouds had thickened, obscuring the sunset and bringing darkness early. It was a good thing, Rob thought. He didn't know if he could continue working at such a pace for even ten more minutes.

Shaw called an end and the two of them drove the wagon back to the barn, unhitched the team of mules, fed, watered, and rubbed them down before trudging back up to the house in the dark. Rob could hardly keep his eyes open, and he was aware that this fact entertained Shaw no end.

Alafair met them on the back porch with a pitcher of hot water, and the men washed up before stepping into the kitchen. The room was cheerful with the yellow light of kerosene lamps, and fragrant with the smell of potatoes, gravy, and hush puppies fried in drippings.

A tall, lanky, young man with a shag of dark curls and deep brown eyes with a hint of mischief in them was sitting at the kitchen table. He stood up to shake Rob's hand.

"Gee Dub," Rob said. "You're a sight for sore eyes."

Gee Dub was dressed in khaki trousers, a faded blue collarless shirt, and a dark brown vest. He towered over his slight uncle. His smile was warm as he murmured Rob's name.

"I heard you're home from college for the summer, bucko. What have you been studying up there at A&M?"

"I've been studying agriculture, Uncle Robin. I've been over at my grandfolks' today, applying all my fancy new learning to Grandpapa Peter's apple orchard."

The men sat down in the parlor as Alafair and the girls set the table. "Last I saw you," Rob said, "you were a boy, Nephew, and now you're a man. But I'd sure recognize you anywhere for Shaw Tucker's son. I see a bit of my brother George in your face, too. You sure got his hair."

"You haven't changed any, Uncle Robin, except for..." Gee Dub swung a finger under his chin to indicate Rob's beard.

"Oh, that. I took a notion to grow one a year or two ago, just to see how it would look, and maybe save myself some razor burn. Didn't realize that it'd come in gray as Aunt Rhodie's goose and make me look twenty years older than I am."

"Why do you keep it, then?" Alafair asked, from her place at the stove.

"Why, it makes me look distinguished, don't you think, Sis?"

"Makes you look like a reprobate."

Rob and Shaw exchanged an amused glance before Rob continued. "Don't worry, Alafair. Someday I'll cut it off."

"I like it," Charlie interjected. "Looks manly."

Rob winked at the boy. "That was my aim."

"I hear Daddy put you to work before you could hang up your hat," Gee Dub said. "How'd you like being a field hand again?"

Rob shook his head. "I enjoyed it. It's good to do an honest day's work with your hands. But I reckon I'm way out of practice or I'm getting old, one or the other, because it nearly killed me. I look to be stove up like an eighty-year-old man tomorrow."

Charlie snorted. "Aw, he did fine, Gee. He slung them bales like he's been doing it all his life."

"I've slung my share of bales," Rob acknowledged, "but I'm afraid I've spent too many years advocating for the working man instead of doing a day's work myself."

"Ironic," Gee Dub said.

Charlie looked up at his uncle. "He's always using words nobody understands since he's been off at A&M."

"I'll buy you a dictionary, Charlie," Gee Dub said. "I wouldn't worry about sore muscles, Uncle Robin. Dad will see to it that you get the kinks worked out in short order."

Mary Lukenbach got right to the point. "Charlie rode over to the house on that hot-tempered roan of his this afternoon and told us all about Uncle Robin coming in. We figured we'd come over and say hey before y'all go to bed."

"I figured he has told everybody he could, Mary," Alafair said. "Robin is the most interesting thing to happen around this farm in a long spell. Y'all better come on in and sit down for some pie."

Mary and her German-born husband, Kurt, followed Alafair into the kitchen. Mary laughed when Rob turned to see who had come in. "You look just the same, Uncle Robin, except for that gray beard!"

Rob laughed, too. "My, but this brush is an occasion for comment. Hello, darlin', glad to see you." Mary introduced her husband, and Rob shook Kurt's hand too heartily, sympathetic to what Kurt was going to have to put up with from his neighbors, if popular sentiment continued in its present direction.

"This pretty little blue-eyed gal trying to crawl under your chair is Judy." Alafair retrieved a white-blond eighteen-month-old from the floor. She cast a glance around. "Where's Chase?"

Mary answered. "Him and Grace are out in the yard hunting fireflies."

Alafair nodded. "Chase has taken a shine to Mary and Kurt, and especially Judy. He spends so much time over there that Mary is practically raising him to suit her."

Rob liked Mary and Kurt at first sight. Mary was as round and gregarious as her German-born husband was straight up and down and taciturn, but otherwise, the Lukenbachs were very much alike. Both were fair-haired and friendly, with wide blue eyes that held no secrets. Kurt never said two words when one would do, but Mary talked and laughed enough for both of them. If Rob hadn't known that their daughter Judy was adopted, he would never have guessed it. She was as fair and open as her parents, her round blue eyes taking in the action.

The conversation was lively, everyone intent on bringing Rob up to date on their lives and curious to hear what he had been up to for the past decade. Eventually Charlie half-turned in his chair to face Rob. "By next Friday we'll know who all is going to get to go to France. I know a bunch of fellows who registered back in June. Pretty exciting, ain't it?"

Rob carefully placed his fork on the table next to his plate. "Can't say I'm excited, pard'. I'm sorry that we've managed to get ourselves into this war after all."

"But we just had to go to war, didn't we, Uncle Robin?" Charlie was amazed that anyone could see it any other way. "After the Germans offered to give Mexico back the whole of Texas if they'd invade us, there wasn't much else President Wilson could do, was there?"

A twitch of amusement crossed Rob's face. "You're expecting that Mexico could wrest Texas back from us, are you?"

"I can't figure out why Germany would do us that way," Shaw said. "I'd think the last thing Hindenburg would want would be for the U.S. to get into the fracas."

"From what I've been reading in the papers, Germany doesn't think much of America's will to fight," Gee Dub put in. "They would rather go to war with us than give up sinking every neutral ship that gets near England or France."

"That's an insightful comment." Rob's tone conveyed his respect for this opinion. "Of course, if this country would stop trying to make a bunch of steel barons richer by selling war goods overseas, rather than seeing to our own folks who have no way to put food on the table, we wouldn't have come to this pass in the first place."

Charlie was scandalized. "As much as you say you care about the downtrodden, Uncle, why ain't you over in Europe, trying to help the poor folks who are being massacred?"

"I've had some experience with this country's 'rescue operations,' Nephew, and if we've gone to war, it isn't to help the Europeans, but to help Mr. Getty and his like get richer than they are, so I reckon we'll just have to agree to disagree on that point."

"I reckon so!" The light of battle was in Charlie's eyes. "All I can say is I hope it lasts long enough so I can turn eighteen and enlist. I'd like to show them Huns a thing or two."

"Your eighteenth birthday is nearly two years away, son," Shaw pointed out. "This business will be over long before then."

"I don't know, Daddy. It's been going on in Europe for almost three years already. Gee Dub'll probably get to go, lucky dog…"

Gee Dub looked up from his plate when Charlie said his name, but didn't comment. Shaw flicked another glance at Alafair. One of her hands was gripping the coffee pot handle with white knuckles. She put the other on his shoulder. He casually reached up and draped his hand over hers as he addressed Charlie. "There's no use to borrow trouble, son. The country is not ready to send troops overseas yet."

"But we will be, Daddy! Why, fellows are joining up by the thousands. And you know as well as I do that there's going to be more than one draft."

Kurt offered an opinion at last. "I did not really think it would happen, us getting into the war. The reason Mr. Wilson got re-elected was because he kept us out of war." He shook his head. "Still, it is done now, and I for one will do my duty as an American."

Mary had not said anything, but she looked so unhappy that Alafair caught Shaw's eye and shook her head.

"And if that happens, Charlie Boy," Shaw interjected, "we'll deal with it then. As for now, the direction this discussion has taken is not good for the digestion."

Charlie could tell by his father's tone that the conversation was at an end. He sat back in his chair, sorry to have introduced such an incendiary topic. He tried to change the subject. "Tell you what, Ma. I'll pay Uncle Robin a nickel my own self if he'll patch the next hole in the roof if it starts to rain again, and save me from having to do it."

"You finish up your supper and go to bed," Alafair said. "It's late and morning comes early, don't you know. Gee Dub, Robin is going to bunk with you out in the shed. Grab a lantern off the back porch, and you can show your uncle Robin the way. Mary, I'll wrap up some of this pie for y'all to take home with you."

The boys left for their respective tasks and Rob looked up at his sister. "I'm sorry, Alafair. I should have kept my notions to myself."

"It's all right," Shaw answered for her. "He's just young and looking for action."

"Well, I'll be quiet from now on. I didn't come to bring a sword, as Dad would say." He sighed and changed the subject. "Gee Dub's made a fine-looking man."

Shaw nodded, trying not to look too proud. "He's just finished his second year at A&M. When he came home for the summer, I was hoping he'd share with his old dad all the up-to-date and modern agricultural and animal-husbandry techniques he had acquired. He ain't disposed to volunteer the information, though."

Alafair had her own explanation of this behavior. "Oh, Shaw, no matter how old-fashioned he thinks your farming is, Gee Dub would never say anything to you, of all people, lest you think he's judging you."

"I expect you're right, darlin'. Which is something of a poser, since I'd be entirely interested to hear about scientific farming." Shaw shook his head. "Sometimes I have to pry the words out of that boy's mouth with a crowbar!"

Chapter Ten

"Come On Boys, Do Your Duty: Enlist!"
—U.S. Army propaganda poster, 1917

Alafair had filled Rob's arms with a pile of pillows and quilts so high that Gee Dub thought he'd have to lead his uncle to the toolshed like a blind man.

The night was brisk and cool, with a fresh gusty breeze that drove tattered clouds across the face of the moon. "Look, there's a ring around the moon, sport." Rob's voice was muffled by a pillow. "I reckon it'll rain before long."

"Why are you so dead set against the war, Uncle Robin?"

They were halfway across the yard when Gee Dub asked his unexpected question. Rob stopped walking and eyed his nephew over the blankets.

Gee Dub continued. "Mama told us that you ran away to join the Army yourself when you were just about the same age as me. You must have wanted to."

"Oh, I did. I was just like Charlie, all piss and vinegar. I was wild to charge right up San Juan Hill with old Teddy. I was just a little squirt, not big and well-grown like you, hotshot, but I found a recruiter in Little Rock who was looking to fill his quota for that month, and he signed me up. My daddy could have had me mustered out for being underage, but he said I had made my bed and I could lie in it. I figure he knew I'd just run off again, and besides, I'd have been old enough the next year, anyway. By the time I finished basic, the Cuban part of the Spanish War was over. They sent me to the Philippines. I spent the next six years of my life wrestling with malaria and foot rot, wading through swamps, picking leeches off myself, and trying not to get my head chopped off by some scrawny little stinker with a big machete.

"I never did know why we were there. The Filipinos were glad to get rid of the Spanish, but they never did cotton to trading one master for another, and wanted us out of there just as bad. Those Moro tribesmen were about as big as a minute, but they sure scared the liver out of me. We all knew that it was better to blow your own brains out with your service pistol than to let yourself get captured."

"Sounds like the Apaches." Gee Dub was a lover of Zane Grey novels.

Rob shrugged. "At least you maybe could see the Apaches coming across the desert and eat a bullet before they got you."

"I think this is different, though, Uncle Robin. The Spanish weren't after ruling the world, but the Germans are. And in the end I'm an American, and when my country calls, I'm going, all right."

Rob broke eye contact and looked out over the dark expanse of Alafair's garden. "You looking to kill some Huns, too?" His tone was neutral, but Rob wasn't best pleased by the announcement.

"They'll take me or I'll go of my own accord like I've got a choice in the matter." Gee Dub delivered this piece of information as a plain statement of fact. "I expect whatever we think about this war, we're all going to have to get behind it. It's win or die, now."

"Well, Gee, each of us has to follow our conscience as best we can. I'd hate to think that we might lose the thing that makes America different than all the other countries—the right to say what we think."

After a brief, awkward pause, Gee Dub said, "So you don't have a good opinion of Army life?"

Rob's expression when he looked back at Gee Dub was oddly compassionate. He knew the young man was anxious to hear something comforting. Rob wracked his brain for a moment. "Well, Army life ain't so bad. They feed you pretty good, and you get as fond of your comrades as if they was your own brothers. And when you're all decked out in your military finery, the ladies think you cut quite a dash." Rob was glad to hear his nephew snort a laugh. He turned and began walking again. "You told your mama yet?"

"No. I figure I'll tell Daddy first. Don't look forward to telling Mama."

Now it was Rob's turn to laugh. "I reckon not."

The beds in the toolshed bedroom were basic, but comfortable. In fact, Alafair had made Gee Dub's "bachelor quarters" into a place that Rob wouldn't mind calling home himself. The furniture was mostly recycled and threadbare, but serviceable and clean. Rob was glad to see that the two cots had iron bedsteads, which made it more difficult for bedbugs to get a foothold. He had spend many an itchy night in bunkhouses and two-bit hotels. Considering the number of animals around the Tucker farm, fleas were still a possibility. But the floor was scrubbed raw and the room smelled vaguely of lye water. If he knew his fastidious sister, vermin steered clear of her domain in fear of their lives. The handmade horsehair mattresses looked new, tufted to hold the filling in place and the edges hand-stitched together. A painted wooden table with two chairs graced the center of the room. A washstand with a pitcher and chipped basin, small chest of drawers, and a Franklin stove in one corner completed the furnishings. There was one window on the back wall, wide open because of the heat. For privacy Alafair had strung curtains made from two worn calico aprons on a leather strap.

"Your ma has fixed this place up nice," he observed to Gee Dub.

Gee Dub cast a critical glance around. "It's home, for the moment at least. Dad made this room up a few years ago so there'd be a place for hired hands to stay, if they needed to. Right now everybody who works for him has his own bunk somewhere else. Handy for me." He gestured toward the table. "Fling your rucksack yonder, Uncle Robin. There are a couple of hooks on the wall there if you want to hang anything up."

Rob made up the spare bed, stripped down to his skivvies, and slid between the quilt and the sheets that Alafair had given him. The pillow was filled with goose feathers and the pillowcase and sheet smelled of herbs. He nearly wept at the luxury of it all.

Chapter Eleven

"Food Gamblers Raise Price of Canned Goods"
—Chicago Tribune, April 1917

As soon as the men left for the fields after breakfast, Alafair hitched up her gray mare, Missy, to the buggy and sat Grace beside her for a trip into town to run errands. On the way she stopped by her daughter Mary's house long enough tickle baby Judy and ask Mary to a family supper tonight. Alafair's seven-year-old nephew Chase Kemp begged to come to town with them. Grace and Chase Kemp were a handful when they were together, but Grace whined for her adored older cousin to be allowed to come, so Alafair loaded him into the backseat and off they went.

Aram Khouri, the proprietor of Khouri's Market, was a compact, dark-haired man of about forty, friendly and kind, with large, moist black eyes that reminded Alafair of her son-in-law John Lee's. Mr. Khouri had an equally attractive wife named Ana and three young children, as well as a fat, garrulous, child-friendly father who lived with them. The Khouris were recent additions to Boynton's fast-growing population, having only lived in town for a couple of years. Alafair had no idea where they were from originally, only that they had bought the market from Mr. Haddad when he retired. They resided in a large apartment above the store, and the whole family, from the seventy-year-old grandfather to the six-year-old baby of the family, pitched in at the market to clean, stock, and wait on customers.

It was Aram himself who was behind the counter today, and he broke into a beaming grin when he recognized Alafair Tucker, her pert little daughter Grace, and her nephew Chase Kemp.

"Hello, Miz Tucker, hello. Why, you're looking pretty, Grace. And Chase! How you've grown since last week! What can I do for you today, Miz Tucker? Don't get to see you so much since the food rules went into effect. I swear, even the townfolks are growing their own vegetables and meat these days."

Chase tugged on his aunt's skirt before she could reply. "Can I go outside?"

"All right, but don't wander off. Stay where I can see you."

Chase sped off and Grace tried to follow, but Alafair caught her by the collar and lifted the giggling little girl into her arms. Leaving Grace below eye-level was an invitation for her to get into mischief. "Have the new food rules hurt your business, Mr. Khouri?"

"It's different, Miz Tucker. I buy folks' extra that they grew too much of, and sell it to somebody that grew a bunch of something else. Better that way than when the war first started and all the housewives here in town were hoarding canned goods. Why, for a month or so there, I couldn't keep anything on the shelves. I could have charged three times the price and they'd have paid. Never would do it, though. It's evil to take advantage of people's fear. Still, I have to charge an outlandish price just to break even!" He leaned over the counter and his voice dropped. "Sometimes I just trade one thing for another—a chicken for a peck of peas, that kind of thing. Don't know if that's a thing to be doing, but in these times I think we've got to help one another however we can."

"Sounds like a patriotic way to do business, to my mind." Alafair felt a small pang of guilt, since she was one of those who was growing her own and no longer buying extra. It seemed like you couldn't do even the best-intentioned thing without affecting someone in a way you didn't anticipate.

"What can I do for you, Miz Tucker?" Mr. Khouri repeated.

"I came into town to pick up mail and visit with my daughters and my grandbaby for a spell, but I figured that while I'm here, I may as well come by and see if you have some round steak for sale today. I'm fixing to cook up a special dinner today and I expect that a bit of beef would fill the bill. We don't much partake of beef these days."

"Well, you're in luck! I just bought a whole beef from Mr. Eichelberger this very morning. He's been raising calves to sell to the co-op but I talked him into selling one to me for the benefit of his hard-working neighbors."

"I know beef isn't that easy to come by these days. I hope it isn't too expensive or I'll have to revise my plans."

"I can let you have some nice bottom round steak for twenty cents a pound."

She sucked in a breath. "That's dear."

"Is this for a special occasion?"

She hesitated. As a union organizer, Rob was a divisive figure, but she knew that the longer Rob stayed with them the harder it was going to be to keep his presence a secret. She had too many gabby children to keep anything under wraps for long. But under the circumstances, there was no reason to go out of her way to advertise the fact that he was visiting. "We've been so austere lately that I reckon the family deserves a nice meal. Besides, we have a birthday coming up." Not really a fib. With ten children, in-laws, and grandchildren, somebody's birthday was always coming up.

Khouri smiled and lifted a shoulder. "Like you said, beef is hard to come by these days. But since it's a special occasion, I'll let you have it for eighteen cents a pound. How's that?"

"How about seventeen cents a pound and I'll bring you a half-dozen quarts of peaches I canned last month next time I'm in town?"

"Deal!" Khouri's eyes lit up. He disappeared into the back room. Alafair heard the mechanical creak of the refrigerator door, the rustling of paper and a couple of thumps, before Mr. Khouri reappeared with the back end of a side of beef flung over his shoulder. He clunked it onto the marble cutting surface, pulled a cleaver from under the counter, and hacked the bottom round away from the bone. He picked up a long, wicked, carving knife. "How much you want, Miz Tucker?"

"I'm tempted to take the whole round, Mr. Khouri. You know what a herd of folks I have to feed. I'll cut the steaks myself."

He carved an enormous slab off the bone and wrapped the meat in a piece of butcher paper. "How's the family, Mr. Khouri?" Alafair asked,

"Oh, doing very well, thank you, ma'am. We're starting to feel right at home here. The children have made so many friends at school. Nathan will be starting fifth grade next year. I can hardly believe it! He's been selling more Liberty Stamps to customers here in the store than I have! Oh, I love the West! So much more opportunity than back home!"

"Where did you move in from?"

"From Chicago. Such a big town, you wouldn't believe. My wife misses her family, of course, but we wouldn't go back to all that noise and crowds."

"I'm glad you came out, Mr. Khouri. Thank you for the nice piece of meat."

Old Nick treated himself to a sundae at Williams' Drug Store downtown, then took a leisurely stroll up and down the main thoroughfare, looking into the shop windows and killing time until dark. He had big plans for the evening, for he figured that Rose's place would be hopping at around midnight. And her customers were likely to be just the kind of men who could be tempted to avail themselves of Nick's special talents.

But it was a long while until midnight, so Nick used the time to look around and see if any other opportunities presented themselves. The street was busy, and it wasn't hard for him to lose himself in the crowd. Most of the housewives, businessmen, and overalls-clad farmers that he passed were plain, decent people who held no interest for him. After an hour or so he was ready to find someplace to hole up and wait for dark. Until a round, natty man in a black suit came out of a door marked "W.E. Clare Insurance Agency, Upstairs." The face was pinched and anxious, sporting hectic red cheeks. He clutched a sheaf of papers in his hand. The round man kept his eyes on the sidewalk as he hurried up the street, thinking his own thoughts, until he came upon Khouri's market and looked up sharply. He stood outside for a moment, carefully inspecting the signs Khouri had posted in his window. The price of a peck of green beans, a pound of butter, quart of sweet cream.

The round man's mouth grew more pursed by the second as he scanned the window. Finally he drew himself up and marched inside, followed by a big-eyed, buck-toothed little boy who had been playing on the sidewalk.

Old Nick sucked in a satisfied breath and let it out. It looked like he would have plenty to keep himself amused this afternoon.

Chapter Twelve

"I am glad to join you in the service of food conservation for our Nation and I hereby accept membership in the United States Food Administration, pledging myself to carry out the directions and advice of the Food Administration in my home, in so far as my circumstances permit."

—Housewife's pledge card,
United States Food Administration, 1917

Mr. Khouri and Alafair turned to see who had entered the store. Alafair smiled, but Mr. Khouri drooped when he recognized the plump, well-dressed man steaming toward them. Chase Kemp had followed the man in, copying his hurried stride and determined expression with such verve that Alafair had some trouble keeping a straight face. Grace had no such compunction and shrieked out a laugh. Alafair put her down and gave her a shove toward the door before the girl could say something undiplomatic. "You children wait for me outside. And stay on the sidewalk." Her tone dissuaded the two children from trying to argue. They were gone in a flash.

"Good day, Mr. Clover," Khouri said. His greeting wasn't as enthusiastic as it might have been.

Emmanuel Clover nodded a businesslike greeting. "Mr. Khouri, Mrs. Tucker."

Khouri crossed his arms. "What can I do for you?"

Alafair sensed a frisson of ill-will between the two men, which surprised her. She had always found both Mr. Clover and Mr. Khouri to be pleasant men.

"I notice that you haven't posted the Food Administration's list of austerity days," Clover said.

Khouri shot a thumb over his left shoulder. "There it is right there, Mr. Clover. Right behind the counter for anyone to see."

Mr. Clover looked as if he'd just had a big gulp of vinegar, Alafair thought. And Mr. Khouri's face had taken on a formidable cast.

"Well, it should be in the front window, as well," Emmanuel Clover said.

Alafair had hoped that if she stood very still Clover would forget her and she could eavesdrop long enough to determine the cause of the unpleasantness between the two men. But her hopes were dashed when Clover turned toward her. His expression lightened and he smiled. "So nice to see you, Mrs. Tucker. Have you already signed your pledge card?"

"Long ago, Mr. Clover."

"Have you heard? The results of the draft lottery will be posted at the Masonic Hall next Friday after the Liberty Sing. I hope you and your family come into town to join the festivities, Mrs. Tucker. Your sons can learn if their numbers have been called."

A "Liberty Sing" was held in the Boynton Masonic Hall every other Saturday afternoon. But this one had been moved up to Friday evening to correspond with the draft lottery. Mr. Kirby, owner of the *Index* newspaper, was sending a reporter to Muskogee to wire the results of the drawing back to Boynton so no one would have to wait for his official draft notice in the mail. This would be the third Liberty Sing the town had held since war was declared, and was as necessary an event for the locals to attend as Sunday church service. The way feelings were running, no one could afford to be counted absent.

"We'll be at the Liberty Sing, but my sons are both too young for the draft." She felt her heart pick up a beat at the very thought of either of them being conscripted.

Clover's eyebrows shot up. "Indeed? I would have thought at least the older one—G.W., isn't it?—had passed his twenty-first birthday."

"Not yet…" she said. She didn't add that Gee Dub's twenty-first birthday was in less than six weeks.

"Well! He shouldn't despair. I don't doubt that there will be another draft within a few months. Besides, any young man over eighteen years of age can volunteer for service, with his parents' permission. Your sons will no doubt do your clan proud."

Alafair felt her cheeks grow warm. She cast a glance at Mr. Khouri before she answered. He looked as uncomfortable with the topic of conversation as she felt. "I'm already proud of them, Mr. Clover. How is that sweet girl of yours these days?"

Clover's business-like demeanor melted away entirely at the mention of his daughter. "Forsythia Lily is fine as maple sugar, thank you for asking. Since I have taken on this important war work she has been residing with her grandmother. I do miss her dearly, but my duty to this great country must come first. I feel everyone should do his part. Our very lives are at stake, you know." A flash of fear crossed his face, and Alafair thought, he really believes that. Clover turned back to Khouri and resumed his stern expression. "I'll bring an extra poster by for you later today. Do you have plenty of pledge cards on hand?"

Khouri pointed them out on the edge of the counter. "I do."

"You must be very diligent, Mr. Khouri. Those who are not native-born run the risk of being seen as insufficiently patriotic to their adopted country."

Khouri drew a sharp breath and straightened, but before he could reply, Grace appeared at the open door of the shop. Since she had been instructed to stay outside, she hollered at the top of her lungs. "Ma! Chase is sticking his toe in the street!"

Alafair clapped a hand to her heart. "Mercy! Grace, come here and quit that bellowing."

Mr. Clover stifled a laugh. "I take that as a cue that I must be going. Good afternoon Mrs. Tucker. Mr. Khouri."

After he had gone, Khouri snorted. "I'm quite native-born, thank you."

Alafair grabbed Grace by the arm and brought the child to heel. "Why, Mr. Khouri, whatever has happened between you and Mr. Clover?" she asked, ignoring Grace's protests. "I didn't know there was bad feeling between you. Mr. Clover has always been a man of great goodwill, though I think that the death of his wife has affected him sorely."

Khouri was not offended by her inquiry. "There didn't used to be ill-will between us, Miz Tucker. But since he joined up with the Council of Defense it seems he's made it his life's work to keep an eye on my family. He bothers the other merchants, too, it's true, but not like me." He paused and sighed. "At least he's not like the other agent, that Avey fellow. Now, he's a bully if ever I saw one."

Alafair was barely aware of Grace tugging to escape her mother's grip or of Chase Kemp standing just outside the door, making faces at his cousin. "But why would they bother you in particular, Mr. Khouri?"

Khouri was surprised that she should ask. "I have a 'foreign' name and I talk different from you, Miz Tucker, and my father was born in the old country. It seems that is reason enough to suspect me and all my kin of sedition."

"Well, that doesn't seem fair."

Khouri smiled at her innocence. "Fair doesn't come into it, not in my experience."

As soon as he saw the round man step out onto the street from Khouri's Market, Old Nick caught his mood from all the way across the street. The round man had been determined when he went inside, and now he was determined, worried, and afraid. Nick didn't know what the man was afraid of, but fear shimmered around him like heat rising from a fire. Something inside the market scared him, something he wished would go away. But was he afraid enough to want what Nick had to offer?

Chapter Thirteen

"The whole nation must be a team, in which each
man shall play the part for which he is best fitted."
—President Woodrow Wilson

Shaw Tucker led a newly broken mule into the barn. Breaking mules to the saddle was hot, tiring work, and he wasn't as young as he used to be. Rob Gunn was in the corral with a yearling. Once Rob had gotten his legs under him again, he had turned out to be a competent hand and a willing, cheerful helper. Rob may have been something of a gadfly, but Shaw had always admired anyone who had the courage to go his own way.

As soon as he entered the barn, he heard Charlie's voice coming from the corner stall. He was talking to the white-maned roan. Judging by the bumps and thumps and the tone of the boy's voice, Shaw decided that Charlie was pleading with the horse to hold still and let himself be saddled.

Shaw didn't interfere. He stabled the mule and wiped it down, listening with a mixture of exasperation and amusement as Charlie tried to wrangle the beast into a saddle. The horse was spoiled, that's what Shaw thought. He had too high an opinion of himself. His original owner, the late Jubal Beldon, may have been a poor excuse for a human being, but he treated that horse like a king, keeping him brushed and polished and trimmed smooth as satin. Shaw was of the opinion that it wasn't good for an animal or a child to think he could get away with doing whatever took his fancy. The animal had to know who was boss, or he'd have nothing but trouble all his life long. Charlie loved him. The boy had always wanted a gorgeous piece of horseflesh, but he had hoped to own one who minded him.

Unfortunately, the white-maned roan had his own ideas.

Shaw was heading out the door when Charlie climbed over the stall gate, sweating but undefeated. He jumped down when he saw his father and strode over to him, ablaze with purpose. "Daddy, I hear that they're putting on an extra shift at the brick plant."

Shaw shot him a mild glance over his shoulder before he turned around. "I heard that too. Mr. Ober is upping production because of the war."

"They're doing the same at the Boynton Pool, too. The Army needs all the oil it can get."

Shaw crossed his arms, resigned. He could see where this was going. "So I hear."

A moment of silence while Charlie took a breath. "I figured I'd get me one of them war jobs."

He half expected Shaw to laugh and dismiss the idea out of hand. But he didn't. "You have a job, son. The Army needs mules as much as it needs oil and bricks, and I need you working for me here."

Charlie almost said, "But you don't pay me." He caught himself in time. It wouldn't help his case to give his father a pert response. "I got it all figured out, Daddy. The shift boss, Mr. Cooper, says that I can work a half shift, in the morning from six until noon. One day a week I could work a full shift. Then after work I'd be free to do my chores at home like I do now."

Shaw was listening intently. "You've already talked to Mr. Cooper about this?"

"Yessir. I seen him at the mercantile a few days ago. That's when he mentioned he's looking for hands."

"Have you fit any time to eat or sleep into this ambitious schedule?" Shaw sounded amused, which worried Charlie.

"I could do it, Daddy." He was anxious to put his case. "I want to do everything I can. Besides, it's just temporary. Now that America is in it, the war will be over by Christmas."

Shaw picked up a curry comb off the tool table and began to clean horse hair out of the grooming brush. "All right, if you think you can manage, go ahead on."

Charlie blinked, hardly daring to believe his ears. "Really?"

"As long as you can keep up with your chores. If the quality of your work around the here suffers, that'll be the end of your clock-punching days. And I'll be the judge of that. When school starts, we'll revisit the situation. Do you agree to my terms?"

"I do! And just you wait and see, Daddy, I'll work twice as hard and get twice as much done."

Chapter Fourteen

*"I didn't raise my boy to be a soldier
I brought him up to be my pride and joy"*
—Anti-war song lyric by Alfred Bryan, 1915

Shaw walked outside to cool off in the slight breeze. He stuffed his gauntlets into his back pocket and wiped his sweat-streaked face with his bandanna. He stretched until his back cracked. He had half a mind to walk up to the house and see if there was any pie left over from yesterday. He could see that Blanche was working in Alafair's truck garden, and he smiled. For a child as work-brittle as Blanche had always been, it pleased him to see how much she loved to garden. And Alafair's garden was a huge affair that took up most of a quarter acre at the back corner of the house. Blanche was squatting down among the rows of cornstalks, digging mulch into the soil at the base of the little mounds. The corn was finally putting on ears, though they were still green so late in the season. The pole beans growing up the stalks were bearing well, and the beans and pumpkins were vining out nicely.

Shaw stood and watched Blanche work, until he heard the rattle of the buggy coming up the drive. Alafair was finally back from town.

He started walking toward her, still thinking of pie, as she pulled up in front of the house and dismounted. Shaw's gait slowed. She would normally drive straight to the barn to unhitch the horse from the buggy. Something was on her mind.

And even if she hadn't varied from her usual practice, he could tell something was wrong, from her stance, from her expression, from the air around her. He was as sensitive to his wife's emotional weather as he was to Mother Nature's.

Alafair lifted Grace out of the seat and started for the house before she noticed Shaw coming up from the garden.

Grace clamored for her father to pick her up and he hoisted her to his hip. "What's going on?"

"I invited all the girls and their fellows to come out to dinner today. They all said they'd be pleased, but for Mary and Kurt, since they were here last night. Grace, get down, now. Run on up to the house and change out of your good dress."

As soon as the child was out of earshot, Alafair answered Shaw's question. "This war business is all anybody can talk about in town. It's fretting me something awful. While I was at Khouri's Market, Emmanuel Clover came in and told Mr. Khouri that since he's foreign-born, he'd better be careful not to be seen doing anything that could be called unpatriotic. I couldn't help but get scared for Kurt and Mary, Shaw. And poor Mr. Khouri, who was born in Chicago, by the way, which last I heard was part of the United States of America. Why, I always liked Emmanuel Clover. How could he talk like that about his own neighbors? If even nice people can turn nasty like that, what about knuckleheads like Win Avey? Somebody around here is going to end up dead if this war doesn't end soon."

Her tale concerned Shaw, too, but he wasn't about to let Alafair know it. "I'm sure folks will calm down directly, sugar. It's always the way that when something big happens, everybody gets all exercised about it, and then the first heat of the moment fades and things get back to normal. Remember what happened when the Spanish sank the *Maine*?"

"That was a mighty big flap," she admitted.

"A big flap that didn't last long," he reminded her. "Less than a year."

Alafair shook her head. "Still, I wouldn't have wanted to be Spanish in that year."

He put an arm around her shoulder. "And nobody cares about Cuba anymore."

Alafair slipped her arm around his waist. "You remember the story my daddy told us about what his dad did when the War Between the States started? My grandfather told his sons that this fight was none of theirs, and he sent them back up in the Ozark hills to hide from recruiters and conscriptors of either side. He told them not come down until it was over. And they didn't." She could tell by his expression that he understood why she was telling him this story.

"You know I won't do that, darlin'." Shaw was firm, but gentle. "Gee Dub's a grown man and will make his own decision. There's nowhere to hide around here, anyway."

"Maybe the war will be over before he's twenty-one."

"Well, I hope so. I'm guessing there will be more lotteries, until they think they have a big enough Army. But even if he don't get called…you know Gee, sugar. Unless the war ends before he gets a chance, I expect he'll volunteer." Even as he said it, his head was shaking a denial. He seized her arm. "But let's don't borrow trouble, honey. Even if he goes into the Army, that don't mean he'll have to go overseas."

Alafair was grateful to him for trying to throw her a lifeline of hope, but she wasn't that naive. "He's a big, healthy, young fellow with no wife, and he can shoot the eyebrows off a gnat, Shaw. He's not as fired up as Charlie, or at least he don't show it, but you're right about him. If his friends and kinfolks have to go, he won't stand by."

"No, he'll do his duty."

His comment pricked her, and she shook his hand off, suddenly angry. "All you men keep saying that. 'He'll do his duty.' Well, as far as I'm concerned, his duty is not to go haring off and get himself killed. And I'm right worried about Charlie, too. He's like to go off half-cocked and run away to join up."

Shaw put a hand on her shoulder. "He's far too young to get called or to enlist, either. He can try but they won't take him."

She scoffed at his naïveté. "He's tall for his age and the Army is desperate for soldiers. He's like to get away with it if nobody looks too close."

"Alafair, young men are rash. No use to wish otherwise. Best just to try and stand back and let them grow out of it." An image of Charlie in an Army uniform popped into Shaw's mind, and he shook his head to dislodge it. "And hope they don't kill themselves or somebody else before they do," he added.

The fire went out of her suddenly, and she sagged. "Oh, Shaw, it's just hard. From the first time they opened their eyes, I've spent every minute of the kids' lives trying to keep them safe. When the war started it seemed too far away to do us any harm, but just lately, I've known that something bad is going to happen. There's a troubled spirit around here that wasn't around before. A fear, a horrible fear. I feel it."

She untied her bonnet and took it off. She was staring at it when she began to speak again. "I remember that when the kids were little, I thought that if I could just keep them from killing themselves until they were big enough to take care of themselves, then I wouldn't be worrying about them so much." She looked at him sidelong. "Turns out I had it backwards. When they were little, I had more charge over what happened to them. But now they're all about their own affairs, and there's nothing I can do about it."

Shaw felt much the same way, but there was no use to wish things were different than they were. So he said, "That was the point, wasn't it, to get them where they could take care of themselves? That's the way of it. Pretty soon they'll be taking care of us."

"Yes, I expect. I never figured it'd be this hard to let them go, though. Especially these boys. Up to now, we've given four girls over to a partner, so they can look out for each other."

"That'll happen with the boys, too."

"I hope so. But they're boys, and they'll do what all boys do before they become men. They'll put themselves in harm's way, and you and me both know there's no guarantee they'll come away unscathed. Or come away at all."

Shaw nodded. She was right that boys had to go through their rite of passage. That was the natural way of things. He was too kind to say it to her, but he was proud that his boys didn't want to shirk their responsibility. This was a man's office, to stand between his loved ones and danger.

"Honey, nobody is guaranteed to live even through today. Every minute of life is in God's hands, so there's no use to fret over it."

She smiled. "You're a better Christian than me, Shaw. I gave life to four boys, and God took two of them from me. I begrudge him another one. I'd fight God or the devil for them, if I had to."

Maybe she was joking, but if Alafair and the devil went head to head for her sons, Shaw wouldn't have laid odds against her. Still, there was nothing more to say on the subject. "I have to go back to work, darlin'. I'll unhitch Missy for you."

She nodded. "You want some pie before you go?"

Shaw smiled. She always could read his mind. "Yes, I do. Oh, and by the way, I told Charlie that he could take a part-time job at the brick plant until school starts. Mr. Cooper told him he could work the six a.m. shift."

She had started for the house with her package of meat beneath her arm, but she stopped in her tracks and turned to face him. "You told him he could do what? Why, he'll have to get himself on the road before dawn to get into town by six. And what about dinner? When's he going to eat?"

Alafair's reaction made Shaw laugh. "If he don't think he has enough time to eat breakfast at five with everybody else then he can eat leftover cornbread and buttermilk from the night before. Don't worry, honey. It'll be good for him. If he thinks he works hard now, he'll change his opinion right fast once he takes on a job at the plant on top of everything. Besides, it'll give him an opportunity to work off some of the ardent zeal he's developed lately. At worst he'll learn himself a lesson."

"I declare, that boy will give me gray hair before my time."

"He's sixteen, Alafair, and full of beans. He'll get over it soon enough."

"I don't remember Gee Dub being such an imp when he was sixteen."

"Gee Dub was born old. Besides, he's had an impish day or two, if you remember."

"Well I just hope that if the war is still going in September, Charlie doesn't decide to quit school."

"I don't think he will, since Gee Dub not only graduated from high school but went on to A&M. Since he was little, Charlie's wanted to do whatever Gee does."

That was a true fact, and made Alafair feel a little better. Still… "He is old enough to quit school if he wants to, though."

Shaw gave her arm a comforting squeeze. "I don't intend to let him know that is an option, darlin'."

Chapter Fifteen

"[Indians] are not citizens. They have fewer privileges than have foreigners. They are wards of the United States of America without their consent or the chance of protest on their part."

—Dr. Carlos Montezuma, 1917

Rob was amazed at how quickly he was able to fall right back into the pattern of farm life. The work felt good to him, a natural thing, in his bones. He and Charlie spent the morning heaving bales of hay out of the soddie-turned-hay-store and into the back of a wagon, hauling the load to the stock in the fields, unloading, spreading, and driving back for another load. Shaw's two long-legged, raw-boned hunting hounds, Buttercup and Crook, and the exuberant young mutt Bacon, followed the wagon back and forth, trotting afield and thoroughly sniffing every dusty, gritty, fragrant bale as it was broken open.

At noon, when Alafair called them in for dinner, Rob was ravenous. He couldn't remember the last time he had been so hungry, or so exhausted, or his hands so blistered from the wooden handles of hay hooks and the rub of leather reins.

Three more of Rob's nieces came in for dinner, the last of Alafair's mighty brood left to reacquaint himself with. As soon as he walked in the door, the women descended on him like a flock of doves. Of all of Alafair's considerable tribe, Rob had known and enjoyed these grown women best when they were children. It made him sad to realize that if they hadn't had a distinctly Tucker look about them, he probably wouldn't have recognized any of them.

He remembered that Phoebe had always been overshadowed by her gregarious twin, Alice, but none of Alafair's children were quite so sweet-natured as little Phoebe. And it seemed that she had found a husband who was cut from the same cloth as she. John Lee Day was a small, dark-eyed man with an easygoing manner. Rob knew about the tornado that had blown through last summer and destroyed the Days' house and barn and nearly killed John Lee. Alafair had told him that John Lee was doing well, even though he still had a gimpy leg and a bad eye that teared constantly. Robin noted that Alafair and Shaw treated John Lee no differently than any of their other children.

Their turquoise-eyed boy Tuck was as loud and boisterous as his sister Zeltha was quiet and dreamy, and both children were doted on shamelessly. Not for the first time since he had come to his sister's farm, Rob was struck with a peculiar longing for the warmth of a family. He shook himself. This kind of thinking was dangerous.

Martha McCoy, the eldest of the many siblings, hugged him as affectionately as if it had been ten days since she had seen him, instead of ten years. She looked so much like a young Alafair that Robin was overcome by a brief, startled feeling that time had become disjoined, and he had been transported back to his own youth.

A tall, attractive blond had draped herself across an armchair and was struggling to contain a rambunctious dark-eyed girl who was desperate to slide off her lap.

"Howdy, Alice," Robin greeted. "My, aren't you a picture? And this must be Linda striving to join the fun."

Tucker daughter number three, Alice Kelley, gave an ironic laugh. "She loves her cousins. I'm sorry Walter isn't here, but he has a standing engagement on Saturday afternoon."

Rob noticed the sour look that passed over Alafair's face when Alice mentioned her husband's "standing engagement," and envisioned a card game. "Too bad Martha's husband Streeter couldn't come, either, Robin," she said. "He's on the draft board, and they're getting ready for the lottery on Friday. You'll like him."

Rob smiled, but said nothing. If Martha's husband was complicit with the draft, Rob figured there were probably too many philosophical differences between them for much of friendship to develop.

"Are Mary and Kurt coming, Ma?" Alice asked.

"They came up and met Uncle Robin last night, honey. We'll all be at church tomorrow, though. Robin, you can meet Streeter and Walter, then."

Rob sat down at the table, to the right of Shaw, the place of honor for a guest. Alafair bustled around for a good ten minutes after everyone was seated, plating dishes and bringing them to the table, pouring drinks, getting the children situated.

Since the U.S. Food Administration had declared that on Saturdays the patriotic housewife should serve one meal wheatless, and one meal meatless, Alafair had decided to go all out for this special dinner and the family could to make do with a bowl of rice for supper tonight. She set a big, bubbling pot of black-eyed peas and fatback in the center of the table, surrounded by bowls of fried okra, sliced tomatoes and onions, sweet potatoes in their jackets, boiled corn on the cob, a dish of wilted lettuce and radishes, and a plate piled high with hot water cornbread, golden little fritters made of cornmeal batter fried in bacon grease.

Alafair smiled when Rob's mouth dropped open at the sight of the chicken-fried steaks piled high on a serving plate.

He looked up at her. "Is that what I think it is?"

"It is, honey. Just the way you used to like it."

"You remembered!"

Alafair tried not to grin, but since she was feeling inordinately proud of herself, it was hard.

Rob was so used to hotels and boarding houses that he had forgotten how family dinners worked. By the time Alafair placed the final dish in the middle of the table, he was hungry enough to bite someone's hand off. When Alafair finally, finally, sat down and Rob moved to pick up a spoon, Shaw folded his hands on the table and said, "Fronie, would you say the blessing tonight?" Oh, Lord, Rob thought, and not with the proper spirit. He looked down at the tablecloth in case any of his kinfolks happened to glance his way and wonder at his lack of piety.

"Oh, Lord," Sophronia began, which caused Rob to smile in spite of himself. "Bless this food to the nourishment of our bodies. In Jesus' name, amen."

Rob waited until the chorus of amens had abated before he reached for the sweet potatoes.

The chicken fried steak nearly brought him to tears. The slabs of round steak had been tenderized to a fare-thee-well, dredged in egg and milk and flour, and fried until they were crisp enough to crackle when you cut them. But then Rob ladled so much silky cream gravy over everything on his plate that it was hard to tell where the steak ended and the corn fritters and vegetables began. He didn't care. Every bite was a delicious, soul-soothing adventure.

The dinner chatter consisted mostly of catching up Rob on what everyone had been up to over the past decade, and though he really was interested, it was hard for him to keep his mind on anything but the food. After half a dozen corn fritters and two helpings of everything else, Rob reluctantly put down his fork, longing for a cigarette.

John Lee noticed that Rob had mentally rejoined them. "Say, Mr. Gunn, I been hearing that the government has been taking Indians and putting them to do war work. I keep half expecting to get hauled off to Tishomingo to get signed up, or explain myself, or something of the like."

"Call me Rob, pal. Tishomingo, the Chickasaw capital? You're a Chickasaw?"

"A fourth. My ma registered all of us when we were born, but I wasn't raised up Indian."

Rob noticed that Shaw, a quarter Cherokee, himself, was giving him a keen stare.

"Well, yeah, John Lee, in May the I.W.W. circulated a copy of the bill to all us representatives. The *federales* are requiring all tribal members who are dependent on the government to do farm work. But since you aren't dependent on the government and you're already farming, I don't reckon you have anything to worry about."

"Streeter says there will be another draft for sure next year and they'll probably raise the age limit," Martha said. She and Alice shot each other an anxious look. Would their husbands have to go?

Alice looked at her uncle. "Have you heard anything about the possibility of a second draft, Uncle Robin?"

Suddenly all eyes were on him, and he found himself really wanting that cigarette. He knew that because of his political activism, his family considered him the best source of information on the mysteries of Washington, D.C. to come to town in a long time. They were probably right about that, he thought, not happily. "Well, during the War Between the States, the Union had three or four drafts and called men between twenty and forty-five."

"Walter's thirty-four," Alice said.

"Streeter's thirty-two." Martha looked back at Robin, her expression carefully neutral.

"This is a big war, sweetheart." Rob assured her. "They're going to need every man they can get. And believe me, girls, there ain't as many men hot to go to war as they're telling you."

Alice puffed. "Are you surprised? Who'd want to get himself killed for that bunch of blasted idiot war-mongers in Washington!"

Robin's eyes widened at her outburst, and he regarded Alice with interest. Perhaps his family wasn't as monolithic in its support of the war as he had thought.

"What about Kurt?" Phoebe shifted Tuck on her lap and removed his hand from the gravy on her plate. "Do you reckon they'd even take a German into the Army?"

"I don't know why not, if he was to volunteer." John Lee leaned forward with his elbows on the table. "He's a U.S. citizen, after all. I'd think it'd be real useful to the Army that he speaks German."

"Well, Kurt wouldn't dare go off and leave Mary out there on that farm all by herself with that baby," Alafair insisted.

John Lee shook his head. "I don't know, Ma. You can see what's going on as well as I can. There's a bunch of firebrands around, shooting their mouths off about anybody who wasn't born here. Kurt may feel like he has to join to show he's as loyal as the next fellow."

Alafair sighed. "Let's pray this folly is over before anybody has to go. Now, let's eat."

Chapter Sixteen

"All hail, all hail! to the Liberty Knights
More strength and more brave to their arm
Give them a strong thrust to humble in dust
The foes that would bring us to harm"
—*Tulsa Daily World*, November 15, 1917

Old Nick whiled away a pleasant evening at the pool hall. He sat in the corner and nursed his root beer for hours, enjoying the sight of a bunch of ignoramuses gambling away their wages on one game after another while swilling bottle after bottle of soda pop that had been sweetened with something from the still that the proprietor kept hidden in the cellar behind his house.

Nick watched the show from the shadows until the hour was late and the would-be pool sharks were thoroughly unsteady on their pins. Then he cocked his bowler hat to a roguish tilt, took up a cue, and proceeded to win enough money to pay for his night on the town. His marks were dejected about their losses, but Nick was so cheerful about it that they found it hard to hold it against him.

Old Nick racked his cue and took a swig of his soda pop. It was a hot night, and the pop was lukewarm at best, but it was wet and felt good going down. He eyed a group of men at a round table in the corner engaged in a heated discussion. One of the arguers was a man whose money was now in Nick's pocket. He walked over. "Mind if I join you, fellows? Let me buy a round of drinks for the table. I don't want there to be no hard feelings."

The man Nick had outplayed seemed to be the head honcho of this group, so nobody argued when he grinned and gestured toward an empty chair. "No hard feelings at all, pard'. Take a seat and join the fun."

Nick turned one the chairs at the table around and straddled it. He had been eavesdropping on conversations all evening, and had pretty well pegged the political leanings of this bunch. "Did I hear y'all talking about the lottery on Friday? From the looks of you fine specimens of manhood, I imagine all of you will be awaiting the outcome with bated breath."

The head man snorted. "You bet we will, but not because we fear the outcome. Every man here has either already signed up, or like myself, being deaf in one ear, can't do military service and has found himself some war work. I joined up with the Council of Defense the day it was formed, and Victor over there is one of our Four Minute Men. His speeches over at the moving picture house have sold many a Liberty Bond."

"Council of Defense," Nick repeated. "Secret Service? So you're keeping an eye on your neighbors for signs of disloyalty, are you?"

The atmosphere cooled instantly. "You got an objection to that?" the head man asked.

Nick laughed. "Lord, no! I know for a fact that there are socialists and unionists and German loyalists hidden in every nook and cranny of this land." He held out his hand. "Call me Nick, by the way."

The head man took it. "I'm Win Avey. This here is Billy Claude Walker, Wilfred DePew, Victor Hayes. Where you from, Nick, and what are you doing in this neck of the woods?"

"Passing through. I'm on my way up to Fort Riley to offer my services to the Army."

Billy Claude found this amusing. "You're long in the tooth for the Army, ain't you?"

Nick was not insulted. "Oh, I may not be spry enough to enlist, but I figure I can turn my hand to any number of things the forces would find useful. Until then, I'm always looking around for something I can do. You all need any more security at the soiree Friday evening?"

"We're not doing the security." Win's expression indicated that he was not happy about that. "The local lawman is a fat old guy who keeps getting hired as constable because he's related to half the town council. He's already deputized a bunch of his kin to keep order. We fellows, on the other hand," he indicated the table with a sweep of his arm, "will be making a note of who all shows up and how patriotic they behave at the Liberty Sing. Also, once the draft numbers are drawn, we'll be seeing that every man called up does his duty."

Nick passed a finger over the scar next to his eye, then removed his derby and fanned himself with it. "Now, that sounds like a worthy endeavor. Who all do you have around here that bears watching?"

"Oh, there's quite a few," Win assured him. "We got maybe a dozen families with German ties living around here. In fact there's one farmer out west of town who came here direct from Germany his own self and married a local gal. I got an eye on him."

"Good thing you can report suspicious behavior to the Justice Department."

"We're going to do more than that. I got a wire today from a pal of mine in Tulsa. They've formed a chapter of the Knights of Liberty up there and they're looking for other places around the state to start units. That's what we were talking about when you come over."

"Knights of Liberty," Nick said. "Yes, I've heard of them. They do good work. They strung up a man in San Jose a couple months ago for unpatriotic behavior. I don't aim to stay around Boynton long, boys, but if you're looking for volunteers, and have an extra black robe on hand, I'd be proud to ride with you for a while."

Win clapped him on the shoulder. "We'd be proud to have you, Nick. We're always looking for right-thinking compatriots."

Nick shook hands all around, thinking that he could have been General Paul von Hindenburg himself infiltrating their group, and these knuckleheads wouldn't have known the difference.

He paid for an extra round of "soda pop" for the house and suggested that everyone cap off the evening with a visit to Rose's place. Nick offered to treat anyone who couldn't pay for a tumble, as long as he was the one who had deprived him of the means. That made him a very popular winner indeed.

Chapter Seventeen

"To provide for the establishment of a division of venereal diseases in the Bureau of the Public Health Service...For the protection of the military and naval forces of the United States."
—The Chamberlain-Kahn Act, 1917

After a late supper, Henry Blackwood stepped out of his uncle's front door for a smoke and a breath of fresh air. It had been a hot, muggy day, but now that the sun was down things were cooling off. It looked like Rose's place was doing a pretty good business. Her grassless front yard served as a parking lot for an auto and several horses. The place was bright with electric lights, and Henry could hear Victrola music and laughter coming from the open windows.

He tossed away his cigarette butt and ground it into the dirt with the toe of his boot. He cast a glance over his shoulder and saw through the open screen door that his uncle was clearing away the supper dishes.

"Hey, Uncle Eric," he called. "I think I'll take a stroll."

Eric Bent looked up. His sharp expression indicated that he wasn't fooled. "Just remember that you're working the early Sunday shift at the plant tomorrow."

"I remember. I'll be there bright-eyed and bushy-tailed," Henry said. "Don't wait up."

◇◇◇

It was busy at Rose's, even for a Saturday night. She put it down to the fact that the draft lottery was next week and these brainless idiots who had not already fled to Mexico or hastily married their cousins to avoid conscription were feeling nervous about it. Whatever the reason, it didn't matter to her. If they wanted a roll in the hay before they were sent off to die, she was happy to provide a distraction for them. Then they could all go to Europe happy and get killed, for all she cared.

There were a number of men here tonight who had never frequented her establishment before. Mostly young fellows, including the blond-haired man with the beat-up puss who had asked after Eric Bent early that morning. That amused her. She had liked Gertrude Bent. Gert hadn't exactly been a friend, but she hadn't treated Rose and the girls like something you'd find on your shoe after a stroll in the barnyard. Unusual behavior for a proper housewife.

But the husband, Eric, was like all the rest of them. While Gert was alive, he cheated on her at Rose's whenever he thought he could get away with it. And while he had never mistreated any of the girls, he had never treated them with much respect, either. Not that they were respectable, but they were human, after all.

Rose decided that this nephew was cut from better cloth than his uncle. He didn't take anyone upstairs right away. Just spent a couple of hours on the sofa in the parlor, drinking enough to be sociable, but not enough to make a fool of himself. He spent much of the evening chatting with whichever girl was not busy with a client. He was intelligent, this one, which didn't make her feel any better about him. The smart ones could be more dangerous than the morons.

She stepped out onto the porch to greet some newcomers who were having a conversation with her bouncer. She knew Dutch Leonard, a dour, middle-aged local who was one of her regulars. But she didn't recognize the two who were with him. They were young, patched and ragged, but clean enough. She stated her prices upfront, expecting that would be the end of their foray into carnal pleasure, but Dutch assured her that he'd stand good for them.

"I don't know you fellows," she said. "What brings you into town?"

The blue-eyed one in the overalls twisted his hat in his hands. "We're friends of Dutch's from Oktaha, ma'am. We're camping over to his place tonight. We're supposed to meet somebody…"

The dark-eyed one in the homespun shirt spoke over his companion. "Got to make plans because of the draft."

Rose had been around long enough to know when someone was skittering around the point and she almost turned them away. If she had to guess, she would have pegged these two as draft-dodgers. She didn't need trouble. But there were already several strangers there tonight, and the two ragged youths looked pretty ineffectual. They had the money and she had no dog in this fight. "All right, but I'm making you responsible for these boys' behavior tonight, Dutch. Y'all keep your politics to yourself or you're out before you can spit."

As soon as they were inside, Rose had a word with her bouncer. Dave was a giant Negro man from Taft who had been with her ever since she opened her own place. He was deadly efficient at his job, and he never asked to sample the wares. She didn't care why not, but she did appreciate his temperance.

"The minute anybody raises his voice, get rid of him."

Dave looked determined. "Yes, ma'am."

"You making sure everybody who comes in knows the rules?" she said.

"Yes, Miz Rose, I always do," Dave told her.

She nodded. He always did, but she thought it prudent to keep him on his toes. Rose's rules of the house were posted on a big piece of cardboard right next to the front door, but probably fifty percent of her clientele couldn't read. Neither did Dave, but he knew the rules by heart and recited them in his *basso profundo* voice to everyone who showed up at the door.

One: No guns.

Two: Ever man who wants to do bisness here has to have had a bath today or yesterday.

Three: No slappin around on the girls. Rioters will be thowd out and can't never come back.

Four: The proprietor can toss out anybody she wants. No argyin.

"Lots of business tonight," Dave noted.

"Lottery coming up. I expect they'll all be back Friday night, celebrating that they didn't get called or that they did, one or the other. We'll probably be hopping all week."

"Yes, ma'am."

She cast him a curious glance. "What about you, Dave? Did you register? Am I going to have to find me somebody else to chuck out the drunks if your number comes up?"

Dave's expression didn't change as he continued to stare out into the night. "No, ma'am, I didn't have to register. I'm too old by a year."

Rose seriously doubted that, but as long as she wasn't going to have to roust up another bouncer his lie was fine with her. But before she could comment, Dave nodded toward the lane. "Look who's come around, Miz Rose."

Rose heaved a sigh. It was Emmanuel Clover. The little fusspot had shown up at her door at least once a week ever since he was named to the Council of Defense. He walked to the bottom of the steps but stopped when he caught sight of her.

"May I speak to you in private, Mrs. Lovelock?" he opened.

Rose didn't move. It suited her to look down on him. "Mr. Clover, why do you keep wasting your time?"

Clover took off his hat. "I'll keep appealing to your patriotism until my last breath, Mrs. Lovelock. Please, please do not ruin these poor boys who may shortly give their all for their country. Especially not now, just before their numbers are called…"

She didn't let him finish. "These poor boys, as you call them, are already pretty dang ruined without any help from me, Mr. Clover. Let them have their fun. They'll be facedown in the mud for their country soon enough."

Clover was not deterred. Rose was not surprised. Clover had not been deterred for months. "We can't afford to send diseased soldiers into the fray, Mrs. Lovelock. What if they don't have the strength to stand up to those monsters who want to kill us all?" His pitch rose a note or two.

Rose's eyes widened. This was a new argument, and an insulting one, at that. "Are you saying my ladies are diseased?"

Clover's tone was pleading. "How can they not be? This evil practice is death to women and men alike. How can we meet the challenge if we cannot keep American womanhood pure and our boys away from temptation?"

Dave clinched his fists. "You want me to send him packing, Miz Rose?"

Rose shook her head in aggravation. The pathetic part of it was that Clover was so sincere in his concern for the welfare of not just the johns, but the hookers as well.

Before she could unleash Dave, Clover pulled a piece of paper out of his pocket and waved it at her. "Mrs. Lovelock, did you know that the House of Representatives has recently passed a bill…" He began to read. "…to study and investigate the cause, treatment and prevention of venereal diseases, and to control and prevent the spread of these diseases?"

Oh, this was too much. "Toss him into the street on his butt, Dave."

Dave started down the steps and Clover started backing up. However, he didn't stop talking. "When the Senate passes this act into law, it'll give the government the power to quarantine any woman suspected of having venereal disease. You and all your women will have to undergo a medical test to determine if you are diseased…."

Dave reached for him and he didn't have time to expound further.

"I'll be back," he called, from his seat in the middle of the dirt road.

"I know you will," Rose called back.

"It's my duty as a member of the Council of Defense to see that we all uphold this country's moral stance." Clover dusted off the seat of his pants, picked up his hat, and strode off into the dark with as much dignity as he could come up with.

Dave looked concerned when he rejoined her on the porch. "You 'spect he's telling the truth? You 'spect we might end up getting shut down, Miz Rose?"

Rose tried not to appear worried, but Clover's information had chilled her. "Nothing surprises me anymore, Dave. But it ain't happening tonight so I don't aim to fret over it."

Chapter Eighteen

"Yesterday marked a golden date on the calendar; a date when the law-abiding people of the community...rose in their mighty wrath and drove from their midst the 'Wobbly.' As a house cleaning makes for better conditions in the home, so does it in the city, and the returning Bisbbites, yesterday noon, sniffed the air with a keen realization that their hope had been realized.

The 'Wobblie' is no more."
—*Bisbee Daily Review*, Bisbee, Arizona, July 13, 1917

He couldn't breathe. He couldn't move. The cattle car was packed with humanity, pressing him into the corner. He was thirsty. His mouth was so dry he couldn't speak. The floor of the car was covered with cow manure. The smell of shit and urine and flop sweat and terror was overwhelming. Don't lose consciousness, for God's sake. Don't faint. They're all looking at you. They're all looking to you to know how to behave, what to do.

Tell them that if we die, we die for something. Do no violence, no matter what indignities they heap upon us. No matter how much you want to retaliate. To smash those vigilantes into the dust. To kill that sadistic bastard in the bowler hat...

Rob jerked upright, gasping for air. It took him a moment to orient himself, to remember where he was. He was safe.

He glanced over at his nephew in the other bed, relieved to see that his nightmare hadn't disturbed the young man. He wiped the sweat off his forehead with the end of the sheet and swung his legs around to sit on the edge of the bed.

It was a hot night, noisy with insects. The apron-curtains stirred in the slight breeze. Rob leaned forward and perched his elbows on his knees. Maybe he hadn't realized just how tired he was. How many times had he thought that he was going to end up shot or beaten to death or dangling at the end of a rope? How many times had he been jailed or run out of town? He should be used to it by now. The thought caused him to chuckle.

He still believed. His religion was a living wage, an eight-hour day, safe working conditions. But after Bisbee he realized that if he kept it up, without a doubt he was going to end up dead. He sighed. Maybe he'd just get tarred and feathered.

He wasn't going to sleep again anytime soon. He stood up and reached for his trousers.

Gee Dub stirred and sat up. "What's up, Uncle Robin?" His voice was hoarse with sleep. "What time is it?"

"It's late, slim. Go back to sleep." Rob pulled on a shirt and fished his tobacco pouch out of his pocket. He began rolling a cigarette, eyeing his nephew's dark form, still sitting up, watching. He was going to have to come up with an explanation. "After that fine supper your mama fixed us, I'm too full to sleep. I'm feeling in need of some air."

"Want me to come with you?"

Rob shook out his match. "No, thanks, I'll try not to get lost. I won't be gone long. It's been a while since I was able to enjoy a quiet night on my own. I'll try not to wake you when I come in."

Chapter Nineteen

"...few people yet understand the real nature of the enemy and the real danger to America."
　　　　　　　　—Oklahoma Council of Defense, 1917

It was nearly one o'clock in the morning and Scott Tucker, town sheriff of Boynton, Oklahoma, was exhausted. There were only a few details left to be worked out with his deputy, Trenton Calder, on the logistics of getting the draft numbers from the Western Union office to the Masonic Hall in a discreet and orderly manner, and Scott was longing for his pillow.

He would be relieved beyond understanding when Friday's Liberty Sing and draft lottery were finished, but as it was, there was no end of preparations to make. Feelings had been running high on both sides about this draft ever since Congress had instated it, and if the town could get through the day without a riot or a brawl, Scott had promised providence that he would become a religious man. He had already deputized eight or ten likely fellows to help keep the crowds in order at the Liberty Sing. Though he never picked exactly the same deputies twice, he did always pick men he trusted, which usually meant his own relatives.

"How many folks know when the wire is supposed to come through?" Trent asked him.

"Most, I imagine. It'll take a long while to get all the numbers drawn in Muskogee, and then for the reporter to get the wire sent. If the news comes in before nine o'clock, I'll be surprised. Probably a lot of families will have already gone home, especially if they don't have any close kin who registered. I hope it'll be a skimpy crowd at the hall when the list is posted."

Billy Claude Walker burst in through the front door, putting an abrupt end to their conversation.

"Fight! Fight!" he yelled. Billy Claude's staggering gait suggested that he had had more than a few.

Scott and Trent leaped to their feet and grabbed for their gun belts. "Where? The pool hall?"

"Over to Rose's! Hurry up! It's some fellow named Pip and Win Avey. The fellow's got a razor! I reckon there's like to be a killing!"

Rose's. Scott's heart sank when he heard that. Scott had run the girls in a couple of times, whenever the neighbors complained of the traffic or the church ladies got on their high horses, but mostly Rose ran a tight ship, keeping the noise and mayhem to a minimum. Scott didn't bother her if she was discreet. And most of the time she was discreet. Many people in town didn't even know there was a bawdy house at the end of Kenetick Street.

Since the house of ill repute was only a few blocks away, the two lawmen took out on foot. Billy Claude had a good head start on them, but being fifteen years younger, Trent outpaced him easily. Being thirty years older than his deputy, Scott brought up the rear.

Trent got to Rose's just as the fight spilled out into the street. Pip's razor had done its job, for Win's clothes were shredded and his arms were slashed. The bloody wounds just seemed to have made him mad, though, for he was chasing Pip all around the yard with an ax handle in his hands, bellowing with rage. Several working women were standing on the porch, taunting and generally doing nothing to help the situation. The yard was full of amused bystanders. One fellow in a bowler hat, standing by the lane, was practically doubled over with mirth.

By the time Scott arrived, Trent had pulled out his Colt and ordered the two to drop their weapons and reach for the sky. Scott jerked the razor out of the young stranger's hand and cuffed him.

One of Win's pals, Victor Hayes, suddenly decided to take his friend's side in the fray and smacked Trent in the jaw. Trent went down, and Victor and Win fled into the night.

Pip began to struggle, but Scott had had enough foolishness to last him, so he parted the man's hair with the butt of his .45 and went over to check on his deputy.

Trent was sitting on the ground, rubbing his jaw, with two or three solicitous ladies of the night bent over him. He looked up at Scott, sheepish. "Sorry, Boss."

"Never mind." He straightened and cast a look around for Rose. He saw her kneeling on the porch, leaning over her bouncer, who was out cold. "Dave all right?" Scott called.

"I reckon he'll be okay," she said. "No thanks to Avey. I've told him a dozen he ain't welcome. But he marched up here with a bunch of his cronies, bold as brass, and started a fight, so I told Dave to toss him out. He aimed to split Dave's skull with that ax handle. Then that boy took it upon himself to even the odds." Her tone was sullen. "I hate that Win Avey."

"You want me to fetch Doc Perry for Dave?"

Rose shook her head. "We'll take care of him." Dave was clutching his sore head and moaning.

Scott rather liked Rose Lovelock, if that was really her name. She was a middle-aged woman, still attractive if somewhat faded. What little he knew of her life story was both interesting and depressing. "Do you want to press charges?"

Rose did not look happy, but she shook her head again.

Scott nodded. Having your clientele arrested for battery was not good for business. "I'm taking this one in for disturbing the peace. I'll go out to Win's house in the morning and arrest him." he said. "I reckon you're closed until further notice, Rose."

Rose straightened with indignation. "Me and the girls got to make a living, Scott."

"Sorry. After this it's best y'all lay low for a while. Now, I have to run this yahoo in."

As soon as they were gone, Rose turned toward Dutch Leonard, standing behind her on the porch, half-clad, with his arm around a soiled dove. "I warned you to keep your pals in line, Dutch. Find your other sidekick and get out. And don't come back."

Chapter Twenty

*"For the total abolition of the crime, disease, and
death-producing practice of rent, interest, and
profit-taking as iniquities that…are now being
imposed upon the working class of the world."*
—Manifesto of the Working Class Union

When they arrived at the jailhouse, Scott flung the brawler into
a cell without ceremony.

"What's your name? I don't know you." Scott tried not to
sound as homicidal as he felt.

The man was blue-eyed, ill-shaven and shaggy-haired, dressed
in worn overalls and a patched shirt. A tenant farmer, Scott
decided. The toe was out of one of his boots. Scott wondered how
he had managed to afford a night at Rose's. Now that he could
see the man in the light, Scott decided that he was younger than
he had first thought. The man lowered himself gingerly onto a
cot and fingered the knot on his head before he mumbled. "Pip
James. It was that other fellow's fault."

"It always is. What was the ruckus about?"

Pip's lip curled. "We had a difference of opinion concerning
the war, and then when the big colored fellow tried to throw
him out, the jackass beaned him with his own axe handle."

"Well, I hope you learned to keep your opinions to yourself. Win is Secret Service and mighty eager to report contrary

ideology. Somebody said you're from Oktaha. Are you in town to hear whether your number gets drawn on Friday?"

Pip looked up at Scott from under his eyebrows and said nothing for so long that Scott began to get a very bad feeling.

"Did you register, boy? Tell me the truth, now."

Pip's nostrils flared. "I ain't volunteering to die for this illegal war."

A draft resister. Scott leaned his head against the bars. He was not wild about the idea of the draft himself. One of his four sons and his deputy, whom he loved like a son, had registered and would learn their fate on Friday. But his personal feelings had no weight here. He made no attempt to talk his prisoner into enlisting to avoid jail time. He could tell by the fire in Pip's eyes that it would do no good. "I'd have let you out tomorrow for rioting, but now I've got to send you to Muskogee for resisting the draft. You know that, don't you?"

"I know it."

"Are you Working Class Union?" Scott asked the question, though he dreaded hearing the answer. The Working Class Union had started out a few years ago as an affiliate of the I.W.W., but since most of its members were tenant farmers and not wage earners, the W.C.U. had gone off on its own. The Industrial Workers of the World were unbending in their beliefs, but the W.C.U. was downright radical. Not that they didn't have plenty of cause. Tenant farmers were often little more than serfs and indentured servants with no hope of improving their lot. Their demand for an end to rent and the charging of interest on loans was too extreme for even Scott's easygoing philosophy of live and let live. In other parts of the state, some of the more hot-blooded members of the brotherhood had taken to night-riding and vandalism, even bank robbery.

Pip didn't answer, which was answer enough for Scott. "How many of you are there? I won't stand for no trouble, you hear me?"

"I'm not here to make trouble, Mister. We…I just come to town to meet with somebody. I don't aim to be any trouble, I promise."

"Well, if it's your plan not to make trouble, you've already done a real bad job of it. You'd better hope your socialist pals don't come by for a visit or make themselves known to me at all, because I'll arrest them faster than you can blink twice. Now sit down and shut up. I'll deal with you in the morning."

When he finally made it home, Scott's wife, Hattie, met him at the door with a mug of hot tea. "I warmed you up some stew," she said. "You shouldn't go to bed on an empty stomach. Go wash up…I declare! You've got blood all over your sleeve! What happened tonight?"

"Me and Trent had to break up a fight. I think we've got a bunch of anti-draft yahoos in town, honey. I've got one of them in jail, but I'm too tired to shake him down tonight. I don't know if they're planning something on Friday or not. He'll lie to me, anyway. Win Avey was the other combatant, but he got away. Probably ran back to his shack. I'll try to pick him up in the morning. Him and his Secret Service friends have lethal objections to draft-dodgers. I'm going to have to deputize half the men in town for the durn Liberty Sing next week. I wish they'd just call it off and let everybody get his draft notice in the mail like God intended." Scott shook his head. "I'll tell you, Hattie, sometimes I despair of humankind."

The moon was down. It was early in the morning, but no light had yet appeared on the horizon. The night was dark and still uncomfortably hot. The last dim yellow light disappeared from Rose's back window, but Nick did not move. He was in no hurry. Endless patience was one of the requirements for his line of work. He'd wait however long it took before he made contact.

He had been recognized, but he wasn't yet sure that his services were required. He had only caught a scent of lingering fury. A whiff of desire for something evil. He didn't know if what he was smelling was desire for revenge, a vendetta, jealousy, or simply a need to make a statement. It didn't matter why. Someone wanted to deal death, and that was enough for him.

A dark figure walked around the side of the house, into the yard, and stopped, back to the man under the tree. Sure he couldn't be seen, Nick observed his subject for a few moments, looking for any sign of nervousness or fear. But there was none. The dark figure stood still and straight, waiting. Nick sensed the heat of determination.

He made his move. He straightened his bowler hat and slid up behind his summoner. When he spoke, his voice was barely audible, smooth as silk. "You know who I am."

His contact straightened, but didn't seem surprised. "Yes."

Nick leaned in close. "Give me a name."

Chapter Twenty-one

"To the work! To the work! There is labor for all."
—1869 hymn lyrics by Fanny Crosby

Before breakfast, Shaw pulled on his hat and made his way across the yard to milk and feed animals. From the kitchen window, Alafair watched him trudge, head-down, away from the house until he disappeared into the barn.

Sophronia ran into the kitchen, interrupting her thoughts, and it suddenly occurred to Alafair that Charlie had not come in for breakfast. He was always the first one into the kitchen after the bacon began to fry. Alafair went into the darkened parlor to check on him. She could just see his long shape on his bed in the back corner of the room, one stockinged foot sticking out from under the covers. She shook his shoulder, and he lifted his head enough to squint at her out of one half-closed eye.

"Is it morning already?"

"It sure is, sleepyhead. You feeling all right? It's not like you to lie abed."

He turned over onto his back and groaned. "I reckon I stayed up too late arguing politics."

"Well, you better get up and around or them cows will go to lowing to beat all. Daddy is on his way to the barn, and I expect Gee Dub and Robin are already there."

Alafair went back into the kitchen, and Charlie swung his legs off the bed and sat himself up. He stretched, yawned, and scrubbed his hands through his mess of blond hair, leaving it sticking up every which way. Blanche sniffed at his appearance as she passed by, a ghostly figure in the half-light. "You look like a pretty untidy haystack."

Charlie curled his lip at her witticism, but made a half-hearted attempt to comb his hair with his fingers. He rubbed his cheek hopefully, but it felt no more whiskery than it had yesterday. He sighed, envious of Gee Dub's newfound ability to sprout stubble. Oh, well, he expected he should be used to trailing along in his older brother's wake by now. He reached for the trousers he had thrown over the foot of the bedstead the night before, stood up and pulled them on before tossing off his cotton nightshirt. Grace and Bacon streaked through the parlor, eager for breakfast, and nearly knocked Charlie backwards onto the bed. He mumbled something under his breath that he hoped his mother had not heard, before he trod into the kitchen in his stocking feet, buttoning his work shirt.

Grace was pouring syrup on her bowl of oatmeal, and Sophronia and Blanche were already well along with breakfast. Charlie felt a pang of irritation that he was the only male left in this nest of females. Alafair looked over at him from the stove. "Grab a biscuit and put on your hat before you go out, son."

The smell of bacon made his stomach growl, but Charlie made do by finishing off the biscuit in two bites. "I reckon I'd better get out to the barn with Daddy and them."

Alafair didn't look at him, but she could feel his aura of discontent from across the room. She frowned over the frying eggs. "Why don't you take your uncle Robin fishing after church? It'll be a nice break for you before you have to start your new job of work on Monday."

"I want to go, too!" Sophronia cried. "Why can't I go?"

"Nobody said you can't." Charlie sounded exasperated, but the idea of fishing intrigued him, and his mood lifted.

Sophronia continued her plaint. "Y'all never let me come. Can I come?"

"Ain't decided to go, yet."

"Looks like it might rain a bit this afternoon," Alafair said. "There's good fishing when it's cloudy and cooler."

Sophronia nodded her agreement. "After a rain, there's like to be lots of crawlers for bait."

"Well, I'll see what Daddy says." Charlie absently picked up a second biscuit and bit it. "I could try out that new pole I got stretching in the barn."

"Right now you've got chores to do," Alafair said, "so y'all better get to it."

Chapter Twenty-two

"Congress has provided that the nation shall be
organized for war by selection; that each man shall
be classified for service in the place to which it shall
best serve the general good to call him."
—President Wilson on the Selective Service Act, 1917

Once the war started, most of the young men in Boynton were full of fire and ready to join up and kill the Bosch. And if some weren't, they generally kept their mouths shut about it. Trenton Calder, beloved of Ruth Tucker and deputy to Scott Tucker, was as hot-blooded about the war as the next young man. But with every able-bodied male in town rushing off to sign up, Scott had asked Trent if he would wait a few months to enlist, just until he could get someone to take the deputy's place who was too old or too married to serve in the armed forces. Trent wasn't optimistic that his boss would find someone who'd do it for what the town was willing to pay, not somebody with any brains, anyway. But Scott had been so good to him over the years that he said he'd wait until after the draft lottery. In the end, both men knew that if Trent's number did not come up, he would be off to Muskogee to join up before the next week was out.

The imminent change in his circumstance had gotten Trenton Calder to thinking. He was sure his number would be picked.

He never for a minute expected that God would allow him to miss his chance to be a hero.

If he went away to war, he'd be gone for two years. He needed to consider the state of his relationship with Ruth.

Ever since she got back from her music course in Muskogee, Ruth had been living with her mentor Beckie MacKenzie, and had taken over Mrs. MacKenzie's business of teaching music to the local youth. Since she now lived so close, Ruth frequently walked into Boynton to visit Trent at the jailhouse, or to have a meal with him at the Newport Cafe. Sometimes he was even invited to take supper at Mrs. MacKenzie's grand house just north of town, or to accompany Ruth out to her parents' farm for Sunday dinner.

He loved her dearly. But until he made something of himself and could support her properly, he had been hesitant to declare himself. He was sitting with his feet on his desk in the sheriff's office, pondering his dilemma, when the object of his consideration walked in. Ruth smiled at him as his boots hit the floor with a clunk.

Something about the way she looked at him with that quirky smile and "you can't fool me" expression made his cheeks hot. He stood up.

"Hello, darlin', you look mighty pretty," he said. "What blows you into town?" He restrained himself from smacking his palm against his forehead at the lame remark.

Ruth stifled a smile and sat down in one of the chairs by the window. "I thought I'd come by and see if you want to escort me to church."

"Oh, I'm sorry, but Scott asked me to hang around the office today and keep an eye on the draft-dodger we got locked up. He rode out to Win Avey's a while ago to arrest him for brawling last night."

"Who's your draft-dodger? Anybody I know?"

"Naw, some fellow from Oktaha name of Pip James."

"Are you going to be at the Liberty Sing on Friday?"

Trent grinned. "I better be there. Wouldn't want anybody to think I was an unpatriotic public servant. Maybe we can go to the shindig together."

Ruth liked the idea. "That would be fine."

"What time shall I come by for you on Friday?"

"I'll be ready about four." Ruth stood, but looked back over her shoulder at him before she left. Her expression was grave. "It could be they won't call your number." She sounded wistful, but that's not the way Trent heard it.

He didn't intend for her to think him a coward. "I'll enlist, then. You won't find me sitting around, trying to think of ways to get out of it. "

"I wish you didn't have to go."

The light finally dawned, and he stood up from his chair and took her hand. "I wish there wasn't a war at all." He said it because he knew that's what would please her to hear, but he was thinking about how exciting it was going to be to see Paris. "But there is, and I can't leave other folks to do my fighting for me."

She looked down at her hands again, unsure how to reply to that. So she changed the subject. "My mother's brother showed up on our doorstep a couple of days ago, and I expect he'll be lingering for a week or so. "

He blinked at the conversational shift. "Your mother must be pleased. I don't believe I've ever met any of your ma's folks. How long has it been since you've seen your uncle?"

"This is the first time in ten years that any of us have seen Uncle Robin. He travels a lot."

"Robin? Your uncle is called Robin?" His tone indicated that he thought that a strange name for a grown man.

"Well, his name is Robert Gunn, but so is my grandfather's and his father's, and his father before him, so the family calls my uncle 'Robin.' I think most everybody else calls him Rob. Just like Robert Burns. Miz Beckie told me Robert Burns was called Robin when he was a boy. Rantin', rovin' Robin." Ruth's laugh was ironic. "Rantin' and rovin' indeed. That's my uncle Robin to a fare-thee-well. He's like a swallow, Mama says, just spends his life on the wing and never alights anywhere."

Trent listened to Ruth's description of her uncle with interest, even though he had no idea who this Robert Burns was. "What does your uncle do for a living that takes him on the road so much?"

"He's a…" Ruth hesitated. Many people had no use for Robin's line of work, and tender-hearted as he was, Trent was quite conservative. But there was no point in dodging the truth. "He served in the Army for a long time, mostly in the Philippines. But for the past several years, he's been a union organizer for the Industrial Workers of the World. The Army took him all over the world, and now the union takes him all over the United States."

Trent's eyes widened. "A Wobblie."

Ruth looked him up and down, gauging his disapproval. "Yes, Trent, and you can wipe that look off your face. It is my opinion that I should allow my fellow humans their peccadilloes and hope they would allow me mine."

Trent did not immediately realize he was being chastised. "I hope he isn't spouting anti-war nonsense to folks who aren't smart enough to see that we have to go to war now, after what the Germans have done to us."

"Now, Trent, Uncle Robin is a good man and he's only here for a short visit to see family. He's helping Daddy with the farm, and he assures Mama that he has no intention of doing union work while he's here."

"I hope not, honey! I'd hate to have to arrest my sweetheart's uncle for rabble-rousing."

Ruth withdrew her hand from his grasp. "I don't agree with my uncle, but it's not illegal to belong to a union, Trent. At least not yet."

Chapter Twenty-three

"Yet will I be avenged of you."
—Judges 15:7

Scott's first order of business that morning was to arrest Win Avey for putting a dent in the head of Rose Lovelock's bouncer, Dave. He would be glad to have Avey behind bars before the Liberty Sing, anyway. Especially now that he knew there were socialists and draft-dodgers in town. Win had no tolerance for liberal thinkers. In fact Win was altogether too free with his fists—and whatever else he could pick up—to mix peacefully with anyone who held an opinion that differed from his own.

Scott backed his automobile out of the shed behind his house that he used for a garage. The auto was a 1913 model Paige touring car that he had bought used from Hattie's cousin's husband, who owned a dealership in Muskogee. He had been petitioning the town council for years to buy an auto for the use of anyone on official business. But the council had turned deaf ears for so long that he finally broke down and bought one for himself. He was proud of his shiny vehicle with its convertible top, and glad that it would remain in his possession after he was no longer in the employ of the town of Boynton. He didn't drive it much. A horse was usually more practical in his line of work. But in this case Scott was pretty sure that it would be easier to transport Win if he was trussed up hand and foot and tossed into the backseat.

If he was lucky, Win's accomplice Victor Hayes had gone home with him, and Scott could pick them both up at once.

Avey rented one of the little cabins owned by Frank Ober, the manager of the brick plant just north of town. Ober had created a small company camp outside the plant for workers who had no families and no homes of their own. The cabins were one-room affairs, but decent, and Ober didn't charge much in the way of rent. As he drove the quarter-mile out of town, Scott wondered if Win would even remember much of the events of the night before. He might have to be reminded. He had been pretty drunk. However, he had managed to give a good account of himself in the fight. If he had his wits about him enough to realize that Scott wasn't going to let it go, Win may very well have legged it out of the county last night.

Most of the renters had left for church or to spend Sunday with kin, so the camp was fairly deserted. Scott thought nothing of it when he saw that the front door of Win's cabin was standing wide open. People often left their doors and windows open on hot nights, and considering how much Win had imbibed the night before, Scott would have been surprised if he was up and about at this early hour.

He parked the Paige and sat there for a moment, watching the open door for activity inside. He stepped out of the car and walked up onto the low stoop where he stopped outside the door.

"Win Avey," he called. "You in there?"

Scott took a moment to listen for movement before he tried again. "Win, I aim to take you in for brawling, and Victor too, if he's in there. Come on out peaceable, now, and don't make me come in there after you."

No answer. He could see part of the interior of the cabin. A table with no chairs, and the foot of a camp bed. No human legs at the end of the bed. Win had likely gotten smart and taken off. Scott frowned and drew his sidearm before he stepped inside. He had been ambushed before and he didn't fancy a repeat of the experience.

Win was there, all right, hanging by his feet at the end of a rope slung over a ceiling beam. His throat had been cut, and he had bled all over the floor like a slaughtered animal. Scott recognized the bulky body and dark hair, and the clothes that Pip James had slashed up with a razor the night before. He wouldn't have been able to identify the face. It had been beaten to an unrecognizable pulp.

Scott breathed an oath and made a cursory search of the room before sliding his pistol back into the holster. Victor was not there. Scott put his hands on his hips and gazed at the floor, thinking. Pip James hadn't done it. He had been behind bars when Win met his maker. Victor Hayes? But why? They were compatriots. Which didn't mean Scott wasn't going to haul Victor in for questioning.

Even so, Scott knew the reason Win Avey had died, as plain as if God himself had whispered the answer into his ear. Win's brutal form of patriotism had outraged the wrong person.

Chapter Twenty-four

*"Woe be to the man or group of men
that seeks to stand in our way."*
—Woodrow Wilson, June 1917

Scott cut down Win Avey's body, laid it on the bed, and covered
it with a blanket before driving to the brick plant and informing
Eric Bent, the Sunday shift supervisor, of what had happened.
Bent sent his nephew Henry Blackwood to the cottage to stand
watch outside while Scott drove back into town. He rousted
Mr. Lee, the undertaker, to retrieve Win's earthly remains. then
sent Trenton Calder to relieve Henry and secure the scene of
the crime.

His next order of business was to call on the newly elected
mayor, Mr. Jehu H. Ogle. Since it was Sunday, he went by the
mayor's home, but Mrs. Ogle told him that her husband had
had an early visitor and the two had gone to the office rather
than discuss business at home.

Mr. Ogle's office was located on Main Street above the Elliot
and Ober Theater, where he practiced law with his partner Abner
Meriwether when he wasn't engaged in the affairs of the town.
Scott climbed the stairs and walked into Mr. Ogle's private
chambers without announcement.

Scott sighed when he saw Ogle's visitor. Emmanuel Clover
stood up from his chair in front of Ogle's desk. A look of relief

passed over the mayor's face when he recognized Scott. Scott wasn't sure how long the relief would last when he gave the mayor his news.

Ogle gestured toward the chair that Clover had just vacated. "Have a seat, Scott. Mr. Clover was just on his way out."

Clover turned to leave, but Scott held up a hand. "That won't be necessary, J.H. I reckon he'd better hear what I have to say. I found Win Avey hanging from a rafter at his house this morning. He's been murdered. Throat cut." There was no use to beat around the bush.

Both men made surprised noises, and Clover sank back into his chair. Scott continued before the questions started. "I don't know what happened yet. I just found him not an hour ago. But he was involved in a scuffle with a W.C.U. member last night. I arrested the Red last night, so he didn't do it, but I fear he's come to town with some of his cronies to make trouble over the draft lottery. I don't know who all the rest of them are, but I'll try to root them out before the lottery. I can't guarantee to get them all, though. So I'm here to...strongly suggest...that the town cancel the Liberty Sing. Win has pals of his own, you know. And after what happened, I expect if those two packs of troublemakers get together there will be a right old hullabaloo. And I'd just as soon..."

Clover interrupted. "Oh, no, Sheriff. We can't let anything deter us from a patriotic demonstration. That's just what the enemy wants!"

Ogle agreed. "I can't call it off now, Scott. It's too durn late. The whole west half of the county is planning to show up. It's been in the paper and everything."

Mr. Clover was too zealous to be persuaded, so Scott directed his argument to the mayor. "Don't make it so hard, then, J.H. Let me lock up the hall and put a sign on the door. The boys can get their draft notices in the mail or read the newspaper to see if their numbers come up, like everybody else."

"But Mr. Tucker..." Clover attempted.

Ogle spoke over him. "Scott, deputize as many men as you need to patrol the Liberty Sing. I'm sure you can keep the peace. I'm afraid if we called it off we really would have a riot on our hands. Folks will come to town anyway to hear from the reporter if their numbers were picked, whether they can get into the hall or not. Better to have everyone in one place where you can keep an eye on things."

Scott bit his lip. Maybe the mayor was right, but that didn't mean he liked it. He shot Mr. Clover a sideways glance. "Emmanuel, I have no idea yet who killed Avey. He was a rowdy in the best of times, so his death may have nothing to do with the fact that he was one of our Council of Defense members. But maybe it does. So if I was you I'd consider laying low for a spell until I can get this thing figured out."

Poor Clover. He already saw enemies around every corner. The mere suggestion that he could personally be a target caused the blood to drain out of his face. He swallowed and leaned back. But Scott was mistaken if he expected that Clover's fear would get the better of him. Clover stood up, shaky but determined. "I'll not hide from adversity, Mr. Tucker. I shall proudly be in the forefront at the Liberty Sing and never give in to traitors and foreign spies and fifth-columnists. No act of terror must ever cause us to alter our American way of life by one jot."

Scott gave Clover a wordless once-over before turning back to the mayor. "If you insist on going through with this assembly, J.H., I'm telling you right now that I can't guarantee there won't be trouble. But I'll try to forestall as many agitators as I can beforehand and if all goes well we'll have a peaceful night." In truth, Scott was anxious to hear about his own son's status as soon as the numbers were drawn. Even if it did mean he may have to bust a few heads during the course of the evening.

Emmanuel Clover's countenance lifted at Scott's surrender. "I'll do my best to keep an eye on things around town, Sheriff, and immediately report any worrisome activity to you or one of your deputies."

"That would be most helpful, Emmanuel."

"Then I shall take my leave, Mr. Tucker, Mr. Mayor. Until Friday."

Clover closed the office door behind him, and Scott looked back at Ogle. "What was he doing here?"

"Oh, he's speaking at the meeting next week. As the head Council of Defense man in the town he gets to read out all the new war rules and regulations. After what happened to Avey, though, I'm surprised he still wants to go through with it. It seems like since his wife was killed in that accident he's gotten afraid of his own shadow."

"Well, that's a hard thing to bear." Scott's tone was thoughtful. "It'll shake a man to his core when he first realizes that trouble and injustice happens to the innocent and guilty alike. Still… he's a man of true conviction and he does plow ahead no matter what." An ironic smile flitted over his lips. "I kind of admire the little pecker."

Chapter Twenty-five

"Resistance in horses is often a mark of strength
and vigor, and proceeds from high spirits;
but punishment would turn it into vice."
—Nolan's System For Training
Cavalry Horses, 1862

The white-maned roan was a fine, smooth ride when he took
a notion to be, but if he wasn't in the mood, Charlie could no
more make him cooperate than he could rope the moon. The
horse would behave like the high-class mount he was for days
on end, lulling the boy into a state of discaution. Then out of
the blue, just when Charlie least expected it, the horse would go
to bucking like he had burrs under his saddle. Charlie halfway
thought that the roan was making a perverse game out of tossing his unwary rider into the dirt. Aside from throwing Charlie
onto his rump with unsettling regularity, the roan had never
tried to hurt more than the boy's pride. It was a good thing. The
animal suffered from a nervous affliction from having survived
a tornado, and Shaw had made it very clear to Charlie from the
beginning that if the horse tried to injure anyone he'd have to
be put down. No reprieve. Charlie expected that the roan knew
that, for he never misbehaved enough to get himself shot.

The horse generally behaved better with Shaw or Gee Dub,
which was all right. Charlie had grown up in the saddle and was

a good rider, but both his elders had enjoyed years more practice with horses than Charlie had. But the awful thing was that when the roan got so riled up that none of the Tucker men could do anything with him, the very sight of Charlie's eleven-year-old sister Sophronia would calm him right down.

The roan was the finest, most valuable, and manliest horse Charlie had ever seen. He never expected to own such a wonderful, fiery creature, especially at the tender age of sixteen. The fact that the horse loved his little sister more than him only added to the boy's general discontentment with his lot in life.

Charlie was in the roan's stall, lovingly brushing the lustrous coat, when the object of his disgruntlement appeared. She climbed up the slats of the stall and hung her arms over the top rail, grinning at him, all a mess of frizzy reddish hair, freckles, and big white teeth.

"Hey, Charlie Boy. You give this horse a name yet?"

He tried to ignore her, but she didn't take the hint.

"Gee Dub said that now you're calling him Lightning Bolt. Does he like that any better than Devil Dancer? Why'd you go with Lightning Bolt? Is it that white blaze on his nose? It's too fat to look like a bolt of lightning."

How did she do that? Sophronia had a knack for knowing just which topic to broach to annoy Charlie the most. Ever since he had come into possession of the roan, Charlie had been trying out one name after another, but nothing seemed to stick. In fact, if he hadn't known better, he would have sworn that every name he tried on the horse thus far just irritated him. He first called the roan Tornado, since it was due to the tornado that tore through Boynton the year before that the horse lost his previous owner. But every time Charlie called him Tornado, the horse tried to buck him off. "Tornado" obviously brought up too many unfortunate memories. So he changed the name to Hercules, but that just got him scraped out of the saddle when the roan decided to run his rider under a low tree branch. Six Shooter earned him a bite on the butt. Devil Dancer shied away every time Charlie tried to mount.

Charlie figured he hadn't come up with a name that properly conveyed the horse's strength, pride, and spirit. The horse would let him know when he did.

He had intended to ignore his sister until she went away, but her question had goaded him. "If you've just got to know, I'm calling him Lightning Bolt 'cause he's fast."

Lightning Bolt snorted and tried to step on Charlie's foot, but the boy skipped out of the way.

"So how's he liking it?"

"He likes it fine." The roan snorted again and knocked Charlie into the rails with his shoulder.

Sophronia chucked. "Yeah, looks like it."

"What do you want, you little flea? Or did you come out here just to get me riled up?"

"Mama says it's about time to go to church and you should come on."

Charlie went back to his brushing. "Tell Mama I'll be there directly."

Sophronia didn't move from her perch on the slats. "You know, you're going about it all wrong."

"I reckon I know how to groom a horse."

"Not that. I mean naming that horse. You keep coming up with hard names, and yonder horse has been through enough hard times to do him. He don't like tough names. You ought to try something peaceful. Something sweet."

This was too much. Charlie glared at her. "Sweet! Now, that takes the cake! This ain't no lady's palfrey. This here is a steed. A war horse. He wants a manly name."

"Pshaw. You're the one wants a manly name for him."

He turned his back on her. "You don't know what you're talking about. Now get out of here before I whop you."

She wasn't bothered. She hopped down off the fence with a chuckle. He could no longer see her, but he could hear her plain enough. "I'm telling you, Charlie Boy. He wants to be called something like Sugarplum."

Charlie rolled his eyes. Sophronia reappeared over the top of the gate, her bare toes curled over a low slat. "Hello, Sugarplum," she cooed. The horse pricked up his ears. Sophronia reached one hand toward the animal's nose. "Come over here and let me love on you."

Charlie gasped, half expecting the horse to bite the girl's hand off. Instead he nodded his big head up and down a couple of times and moved up close enough for her to rub his forehead. "Why, you're just a cuddle pie, aren't you? Yes, you are, you sweetie. You've had enough manliness to last you, haven't you? Well, don't you worry, I'll come by every day and hug you and bring you sweet potatoes and carrots and, and, and, an apple. How about that, mother's little darling?"

Charlie's mouth flopped open as the gelding leaned in to Sophronia's petting and gave a contented huff. For an instant he was dumbfounded, but his amazement transformed in a blink to wild indignation. The finest horse he ever had or was likely to have loved a freckle-faced, frizzy-haired eleven-year-old girl with big teeth better than it did him. Charlie had lavished all his attention and care on that beast for more than a year and Sophronia had never done a thing in the world for him but talk to him in baby-talk. Was there no justice in the world? Was there no reward for devotion? It wasn't right. It wasn't fair.

He emitted a bellow that encompassed all his rage and heartbreak and flung the curry brush at the gate, not really intending to hit his sister, but determined to drive her off. The brush hit the gate hard enough to ricochet and smack him in the shoulder. The horse shied and Sophronia dropped out of sight again. Her laughter taunted him. The sound of her voice receded as she ran out of the stable. "I'll be back, Sweet Honey Baby!"

Chapter Twenty-six

"Pack up your troubles in your old kit bag
And smile, smile, smile."
—World War I marching song
lyrics by George Asaf

After breakfast and chores, Phoebe, John Lee, and their children, along with Mary, Chase, and Judy met at Alafair's house so that the whole family could go to church together. The rain had stopped so the children and Mary and Phoebe piled into the back of Shaw's quilt-lined hay wagon. Gee Dub and Charlie followed alongside on horseback, and John Lee sat on the bench with Alafair and Shaw, since his stiff leg made it difficult for him to sit on a horse gracefully.

No one commented on Kurt's absence. He told them that he had too much work to do if he wanted to get the co-op's order for pork filled in good order, and he figured God would forgive him. The truth was that he had lost faith that his neighbors would still be able to see him as a man like themselves rather than a native son of the ravening Fatherland. Mary, however, was dead-set on going. She had been part of this community almost all of her life, and she was blessed if she was going to let anybody make her feel like an outsider.

After Alafair had wrangled the children into their Sunday clothes and plaited and re-plaited so many braids that she lost count, she set out to find Rob. She found him sitting in a chair at the edge of the front porch, a cigarette in his hand and four dogs arrayed around his feet.

She sat down on the porch swing. "Robin, I'd be pleased if you'd come to church with us."

His mouth quirked, and he flipped ash over the side of the porch. "Sister, the last thing y'all need is to be seen in the company of a Wobblie."

"Nobody around here knows you," she said, "except for kin. And I don't believe any of Shaw's brothers and sisters know what you do. Even if one them did, they wouldn't say anything."

He felt a passing pity for her naiveté. "Oh, somebody knows and somebody will blab. That is, if word isn't all over town already. Believe me, it's best not to be seen with me. Shaw's hired men will find something for me to do."

"Robin, I want you come, now." She sounded determined. "I won't introduce you to anybody if you don't want me to. Church will do you good, and if you don't believe it, then you going to church will do me good. Please, Robin. Do me this favor."

Rob felt himself weakening. He had no good opinion of religion, but if it would make his sister happy…

He crushed the butt under his toe and scraped it off the porch with his boot. "Oh, all right. But don't say I didn't warn you."

Rob climbed into the wagon among much merriment from the children, and they headed out. As they reached the road, Grace began to sing one of her favorite songs to Tuck, and soon everyone joined in the family anthem:

Old Dan Tucker was a mighty man
Washed his face in a frying pan
Combed his hair with a wagon wheel
And died with a toothache in his heel.

Gee Dub trotted beside the wagon on his chestnut mare, Penny, singing along. But Charlie was having trouble controlling his white-maned roan, who skittered hither and yon, tossing his head and generally making a nuisance of himself.

When the horse fell behind the wagon, Sophronia hung over the tailgate and called out over the singing. "Hey, Sweet Honey Darlin', come on up here to Mama, come on up for a nice nose rub and a kiss!"

The roan settled at her voice and nosed her hand with a "whuff." He gave Charlie no more trouble for the rest of the trip, but Charlie felt like strangling Sophronia with one of her own pigtails.

Chapter Twenty-seven

"Compassion will cure more sins than condemnation."
—Henry Ward Beecher

Shaw's mother and stepfather lived in a pale gray two-story house on the outskirts of town. The house was bigger than Alafair's house by far, and only two people officially lived in it. Which didn't mean it wasn't always full to bursting with children and grandchildren and great-grandchildren, either visiting or spending the night or a week or a month. Peter McBride raised apples, pecans, and Tennessee Walkers, and a month under his tutelage was worth a semester of agricultural college.

Shaw pulled the wagon to a halt in the drive and everyone piled out to help Grandpapa Peter and Grandma Sally get ready to go into town.

The boys hitched the horses to Peter's four-wheeled carriage while Shaw and Rob hauled out a crate of apples destined for Khouri's Market and loaded it onto the tailgate. Inside the airy parlor, Grandma Sally directed the females to fetch and load boxes of old clothes and quilts for the clothes drive, and jars of fat for the war effort. Before heading out the door, Alafair waited as Sally stopped in the foyer to crown herself with a feathered and beribboned hat.

"So your scandalous socialist brother Robin has come to visit." Sally's comment was offhand, but there was a bubbling quality to her voice that indicated she was delighted by the fact. "My, it has been years since I've seen him."

Alafair was shocked. She had just assured Robin not half an hour earlier that few people had any idea of his politics. "I didn't know you ever heard about him and the union, Ma."

"Well, of course. Your mama writes to me right along. He joined up with the I.W.W. right after the Army, didn't he? That was a long time ago."

Alafair hadn't considered the fact that her mother and Shaw's mother were friends. "Well, given the times, we've decided to keep quiet about it while he's here. He didn't want to come to church this morning but I talked him into it. I hope I didn't make a mistake."

Sally dismissed her concern with a wave of the hand. "Oh, don't worry, honey, I ain't going to talk. How is he? He looks good."

"I think he's pretty wore out. I hope while he's here he'll get rested and maybe decide to pursue a different livelihood."

Sally laughed at that. "I wouldn't count on it if I was you. I remember what a hard-headed tyke he was. Did he ever make up with your daddy?"

"No." There was no more to say about that.

"Sorry to hear it, for your mama's sake." Sally adjusted her bonnet and ran a hatpin through the crown. "Well, let's get to going."

One large covered basket sat apart near the front door. Alafair bent to pick it up, but Sally stopped her.

"I'm not taking that one today, sugar. It's just a passel of vegetables from my truck garden. I'll deliver it tomorrow."

"Who's it for?" Alafair asked the question idly. "Josie?" Sally often exchanged goods of all sorts with her eldest daughter.

Sally regarded her reflection in the small mirror beside the front door. "No, I'm taking a few things to Rose Lovelock and the other poor creatures who must toil in such cruel circumstances."

For a moment Alafair had no idea what she was talking about. Sally McBride had been raised by her Cherokee mother and white father in the deep woods of Arkansas, and had a wildly different understanding of reality from most of the ordinary people Alafair knew. It was not unusual for Alafair to have to take a moment to get her bearings with Sally. Her first thought was who is Rose Lovelock? But as she uttered the word "who's", the light dawned.

Sally's sharp black eyes were gazing at Alafair's image in the mirror. Her expression was amused and not a little ironic. "Close your mouth before you eat a fly, Alafair."

"You mean those harlots in the house at the end of Kenetick Street?"

Sally turned to face her and broke into a grin. "I'm surprised you even know such a place exists, honey."

"But, Ma, what if somebody finds out you've been talking to those fallen women?"

"I'm careful about when I go by there. Besides, I ain't planning to tell any of our upstanding neighbors about it. Are you?"

Alafair's eyes were so wide that it almost hurt. "Gracious, no! Does Grandpapa know what you're up to?" She cast a glance toward the door to make sure none of her children were close enough to hear this shocking conversation.

Sally raised a warning finger. "Now, Peter don't have to know everything I do and I don't expect you to tell him. Or Shaw neither. Don't make me sorry I told you, now."

"Oh, of course not, Ma. But why on earth would you associate with those women? Is this your way of bringing them the Lord's word in hopes they'll change their ways?"

Sally hung the basket of loaves for the food drive over one arm and threaded the other through Alafair's. "I've always thought that women are too hard on each other, shug. We have enough trouble with men and their foolish notions about how things ought to be. We don't need to be so mean to one another. Now, let's go before the fellows wonder what we're up to."

Alafair dug in her heels, unwilling to drop this sensational bit of information. "Wait a minute, Ma…"

Sally cut her off. "I'll tell you later how this all came about. But don't be so quick to judge, darlin'. If you heard some of those poor girls' stories you'd have more compassion for them. Just think about how folks judge your brother and they don't even know him or why he is like he is." An impish smile lit her face. "Maybe you should come with me to Rose's next time I visit."

Alafair's stomach flipped at the thought. "Oh, my," she managed, before Sally dragged her out the door.

Chapter Twenty-eight

"No Conscription! No Involuntary Service!"
—Army veteran Bruce Rogers,
anti-draft pamphlet, 1917

Rob couldn't remember the last time he went to church. Most likely the last time he had visited a relative and couldn't get out of it. Rather like today. Since he had converted to the socialist philosophy, he found it hard to accept the doctrine that poverty and class differences were God's will.

The congregation was abuzz with the news that Win Avey had been found murdered that very morning. Scott was not at church since he was transporting his prisoner to Muskogee. Deputy Trent Calder was there, though, and was the center of attention. The circumstances of Avey's death were whispered around—a brawl with a draft-dodger. Still, the fact that the brawl had occurred at a brothel was of more interest than the victim's politics.

Rob enjoyed himself more than he had expected. He met Martha's husband, Streeter McCoy, and Alice's, Walter Kelley, and liked both of them very much. He also met Ruth's beloved, Trenton Calder, tall, thin, and sincere, and so redheaded that it was startling. Rob could tell by their attitudes as they shook his hand which of his nieces' menfolk knew his background and which did not. Walter Kelly was so hail-fellow-well-met that he either knew nothing or didn't care. Streeter McCoy greeted him warmly but gave him a speculative once-over, reserving judgment for the moment. Trenton Calder looked at him like he was itching to clap him in irons, but gave him a firm handshake and a nod, determined to be civil for Ruth's sake.

Rob loved singing the hymns from his childhood, and he enjoyed the sense of community that bound a group of like believers. When the preacher gave his fiery, guilt-inducing sermon, Robin took the opportunity to catch a quick nap. At the last 'amen,' he awoke refreshed and still in a good mood. He allowed Alafair to introduce him to some of her neighbors as the parishioners filed out of the sanctuary, but managed to escape before the preacher made his way down the aisle.

Afterward, he leaned against the wall of the First Christian Church, in the back of the building where the autos and buggies were parked and waited for Alafair and Shaw to round up their children for the trip home. He intended to smoke his gasper in peace, but before he could finish, two men he didn't know came striding toward him with a will.

His half-smoked cigarette was pinched between his finger and thumb, and he watched the men's purposeful approach with trepidation, fearing either a lecture on the duties of a patriot, or Christian witness for the benefit of his soul.

One of them was a little guy, mostly Indian. He was young and good-looking, in clothes that had seen better days and were none too clean, rather like their occupant. He had a stiff brush of black hair and black eyes that shone with zeal. The other one was tall and lanky, middle-aged, with stringy blond hair and a permanent scowl.

The duo came to a firm halt in front of Rob. "You Rob Gunn?" The older man spoke first.

"I am, neighbor. What can I do for you?"

"We've been looking for you. I've heard your name before. Is it true that you're a union man and a socialist?"

Rob's heart sank. So much for remaining incognito. He felt for the cosh in the front pocket of his trousers, just in case. "I am, friend. But I'm not here on union business. I'm just passing through long enough to visit some of my folks." He kept his tone mild and non-confrontational.

His accoster nodded and glanced around to check for eaves-droppers. His young companion spoke up. "My name is Dick Miller, from down around Pottawatomie County, and this here is Dutch Leonard. He lives just east of town, here. I'm with the Working Class Union."

"And I belong to the I.W.W., same as you," Leonard said. "I work over to the brick plant. Friend of mine with the I.W.W. office in Tulsa told us that there was a national rep here in Boynton. Dick and another fellow and I come here yesterday to try and find you."

Miller leaned in and slipped Rob a handbill. "All the folks around here from the W.C.U. and the Oklahoma Socialist Party will be having a secret meeting next week to plan a way to stop this country from hauling honest men off to fight in this damn war against their will. I'm hoping you'll go down to our encamp-ment with me, and confab with us on behalf of the I.W.W."

Rob blinked at him. This was not what he had been expecting at all, though it occurred to him that he shouldn't be surprised. Oklahoma was full of unionists and socialists. Not all of them would have abandoned the cause the minute the war began. He slipped the handbill into his vest pocket. "What do you expect I can do, Brother Miller?"

"Talk to us," Miller said. "We want to know what plans the Wobblies have to stop this draft madness in its tracks. We want the I.W.W. behind us when we rise up. Lend the strength of the I.W.W. to our cause, Brother."

Rob flipped his cigarette into the dirt. "Come on, Brothers. Let's take a stroll."

The three men wandered away from the hall. They were well down the road before Rob spoke again. "So a few fellows from the W.C.U. have a plan to get us out of the war."

Miller was alight with enthusiasm. "More than a few fellows, Mr. Gunn. They's hundreds of us. And not just Working Class

Union members, neither. All the tenant farmers of every color, and Holy Rollers and us Injuns and ever man that ever had to work for a living. Why, near to the entire state of Oklahoma is a'gin the war, and I reckon most of the rest of the country is, too."

Rob gave Miller a sidelong glance. "You think so? What newspapers have you been reading, Brother?"

"I don't need to read no papers, Brother Gunn. I got ears and eyes, don't I? I hear what my neighbors are a'saying. And I'm here to tell you that we aim to stop this damned war that them criminals out East has thrust upon us."

Rob clasped his hands behind his back and kept his eyes on the road. He expected that Miller didn't "read no papers" because he couldn't read at all. "And just how are you aiming to do that, Brother Miller?"

"We're aiming to rise up and take over the government. We're a'going to start by blowing up the railroads and the bridges and taking over the banks and the newspapers. Then, we're going to march east, all the way to Washington, and all the working men betwixt here and there will join up with us until we're stronger than any Army. And when we get to Washington, we'll hang all them rich brigands that call themselves the government and take it over ourselves."

Rob addressed the older man. "What do you have to do with this?"

"I told Dick I'd help get the I.W.W. behind them, if I could."

"And when is this uprising supposed to happen?"

"Upon our signal," Miller said. "We're almost ready to go. Maybe next week."

Rob stopped walking and turned to face the men. "Have y'all thought this through? Are you prepared for what will happen if you take up arms against the United States government?"

"We'll do what we have to do to take back the United States government for the people." Miller was straining forward eagerly, thrumming with passion. "And besides, we won't fail!"

Rob stood still and gazed at the eager face and the face set with grim determination for a long minute before they turned around and started walking back toward the church. "You say this meeting is secret?"

"It is," Leonard replied.

"How do you know that I'm not Secret Service?"

Leonard snorted in derision, but Miller looked stunned. "I heard you was a Wobblie organizer and a right well-known one."

"Well, I don't know about well-known, but I'm a Wobblie, all right. If you intend to keep this plan secret, then I suggest you be more careful about who you go to blabbing to about it. Next time, ask to see a union card."

Miller emitted a nervous laugh. "Shoot fire, don't go to scaring me like that, Brother. So are you telling me that you won't join our cause?"

Rob's gaze slid off into the distance and they walked in silence for a while. Finally he shot Miller a narrow glance. "When is y'all's next meeting?"

"We put out a call for all right-thinking folks to come out and join us at our meeting place next Saturday," Miller said.

"Will you send somebody to carry me in?"

Miller grinned. "You bet!"

"Will you let me talk to y'all before you commence this march to Washington?"

Leonard nodded. "That's what we're hoping for."

"Then I'll wire the I.W.W. regional headquarters for instructions. Give me a day or two. I'd rather not send the wire from Boynton. If they give me the go-ahead, I'll come. How can I get in touch with you?"

"Send the wire from over at Morris," Miller said. "When you get the answer, leave a message for 'Mr. Jones' at the post office there. Just say yes or no. If it's yes, I will meet up with you after the Liberty Sing on Friday and we'll make arrangements."

Dutch Leonard lowered his voice. "Try to keep yourself on the down-low until then, Brother Gunn. There was a spot of trouble last night at the local bawdy house and one of our number got hisself arrested. Our boy's a good fellow, but if Sheriff Tucker has got him to spill that the W.C.U. is in town, he'll be on the lookout to arrest as many unionists as he can find before Friday."

Rob frowned. "Brother Leonard, I've been watching out for myself longer than I care to say. I warn y'all to do the same."

Chapter Twenty-nine

"Eat More Fish. They Feed Themselves"
—U.S. Food Administration poster, 1917

After church, Shaw gave his permission for Charlie to spend Sunday afternoon on the banks of Cane Creek with Rob and Gee Dub, but the price Charlie had to pay was to include Sophronia. Sophronia was delighted, Rob was cheerful, Gee Dub was amused, and Charlie accepted the stipulation with as much good grace as he could muster.

It had rained a bit, but stopped shortly after dinner. By the time the four of them stretched out on an old blanket next to the bank and arranged their poles in the water, puffy, rain-laden clouds were scudding across a bright blue sky, driven by a fresh breeze. Branches of spindly sassafras, pin oak, and locust, still wet from morning showers, overhung the bank, and with every breezy burst, fat droplets of water rained down. To protect them from the intermittent spray, Rob rigged a lean-to out of a horse blanket propped over two long sticks with rocks on one edge. Bacon complicated matters by sniffing around in the wet undergrowth, then vigorously shaking off his wet coat in their direction before flopping himself down between the bodies on the blanket.

Sophronia, who had ditched her Sunday frock for a pair of Charlie's outgrown overalls, baited all four hooks with night crawlers and staked the poles in the muddy bank. The males were content to let her take over the fishing enterprise with just an occasional teasing word of advice. Eventually they fell into a desultory conversation.

"How much longer are you going to be here, Uncle Robin?" Charlie asked.

"Not much longer, cowboy. A few more days yet."

Gee Dub was reclining on the blanket with his hands behind his head and one ankle crossed over his knee. He appeared to be asleep, his hat covering his eyes, but he wasn't missing any of the conversation. "How come you're not up on the stump while you're here?" he asked. "You could do some satisfying recruitment for the I.W.W. around these parts."

Rob adjusted his position and didn't answer for a moment. "Well, Gee, don't think I haven't ruminated on it. Y'all have some good organizations around here, active too."

"So why…?" Charlie began, but Rob anticipated his question.

"I don't want to take advantage of your folks' good nature, sport. What I do ain't exactly popular with the powers that be, you know, especially right now. I admire your daddy and mama. I don't mind bringing the house down on my own head, but I'd just as soon not worry your folks with it."

"Everybody around here knows our folks and what they believe in, Unc. The neighbors aren't going to think that your Red thinking has rubbed off on Daddy." Gee Dub's delivery was deadpan, but Rob could hear the hint of teasing in his voice.

Rob didn't laugh. "You'd be surprised what the neighbors might do, Gee. I've seen men turn on each other like rats for more unlikely reasons than having a Wobblie in the family."

"That don't seem right," Charlie said.

Rob's eyes crinkled. "You know what they say, pal. Lie down with dogs, get up with fleas."

"You being the dog we're lying down with."

"That's right. Your neighbors are entirely like to think that the old nasty flea of unionism will jump on anybody who gets near me."

They were interrupted by Sophronia, who had grown tired of staring at the corks bobbing in the wind-ruffled water and rushed back up the bank. She threw herself down on the blanket between Rob and Gee Dub. "What are y'all talking about?"

The two men eased themselves over enough to give her some room. "Mr. Woodrow Wilson," Rob answered, "president of these here United States of America."

"We studied the presidents in school."

Charlie was annoyed at the change of topic. "Fronie, nobody cares about that. We're talking about important stuff…."

Rob held up a hand. "Well, now, wait a minute, slick. Presidents are important stuff. What did you learn about presidents, sugar plum?"

Sophronia made a face at Charlie before she replied. "I learned that Teddy Roosevelt was president when I was born."

Gee Dub lifted his hat off his eyes and winked at her. "Why, that's right! Fancy you remembering that."

She elbowed Gee Dub in the ribs. "Who was president when you were born, Uncle Robin?"

"I had so much on my mind on the day I was born that I didn't think to ask, Fronie. But later it came to my attention that Rutherford Birchard Hayes was in the White House at the time."

"How about you, Gee?"

"George Washington."

Sophronia sat up straight, indignant. "You'd have to be more'n a hundred years old!"

"Why else do you think Mama and Daddy named me after him, then?"

"You're not named after him!"

Charlie forgot his impatience for a moment and sputtered a laugh. "What did you think Gee Dubya stands for, then?"

Sophronia gasped. "Gee Dubya!"

"The light dawns!" Gee Dub exclaimed.

"Oh, Gee!" Sophronia jumped on her brother and tried to pummel him, but he held her off with one hand as she flailed the air in front of his face. "No kidding, now! Who was president when you were born?"

He was enjoying her ineffectual attempt to get at him. "I don't remember. I was just a baby at the time. You figure it out. You're the president expert."

She quit struggling and rolled back onto the blanket. "Let's see, now. Washington, Adams, Jefferson, Madison … oh, never mind! This is boring."

"At last!" Charlie threw up his hands. "Go check the lines again and quit bothering us."

Sophronia stood and flounced off, her long, reddish, damp-frizzed hair streaming behind her and the wet hound close on her heels.

Charlie turned back toward Rob. "Are you a traitor?"

Rob blinked at him, taken aback by the sudden mood shift. "Well, now, Charlie, just because I disapprove of this war don't mean I'm a traitor. I think of myself as a patriot, and a patriot of the real kind. This is my big, messy country. I love it. I want for it to be the best country there is. If it suffers ills, I want to cure them. I want for every citizen to enjoy all its rights and privileges, and I believe it is my duty to try and help that happen."

"But who are you to decide what's right, Uncle? If the president says it's so, don't he know best? We can't all be running off in all different directions. We'll never get anywhere that way!"

Rob sighed. "Charlie Boy, that's for every man to decide for himself, and woman too. In this country we're free to think whatever we determine is the best thing to think. At least I hope that's still the case."

"I'm volunteering as soon as I turn eighteen. I just hope this war don't end before I can get into it and kill me some Huns."

"That so? You'll have to have your mama and daddy's permission to enlist before you're twenty-one. You think your ma is eager to see you go get your yourself killed?"

"My parents won't stand in my way, nor Gee Dub's way either. Tell him, Gee. Tell him how you're going to show 'em a thing or two."

Gee Dub sat up and wrapped his arms around his knees. He gazed at Rob for half a minute before nodding toward the knife hanging in its sheath from Rob's belt.

"I been meaning to ask you, Unc. Where did you come across that Arkansas toothpick, there?"

Rob was more than willing to change the subject. "What, this little old pig sticker?" He pulled it out of the sheath to reveal a slightly curved, single-edged, six-inch blade.

Charlie sat up straight, instantly diverted. "Whoa!"

"I got this from a young fellow name of Buck, up in Washington state. He makes them out of old rasps. I never had a knife that held an edge better than this one. I use it for everything from dressing game to peeling peaches to shaving my fair and tender cheeks as smooth as a baby's bottom, when shave I did. Not only that, this here buck knife has got me out of more than one skinny situation, and I've amused myself on many a lonely night on the road by playing a game of mumbledepeg with it, or carving works of art or flutes from a handy stick."

The boys were laughing when Sophronia made her way back up the bank toward them. She stood and looked at them quizzically for a moment, aware that something was up. Rob looked up at her and smiled.

"You get a fish, popover?"

She shrugged. "Fish ain't biting, boys. They've all gone to the bottom."

"Honey bun, why don't you go ahead on and pull in the lines?" Rob said. "It's time we got home, anyway."

The males stood to gather up their gear while Sophronia returned to the fishing poles. They had just taken down the lean-to when a light rain began to fall. They exclaimed and pulled their hats down, and Charlie hurried down the bank to throw a half-dry blanket over Sophronia's head and relieve her of the poles. She came at a run, enshrouded in the blanket head to toe, and punched Gee Dub in the arm. "Grover Cleveland!" she yelled.

Chapter Thirty

*"Is there aught we hold in common with the greedy
    parasite*
Who would lash us into serfdom and would crush us
    with his might?
Is there anything left to us but to organize and fight?
For the union makes us strong"
          —"Solidarity Forever," I.W.W. anthem
          by Ralph Chaplin, 1914

Supper was over and the children were scampering around the yard trying without much success to capture lightning bugs in a jar. Charlie, Blanche, and Sophronia joined the little ones and soon they were gathered around in a circle listening to Charlie tell scary stories by the illumination of half a dozen lightning bug lanterns.

"Charlie, if them young'uns can't sleep tonight, you're going to have to let them crawl into bed with you," Alafair called from her seat on the front porch. The night was warm and sticky, punctuated by the loud whirr of cicadas. Alafair, Shaw, and Rob were arrayed across the porch in kitchen chairs, watching the children play.

No one said anything for a while, content to watch the youngsters. Alafair fanned herself with a dishtowel. Eventually Rob rolled a cigarette and lit it up. The flash from the match roused Alafair enough to turn her head and regard her brother's shadowy figure on the chair next to her.

"You heard from Mama and Daddy lately?' she asked.

Rob took a drag and gently exhaled the smoke into the air before he answered. "Not for a while."

"So you aim to see the folks any time soon?" Alafair could tell Rob didn't want to talk about their parents, but she wasn't going to let him off the hook.

"Sure would like to. I'd like to visit with Mama, at least."

"You haven't been home in close to a dozen years, Robin. I'm sure Daddy would like to see you, as well."

She heard him chuckle. "I doubt it, Sis. Neither one of us has changed our opinion on how the world ought to be run."

Shaw finally offered an observation. "Y'all are too alike. That is the difficulty. Neither one of you will bend an inch."

"Why, I take exception to that remark, Shaw. I never did try to foist my beliefs off on Daddy. Always did my best to keep my thoughts to myself when I was in his presence. But he won't be content unless I bow to his superior wisdom in all things and agree to each and every point of his philosophy."

Alafair smiled. Rob's assessment of their father's attitude was right on the mark. "Daddy is just old-fashioned, Robin. He was taught that it is his duty as a father to guide all us children down the path of righteousness. Wag your head up and down and say, 'yes, Daddy,' a couple of times and peace will be restored."

"I ain't a liar. I won't pretend to ascribe to a doctrine I don't believe." Rob's tone was sulky.

Alafair and Shaw exchanged a glance. Too alike indeed.

Several tykes pounded up the steps and clamored across the porch in a noisy game of chase. Zeltha, currently "it," took shelter under her grandfather's chair and was promptly set upon by her pursuers. Shaw joined in the game by shifting his arms and legs to keep the children from tagging their prize, much to the merriment of the participants. Zeltha's brother Tuck, just beginning to walk, was stuck at the bottom of the steps and loudly voicing his displeasure at being left behind.

Alafair stood and beckoned to Rob. "Mercy! Come on, Brother, let's take some air and leave these ruffians to their brawling."

They strolled away from the house and into the woods with the old shepherd, Charlie Dog, wagging along at Rob's side.

"That old dog likes you," Alafair observed. "That bespeaks well of you. He has a sense of how folks are."

Rob rubbed the silky ears and was rewarded with a wet nose to his palm. "I liked your sons-in-law, Sis. Seems like the girls all picked well."

"Mostly they did."

Her tone caused him to slide her a glance. "Oh? I get the feeling that at least one of them don't meet with your approval."

She shrugged. "Well, Alice could have done better, I think. But then not everyone has the same requirements for husband as I do. He seems to suit Alice. Now, tell me the truth, Robin. What have you been up to, and what really brings you here after all this time?"

"Well, Sister, I'm wounded that you would think I have a purpose other than a long-held desire to reconnect with my kinfolks."

"Oh, I'm sure that figures in to your calculations." Her tone was more than a little ironic. "But after church I saw you talking to Dutch Leonard, who makes no secret of his anti-government views. So unless you've changed right down to your heels since last I saw you, there must be some wrong that needs righting around here and you think you're just the man for it."

Rob had fallen behind as they wound through the pin oaks, Alafair doing the talking as they strolled. When he didn't respond to her jibe, she glanced back over her shoulder.

He had stopped and was studying his boots, hands in his pockets, a thoughtful look on his face.

"Robin?"

He looked up. "Alafair, I've spent most of my life fighting for the working man, and in spite of the awful abuse I've endured and seen other men endure, I've seen a lot of progress, too, when it comes to the rights of the downtrodden. But this war has changed everything, and I'm afraid we're going to lose everything we've fought so hard to gain."

His sudden declaration of despair almost brought tears to her eyes. Robin had always been full of fire and fight when it came to his principles, and so sure that what he considered right would prevail in the end. She shook her head. So many start out with a burning yen to make the world a better place, and it is always a bitter disappointment to realize that it can't be done. "Brother, you can't change the world. You can only change what's right in front of you, and sometimes not even that. But I'm sure you've helped many a man find dignity in his work."

Rob's laugh was bitter. "I'd just like to help more than a few men find wages enough that their families don't have to live like dogs."

"Well, why would anybody work at a job where they don't make enough to live on? They ought to quit and find a better-paying position."

Rob blinked at her naiveté. "Sorry to say it don't work like that, Sis."

"Oh, honey, I wish I knew something to say to make you feel better."

"I know you do. That's why I'm here. Even if you don't agree with my beliefs you never have desired to shoot me for them. It does me good to spend a little time in the company of decent, good-hearted folks for a change."

"I wish you'd give up this dangerous life. It'd break my heart if you got yourself killed. It'd break Mama's heart, too, and Daddy's, make no mistake. No matter how much y'all have butted heads over the years. Don't go back to the union. Stay here. Let me fatten you up a while. We'll find you a good wife. You must be lonesome all the time, flitting hither and yon without a place to lay your head."

"You tempt me, Alafair. But I can't quit. Like Dad always says, keep fighting the good fight. Somebody's got to do it and I reckon it's me." He sounded sad about that. Yet he perked up when he said, "But I'm right happy to let you fatten me up a mite."

Chapter Thirty-one

"Remember the Maine
To Hell with Spain!"
   —Spanish-American War slogan, 1898

While Robin and Gee Dub were making their way to the shed for the night, Alafair was raking out the stove and preparing it for breakfast in the morning. She had just wiped the ashes off her hands when she noticed Charlie leaning on the doorframe, clad in his nightshirt and ready for bed. His arms were crossed over his chest and his head cocked to one side as he gazed at her with a speculative expression.

She started. "Gracious! You gave me a start. You could have offered to tote in the kindling for me rather than stand there like a post, you know."

His lips twitched. "I might have, if you hadn't already done it, Ma."

Alafair dashed the ashes off of her hands. "Something on your mind?"

"Uncle Robin is younger than you, ain't he, Mama? How old is he, anyway?"

She carried the ash bucket to the back door and set it on the floor before she answered. "Oh, let's see, he must be close to forty now! Can that be?"

"Why is it that him and Grandpa Gunn don't get along?"

She sat down at the table, prepared to tell her brother's story to her son, and perhaps to remind herself of why Robin was the way he was. ""Well, honey, he's the oldest boy in my family, and Grandpa kind of hoped that he'd go into the ministry. But from his first breath, Robin has gone his own way. He has sunny ways but he's just marched to his own music from the moment he was able to hoist himself up onto his own two feet. Robin has high principles, but he has never taken to religion in any way that suits our daddy. It's all very well to help the poor, but Robin does carry things to the extreme. Every man's trouble is his own, and every man don't have to be white, or Protestant, or respectable. Or a man."

"That's a good thing, ain't it?"

Alafair's expression didn't change, but there was a glint in her eye. "I reckon Jesus would think so, but your Grandpa Gunn has his own ideas on how things should be gone about."

"I remember that he was in the Army, first time I ever knew anything about him."

"Oh, mercy, that was a right old set-to when he enlisted. He just up and joined when he was about twenty without so much as a by-your-leave. I thought the folks would both have an apoplexy. But he was off to help the poor set-upon Cubans gain their freedom from Spain, and he never came back to live in Arkansas again."

"How long was he in?"

"Five or six years, I reckon. Never did get to go to Cuba, either."

"And he never married?"

"Married only to his causes."

Charlie's questions depressed her a bit, and she didn't really know why. Probably just bringing up all kinds of childhood feelings. How she had always loved Robin. He had been a stubborn and inflexible child, but quite good-natured about it. Like Charlie, she realized with a pang. She had spent much of her youth trying to act as a buffer between Robin and their father, though Robin didn't seem to care whether his father approved of him or not.

After all this time, she expected that Robin and Elder Robert Gunn would never see eye to eye. That fact grieved her, because even though Robin was unconventional in the extreme, he lived his principles in a way most people could not.

Alafair realized that Charlie was speaking to her, and put her reverie aside. "What's that, honey?"

"I said, I like Uncle Robin, but he's dead wrong to talk against this war, and I wish he wouldn't do it. It's unpatriotic, not to mention that he's like to get arrested. He gave her a sidelong glance, worried that she might not take kindly to such harsh criticism of her brother, but her mild expression of interest encouraged him. "I hate to say it, Ma, but I'd just as soon not get tarred with the same brush that he's going to."

"Charlie Boy, I don't think anybody in all of Oklahoma is going to take you for a pacifist. Now quit standing there in the door in your nightshirt and go to bed." She turned back to her chores, troubled. She was wishing that she hadn't told him the story of Robin running away to join the Army. Charlie had a disturbing tendency to act first and think later.

Dear Charlie, full of life. Energetic, impish, funny, and desperate to keep up with his adored older brother. Always on the lookout for action. But in spite of his tendency to trouble his mother with his headstrong ways, Charlie had a great heart and Alafair loved him to distraction. In fact, if someone had threatened to drown all her grandchildren if she didn't choose, she might say that as much as she adored every one of her offspring, Charlie was her favorite. Whether he liked it or not, there was nothing she wouldn't do to save him from rushing headlong into trouble.

Chapter Thirty-two

*"The brick industry has made rapid strides in
Oklahoma…and the opportunity it offers for
profitable investment of capital can hardly be
equaled…"*
—*Oklahoma Almanac and Industrial Record*, 1907

The Francis Vitric Brick Company, located less than a mile
northeast of Boynton, backed up to a range of small hills that
were rich with an excellent quality of clay, perfect for making
a sturdy, durable brick for paving and building. A spur of the
St. Louis-San Francisco railroad line that ran through town
reached up to the plant like a finger. Several times a week an
engine hauled boxcars full of finished brick destined for the
Army training camps that were springing up all over the country.
Some Francis bricks would even travel to Europe for the use of
the French Army,

Charlie had been curious about the plant since he was a tad,
and had always wanted to go onto the grounds and have a look.
But he'd never been able to convince his father that it was a good
idea to ask for a tour. Charlie knew that the two enormous,
solid brick towers that could be seen from the road were used
for an overhead crane. He could hear the roar and grinding of
machinery when he passed. He was acquainted with the steam
shovel operator, Mr. Frasier, a friend of one of his uncles. Maybe

he'd try to have a word with him if they crossed paths. Charlie would love to have a go at operating the giant steam shovel that excavated the clay from the hill behind the plant.

Charlie's first day at work was a full shift, so his introduction to wage earning was something of a baptism by fire. Literally, since Charlie was put to stacking bricks fresh out of the kiln, alongside a young man from Texas by the name of Henry Blackwood, who had only been at the plant a few days himself. The newcomers were under the supervision of Jack Cooper, a hefty, dark-visaged man with more muscles than Charlie had ever seen on a single individual. In spite of his intimidating appearance, Cooper was a mild-mannered and indulgent overseer who spent quite a bit of time giving his young worker advice on the proper way to lift and transfer pallets of brick. Back and legs, back and legs, as much as you can, and save your arms.

When the whistle blew for lunch, Charlie and Henry moved away from the long kiln in hopes of picking up a breeze, and flopped onto the ground beside the rail spur. In spite of Jack Cooper's good advice, Charlie felt like the bones in his arms had liquefied, leaving nothing on which to hang his trembling muscles. He could barely lift his lunch bucket to examine the contents. He glanced at his companion, hoping that Henry's condition was as alarming as his own.

If it was, Henry didn't show it. "I packed me up some of the squirrel stew with dumplings that my uncle made last night. I miss my ma's cooking. Eric isn't a very good cook, but this is tasty!" He looked up at Charlie with a grin. "I swear I could eat a rhinoceros!"

"Me, too. I'll tell you, I'm going to have arms like tree trunks by the time this war is over."

"I hope you won't have time to develop those tree trunks, Charlie. I'd just as soon the war would come to a speedy and honorable end and Mr. Ober won't have need for extra hands."

Charlie almost missed the comment. The slab of pie that his mother had placed on top of his lunch had captured his attention. He had taken a bite before it dawned on him what his companion had said. "Are you against the war, too?" He tried not to sound accusatory.

Henry's blue eyes widened. "I hope no person of goodwill wants war."

Charlie sighed. "Well, no…" he said, though he wasn't entirely sure he meant it. "But it wasn't our fault that we had to get in it."

Henry's gaze slid away and he shrugged. "I hope it's over soon, whatever it takes. I did register for the draft so if my number gets called I'll go if I can. Though when I tried to volunteer they wouldn't take me because I got the asthma."

Charlie gave his companion a critical once-over. Henry was a good-looking young man, tall and well grown, older than Charlie by maybe eight or ten years. "You afraid of getting shot?" Charlie asked.

Henry didn't look up from his squirrel stew. "Naw. I been shot at before. I just don't fancy living in a mud hole for months on end with a passel of overripe soldiers." He shot Charlie a sly glance. "Of which I would directly be one."

"Who shot at you?"

Henry shrugged. "Some Mexican. Sometimes the Mexicans like to take a little target practice across the border. Or maybe some drunk Texican. Who knows? It was just a rough Saturday night in Brownsville. A bullet whizzed by my ear and I hit the dirt. Never did know where it come from. Didn't have my name on it, though."

"You ever shoot back at the Mexicans?"

"Sometimes. They don't much like us gringos, and us gringos return the favor." Henry didn't sound overly concerned that citizens of the two countries made a habit of taking potshots at one another. "I think America should be more worried about Mexico than Germany, though. They're a lot closer and hate us a lot more. I don't think Germany wants to tussle with us."

If there was anything Charlie loved, it was arguing about the war. "Well, then why—?"

Henry did not feel the same way about debate. He cut Charlie off. "Hey, what do you think about old Win Avey getting his throat slit like that?"

He could not have chosen a better topic to distract Charlie. "Ain't that something? My ma says Avey was always knocking heads with somebody and it's no surprise that he came to a bad end."

"He worked here, you know. He was one of the supervisors on this very shift. My uncle is of the same mind as your ma, that Avey was a scoundrel."

"He was a Council of Defense man, though," Charlie said. "And I heard he was starting up a branch of the Knights of Liberty around here. So it's mighty suspicious what happened to him. Scott thinks he ran afoul of the socialists and they killed him. He got in a fight with one of them the very night before he died."

"So is Sheriff Tucker kin to you?" Henry seemed more interested in Charlie's familiarity with the lawman than in Win Avey's demise.

"Yeah, he's my dad's cousin. His daddy and my grandpa were brothers."

Henry grinned. "So y'all must know all the dastardly deeds that happen around town and who all did them."

"I wish we did, but Scott plays it close to the vest. Besides, we live so far out in the sticks that sometimes I think we're the last to hear anything."

"Sometimes it makes life easier if you don't know what's going on."

"Is that why you came up here to nowhere from all the action in Texas? So you wouldn't have to know what's going on?"

"Well, young'un, I came up here because, like I said, I probably can't get into the service, so my uncle Eric Bent said he could get me some useful war work here at the brick plant." Henry's tone was teasing, but Charlie took the hint.

He felt his cheeks heat up. "Sorry. I didn't mean to act like I think you're a slacker."

"You can't tell a fellow's situation just by looking at him, Charlie. You never can tell but what he's making some important contribution to the war effort in secret."

Charlie's eyes lit up. "Wouldn't that be crackerjack? To be a secret government agent on the lookout for fifth columnists here in America? Or to go over to Europe and be a spy?"

"Might end up on trial for your life that way, like poor old Mata Hari." The exotic dancer was still on trial for espionage in Paris, but according to the sensational accounts being published in the papers, her prospects for acquittal were dim.

Charlie's bottom lip jutted out. He liked the look of Henry Blackwood and had hoped to make a new friend, but Henry seemed to enjoy making sport of everything Charlie said. Henry caught the look of hurt that passed over the younger man's face, and he gave him a friendly clap on the shoulder. "I don't mean nothing. It's just my way to josh with my pals. I'm a mite put out because I can't get into it like all the other fellows my age. But we do what we can, don't we?"

Charlie's mood lifted and he smiled. "We sure do, Henry. We do whatever we can."

◇◇◇

"Hey, is that Charlie Tucker?"

Charlie wiped the sweat out of his eyes and turned around to see who had called him. Billy Claude Walker was passing by the clay pit on his way to the machine shop. Charlie gave him a wave.

Billy Claude grinned. "Why, it sure is! Nice to see one of your bunch working a proper job for a change."

"Just doing my bit for the war effort," Charlie called.

"I figured you for a German sympathizer, what with that krauthead your sister married. Glad I was wrong."

Charlie's mouth dropped open, blindsided by the comment. He glanced at Henry, who was shoveling clay into the dump car alongside him. Henry glared at Billy Claude. "Leave the young'un alone, Walker," he hollered. "He ain't the only person in the world with a German in the family."

Charlie found his tongue. "Kurt can't help where he was born, Mr. Walker. He came to this country to get away from Germany. He's a loyal American now."

Billy Claude laughed. "A loyal American, is he? Well, we'll see about that. Enjoy your digging, boy!"

Henry stabbed his shovel into the dirt and straightened. "You don't need to defend your kin to the likes of him," he said in an undertone.

Charlie nodded, but didn't reply. He went back to his digging, his good mood gone.

Chapter Thirty-three

"The fine and noble way to kill a foe
Is not to kill him; you with kindness may
So change him, that he shall cease to be so;
Then he's slain."

—Charles Aleyn

The beans were about to take over Alafair's truck garden. The warm, dry, summer had produced a bumper crop of beans of every ilk. The pole beans were so prolific that they were pulling the vines down off of the stakes. Blanche and Sophronia were crawling along the rows, on their knees among the vines, harvesting beans and piling them into bushel baskets while Alafair finished hanging the last of the Monday wash on the line. Chase Kemp and Grace were there, too, though whether they were helping the girls in the garden or not was a matter of interpretation. Alafair had put them to picking beetles off the bean plants and drowning them in kerosene. If their loud expressions of delighted disgust were any indication, they were enjoying themselves very much. Alafair picked up her empty clothes basket when Sally McBride drove up in her carriage and hollered at her from the drive. Alafair walked over to the fence, a bit worried. Her mother-in-law seldom just turned up without a good reason.

"What's going on, Ma? Is somebody sick?"

Sally grinned down at her from the driver's seat. "Don't look so worried, honey. Nothing's wrong. Remember the conversation we had at the house on Sunday? About the folks I take food to every once in a while? I can tell by how your eyes are about to pop out that you do. Well, I'm on my way over there right now and I figured to take you along."

"Oh, no, I couldn't." Alafair's insides shrank at the very thought. "We've got to get these washtubs put away before I start dinner. Besides, I couldn't leave the little'uns here on their own…"

"Alafair." Sally interrupted her in mid-ramble. "It's two hours before you have to start dinner. You have plenty of hands for the task and we won't be gone more than an hour. Blanche is old enough to keep these ruffians in line for that long."

Alafair climbed up into the buggy, but only so she could protest in an undertone. "Ma, why are you wanting me to do this so bad? Why, it'd be awful if we were seen to consort with such types. What would everyone think?"

Sally was five feet tall and round as a dumpling. But anyone who crossed her soon regretted his mistake. She drew herself up. "Alafair, the Pharisees asked Jesus why he was keeping company with criminals and prostitutes. And he said, did he not, that it was the criminals and prostitutes who needed the grace of God and not the righteous people? Well, I don't aim to let the judgments of the Pharisees in town get in the way of doing a small good deed to our local criminals and prostitutes. And I don't want you to do so, either, if I can help it. These are human women, sugar, who have fallen as low as they can go. How can it hurt to show them some kindness?"

Alafair bit her lip. What could she say? That she had to live in this town? That her actions would reflect on her children, and she'd do anything to keep from causing them grief? What if she was seen and she had to explain to her family what she and Grandma were doing talking to a bunch of whores?

Sally was regarding her with keen black eyes, waiting to see which way Alafair would jump. Alafair didn't want to pay a call on a passel of soiled doves, not even as an act of Christian charity. But even more, she didn't want her beloved mother-in-law to think less of her.

Sally's expression softened. She could tell that Alafair was weakening. "You don't have to speak to any of them. You don't even have to get out of the carriage. I always put the top up and come up the back way around town. Nobody will see."

"You promise we'll be gone less than an hour?"

"Less than an hour." Sally's eyes crinkled with amusement. "Even if I have to throw this food basket into the yard as we gallop by. Come on, honey. It's good for your soul. You'll see."

"But look at me. I'm in my washing clothes and have soap on my sleeves. Let me take off my apron and change my hat, at least."

"No excuses, now. You think the girls will turn up their noses at your outfit? Besides, you ain't even going to talk to them, remember?"

Alafair's resistance collapsed in the face of the juggernaut that was Sally's will. She climbed down long enough to charge Blanche with keeping her siblings on the job while she and Grandma ran a brief errand. Grace whined to go along, but Alafair refused with such force that she dropped the subject and hastily resumed drowning bugs.

Sally turned her horses onto the section road and headed toward town at a breezy trot. The two women rode in silence for a time, Sally secure in the rightness of her path and thus happy as a puppy with two tails. But Alafair was bitterly ruing her decision to go along with this ill-considered errand.

They reached the main road, but instead of turning right into town, Sally turned the carriage left and drove north for a quarter-mile, until she reached a rutted farm path that circled around Boynton to the east. Alafair shrank back into the seat when they passed in sight of a farmhouse, but they saw no one.

Alafair finally ventured a comment. "I cannot imagine what would drive a woman to a life like that, not to mention run a business that shames others of her own sex, some of them barely girls. Why has Scott never closed down her institution?"

Sally kept her eyes on the road. "I asked him the same question not long after she came to town. He said that she's real protective of her girls and runs a clean house. He told me that for years there was a similar establishment out in the country, south of town. Did you know that?"

Alafair's eyebrows shot skyward. "No, I didn't." She wasn't surprised that none of her men had mentioned that fact to her, but there weren't many women in town who would have kept that titillating bit of information to themselves. The minute Rose's place opened last year, churchwomen of all denominations had sent a delegation to the mayor to demand that the fallen women be immediately run out of town. The mayor and town council had promised to consider the problem, but nothing had ever come of it.

Sally continued. "Rose was one of the girls at the old place. The previous bawdy house was a den of iniquity, according to Scott. It was run by a devil of a woman called Star Karsten who used her strongman to keep her girls in line, then she robbed them of their shameful wages on top of it. Finally she got stabbed during some big dust-up at the house. The woman didn't die, but never quite recovered, either. I reckon when she closed down, Rose saw a business opportunity."

"Well, why does he let her stay and not that other woman? I don't care how nice she treats her poor girls, that's a horrible life for them."

Sally shrugged. "Scott seems to think that if it ain't her, it'll be someone worse."

Alafair wasn't going to accept that explanation. "But why must we have such a place here at all? What about our children?"

Sally chuckled, amused at Alafair's righteous indignation. "You'd better ask the town council about that, hon. I blame the men. As for the women, who knows? Rose has had a pretty sad life. Don't judge her without knowing what drove her to it."

Alafair was feeling cautiously relieved as they drove up the dirt path that ran along beside a few houses at the edge of town. Just before they reached the turn to Kenetick Street, Sally guided the carriage into a wide drive behind a plain, two-story clapboard house that edged up to an empty field. She reined at the back door just as an enormous Negro man came down the steps to greet her. He offered her a hand down and a big smile. "Hello, Miz McBride. Nice to see you."

Sally retrieved the basket from the backseat and passed it to him. "Hello, Dave. I brought y'all some dried apples, a sack of pecans, and a few loaves of fresh bread to go with the extra jars of jam I had in the pantry. Is Rose up and about?"

Dave was eyeing the jam jars with anticipation. "Now, ain't that nice? Thank you, ma'am. Last I seen Miz Rose was at the breakfast table. I'll tell her you come by."

Alafair's eyes were glued to the back door, where an attractive if somewhat frowsy older woman stood at the screen, watching. She was clad in a dressing gown and holding a tea cup in one hand. The expression on her face was anything but welcoming.

Sally was aware that she was being watched. Before she stepped back up into the carriage, she nodded at the woman. "Good morning, Rose. Hope y'all enjoy the eats."

"We don't need your charity, Miz McBride," Rose said.

"I know you don't need charity, Rose, so just think of it as a neighborly gift."

Rose made a disparaging noise and disappeared back inside as Sally turned the carriage and headed out.

She snapped the reins and the horses picked up the pace. "See, now, Alafair, I told you this trip wouldn't take but a blink."

Alafair was aghast. "Why, Ma, you made me think that you and that Rose woman were best of friends. She didn't appreciate your charity a bit, or that a respectable woman would even speak to her, much less bring gifts!"

"Nobody likes to be pitied, Alafair. Besides, the Lord wants us to try. He don't care if we succeed."

That gave Alafair pause. She mulled over the sentiment in silence long enough for Sally to make the turn onto the road north of town. "How did you come to meet that woman, Ma?"

Sally clicked her tongue at the horses and they picked up the pace. "Do you remember Gertrude Bent? No? Well, she was a real nice woman who used to belong to my ladies' sewing circle. She got the cancer and I went by regular to sit with her and bring food so her and her husband wouldn't starve. Her house is right across the lane from the brothel. Rose's place looks like any other house during the day, so I hadn't even given it a glance. But then once while I was visiting, Rose and a couple of her girls came over to look in on Gert. They brought a real pretty wool blanket for her since she was always cold. Rose took one look at me and left, but the two sporting girls walked right in and made themselves at home. They were bawdy, all right, but I liked them for the way they teased and joked with Gert. After they left Gert told me that they had all kindly looked after her ever since she got sick, and several of them had told her their stories. Even sinners can be kind. So after Gert passed on, I resolved to try and be kind myself, for I expect them women don't get much kindness in their line of work."

"But she doesn't even appreciate what you're doing, Ma. You could become a subject of gossip if word gets around. Why do you insist on taking food over there to them if they don't need it or want it either?"

Sally emitted a derisive *pfft*. "I'm too old to care what anybody thinks, Alafair." That seemed to be the end of the conversation, but not long after Sally turned the carriage off the main road toward Alafair's place, she said, "You know that after Shaw's daddy died, me and the young'uns were left in bad spot."

"Yes, I know it."

"I had six children under twelve, one just weaned. Jim had taken out a loan to buy ten more acres of hillside for logging. He wasn't cold in the ground before the bank called in the loan. I had the cabin and yard, and fifty acres of woods. I could have found a buyer if the bank had given me time, but I think old

Plummer, the banker, smelled an opportunity, so he foreclosed. I was in a bad way. Jim was gone and all those babies and I hadn't had time to take a breath. I was left with the cabin and yard, but no means to make a living."

As Alafair listened to her mother-in-law's story, she felt a chill envelop her heart. "You don't mean to say that you…?"

Sally shot her an amused glance. "I did not, honey. You can be at ease. Jim's brothers and sisters came to my rescue. But I know only too well how fast a woman can be left with no options. In fact, in the course of my long life, I've known many good people who have been driven by circumstance to do an evil thing. I long ago decided that I should be kinder with my opinions and to leave judgment in the hands of the one who knows a sinner's heart."

"Are you trying to make a Christian out of her?" Alafair could understand that motive.

Sally disabused her. "No. I'm trying to make a Christian out of me."

"But she wouldn't even come out and say hello!"

"No, not yet. But I haven't given up on her. Besides, me and Dave and a couple of the girls have got to be friends."

They were home by this time, and the instant Sally pulled up in front of the garden, a gaggle of children tumbled out the gate and ran to meet them, all talking at once.

WhereyoubeenwhycouldntIgoChaseateabugIdidnotMaItried togethimtowegottwobushelsMadoIhavetohelpstringthebeans…

Alafair climbed down to adjudicate. Sally laughed and glanced at the sun. "I told you I'd have you home right quick," she said over the chatter. Alafair only had time to give her a wave before Sally circled the drive and headed out.

Chapter Thirty-four

"Hear, my son, your father's instruction,
and forsake not your mother's teaching,
for they are a graceful garland for your head
and pendants for your neck."
                                            —Proverbs 1:8-9

Alafair saw Charlie coming from the kitchen window and had time to chip a handful of ice from the block in the top of the icebox before he made it into the house. His face was red from the heat. She handed him the glass. "How was your first day as a brickmaker, son?"

Charlie hung his hat on a hook by the back door and flopped down at the kitchen table. His mother was cooking and it was hot in the house. He wiped his forehead on his sleeve. "It was good, Ma. Most of the fellows on my shift are swell. Mr. Cooper put me with another new man by the name of Henry Blackwood. You know Eric Bent who lives in town? Henry's his nephew from Brownsville. He's a good guy."

Alafair made a surprised sound. She had never heard of the Bents before, and yet today they had been brought to her attention twice.

Charlie went on. "It was hard work, though. I thought I was pretty strong, what with all the hay bales and newborn foals I've toted, but shoveling clay all day will plumb wear you out."

Alafair watched him gulp down the tall glass of iced sweet tea. "Now, if the job is too much for you, you don't have to be doing this, you know."

He set the glass down and Alafair refilled it from the pitcher. "It's not too much for me, Ma. I just have to get used to using a different bunch of muscles, is all. Besides, I'm doing my bit for the war effort."

"But all the mules your daddy raises and trains are for the war effort, Charlie. I don't understand why working for Mr. Ober at the brick plant is so much more patriotic than working for your dad."

Her comment irked him. She just would not believe that he was smart enough to make his own decisions. "I can do both," he said. It came out sharper than he intended, and Alafair drew back, stung.

Charlie had surprised himself with his tone. He was about to say something conciliatory when Gee Dub appeared at the back door.

"There you are," Gee Dub said. "I thought I saw you ride up. You'd better turn your horse out and head on up to the stable. Dad and Uncle Robin are bringing in those mules we've been working with. Captain Worley from Fort Reno is coming tomorrow to look at 'em, and Dad wants to clean them up and put them through their paces once more before he shows up."

Charlie stifled a moan. He had no intention of letting his parents see how tired he really was. He straightened and shot his mother a defiant look before he stood. "I'm on my way, Gee."

Gee Dub pushed his ancient flop-brimmed black Stetson back off his forehead with his thumb. "Slug down that tea and come on along then. I'll help you with the roan and walk up to the stable with you."

The boys were down the steps and walking toward the roan before Gee Dub said, "What's eating you, Charlie Boy?"

"Nothing. What makes you say something like that?"

"I heard you snap at Mama. That was uncalled for. She's just worried about you trying to take on two tasks at once."

Charlie stopped walking, his irritation bubbling up. "She treats me like a baby and I'm tired of it, Gee. She don't treat you like you ain't got a brain in your head."

Gee Dub laughed, which didn't make Charlie feel any better. "She don't treat you like a baby any more than she does the rest of us, knucklehead. I've never known her not to fuss over us, each and every one."

Charlie raised his hands to his hips and studied his boot tips. "Dang, I know it, but it does get on my nerves. I reckon I'm in a bad mood because old Billy Claude Walker gave me a hard time about having a German in the family. If I thought he was teasing that would be one thing, but he was pretty mean about it. And I heard that he's taken over for Win Avey on the Council of Defense."

"I hope you stuck up for Kurt."

"Of course I did, but I didn't like having to do it. It's not fair. Kurt chose to be an American. He can't help where he was born."

"Durn right."

Charlie looked up, his forehead wrinkling. "What if Billy Claude finds out about Uncle Robin? Will we get in trouble for harboring a Wobblie? Maybe Dad ought to talk to Scott about it."

Charlie's attitude disturbed Gee Dub more than Robin's leftist tendencies. "Don't go borrowing trouble, now. Let Mama and Daddy worry about Uncle Robin and you mind your own business. Let's get that horse unsaddled."

Chapter Thirty-five

"I.W.W. and pro-German Activities in Tulsa,
Oklahoma and Surrounding Territory Coming to the
Attention of the Tulsa County Council of Defense."
—*The Daily Oklahoman*, 1917

Scott and Trent had just finished the soup and cornbread that Hattie Tucker had packed for their lunch when John S. Barger, the duly elected sheriff of Muskogee County, came sauntering in to the jailhouse.

Scott could count on one hand the number of times the county sheriff had been to Boynton. As a rule, Scott went to Muskogee to see the sheriff, usually for the monthly meeting Sheriff Barger held at the Muskogee County Courthouse for all the constables and undersheriffs in his jurisdiction. Since it wasn't anywhere near election time, Scott and his deputy were surprised by his unannounced visit.

Scott jumped up and held out his hand. "Howdy, Sheriff," he said. "What the heck are you doing out in this neck of the woods?"

Barger returned the greeting, nodded at Trent, poured himself some coffee, sat down, lit a pipe, and asked Scott about Hattie and the boys. He made innocuous small talk until Scott finally asked him what it was he didn't want to say. "You're sure going round and round the mulberry bush."

The sheriff laughed and placed his coffee cup on the desk. "Well, this does have to do with monkeys and weasels, I reckon. I got a wire from your local Secret Service agent, Mr. Emmanuel Clover."

"Oh?"

"Seems he thinks you're not as diligent as you ought to be when it comes to enforcing the Espionage Act."

Scott grew still. "That so?"

"Says you ain't keeping an eye on aliens living around town, and you're looking the other way when folks talk against the war."

"I can't say as I've heard anybody talking against the war now we're in it."

Barger ran a finger over his impressive mustache and adjusted his fedora. "You have at least one German-born fellow who lives around here?"

Scott felt a thrill of alarm and struggled not to show it. "Well, yes, if you're talking about who I think you're talking about. But he's an American citizen and I'd trust my life to him anytime. He's married to a relation of mine."

Barger pondered this bit of information, and nodded. "Clover says you have some other people in town who have kin in Germany? Any resident aliens?"

Scott's forehead furrowed. "You're joshing me, aren't you, John? I don't care if somebody ate sauerkraut yesterday. That don't make them traitors."

Barger pulled a piece of paper out of his jacket pocket and shook it open. "Who's this Robert Gunn? This letter says that one Robert Gunn, a socialist agitator, was seen in the vicinity recently." He looked up. "Believe me, ever since this American Protective League thing started, I've seen plenty of people try to get even with their neighbors for some scrape they got into twenty years ago, so I don't usually pay much attention to this kind of thing. But the other day I got a note from Sheriff Duncan over in Pontotoc County. His spy inside the Working Class Union says there is a large group of draft-resisters gathering outside of Sasakwa. Says that a I.W.W. agitator who was deported from Bisbee is known to have bought a ticket to Muskogee after he was released from detention."

Trent, who was sitting in the corner in bug-eyed astonishment, exclaimed something unintelligible.

Scott spat out an oath. The next time Emmanuel Clover crossed his path, he was going to wring his chubby neck.

The sheriff tamped down his pipe, put it between his lips, and re-lit it. "Clover also says he saw your wife sell a sack of flour at the Mercantile on a Wednesday."

Scott's mouth flopped open. "You mean to tell me that you come all the way over here from Muskogee because my wife sold somebody a sack of flour on Flourless Wednesday? Now that's the damnedest thing I ever heard in my life. In the first place, last I heard these food and gasoline restriction were voluntary, and in the second place, my wife, Hattie, is as straight as they come. She follows the Food Administration's guidelines to the letter, and if anybody casts dispersions on her patriotism in my hearing I'll pull his lungs out and make balloons out of them!"

"Hang on, pard'!" The sheriff raised his hands in surrender. "No need to get yourself all tied up in a knot. I take everything I hear with a pretty big grain of salt. Now, I don't know this Clover fellow, or what his reasoning is. I just figured you ought to know what kind of over-enthusiastic fellow you've got on your hands. He can stir up some trouble for you if he's a mind to. Judging by some of the directives I've been getting out of Oklahoma City, the government is apt to throw dissenters in jail first and sort out the legalities later. So if I was you, Scott, I'd be walking pretty ginger right about now, especially since it seems everybody Clover fingered is kin to you in some way. Might want to have a word with some of these folks, let them know that it'd be in their best interest to toe the line a little closer."

Only somebody who knew Scott as well as Trent did would have been able to see how Barger's warning had affected him. The skin over his cheeks was pulled so tight it looked as though the bones were going to cut right through. But somehow his tone of voice was entirely pleasant when he answered the sheriff.

"Thanks, John. I appreciate it that you made the trip in person to tell me this. I'll sure think about what you said. Now, why don't you come along home with me for some dinner and catch me up on all the war doings in Muskogee?"

"I appreciate it, Scott, but I was just on my way down to Council Hill to pick up a felon they got locked up in a chicken coop. I figured I'd take a detour so I could put a bug in your ear about this Secret Service man you got on your hands."

Scott walked to the door with Sheriff Barger and let him out. He stood without a word for a long while, watching out the front window, until the sheriff got into his motor car and drove off south, toward Council Hill.

When Barger was completely out of sight, Scott turned and faced Trent. "Damn!" he spat.

"Why didn't you tell him about Rob Gunn out at your cousin's place?" Trent asked the question even though he knew why. You don't rat on family.

Scott gave Trent a sour look. "Trent, I've known Rob Gunn from when he was a little shaver living in the same town as me over in Arkansas. If he's been agitating, I haven't heard about it. Don't see any point in making a problem out of no problem."

Even as he explained his reasoning, Scott was reaching for his hat. "I'm going out to Shaw's place to have a word with Rob Gunn. Hold down the fort, and if Emmanuel Clover strolls by, go out and knock him three ways to Sunday for me.

Chapter Thirty-six

*"Join the Red Cross.
All You Need is a Heart and a Dollar"*
—American Red Cross recruitment poster, 1917

Martha McCoy could hear a persistent pounding coming from the back of her mother's house. She pulled open the screen and stepped into the parlor. "Hey, Mama!"

The pounding didn't stop as Alafair's voice greeted her. "I'm in the kitchen, honey."

Martha paused in the kitchen door. Alafair was standing at the big table, assaulting a piece of meat with a mallet. "You getting ready to fix dinner?"

Alafair finally forbore from pulverizing long enough to wipe her brow with her apron tail and smile at her daughter. "I've got a bit of this round steak left. Thought I'd fix it up for your daddy's dinner. I am glad to see you, honey, but I sure never look for you to travel all the way out here at this time of day. You want to stay and eat?"

"No, Mama, I have to go to a special Red Cross meeting in a bit. I just decided to stop by on my way over to Mary's."

"Oh, I'm sorry! I don't see enough of you these days. You want to say hey to your uncle while you're here? I think he's in the stable with your daddy."

"No time today, Ma." The hammering started again as Martha seated herself at the end of the table. "I heard a thing from Streeter last night that concerns Uncle Robin, and I thought I'd better tell you before you get wind of it somewhere else."

Alafair hesitated and looked up.

Martha met her gaze. "There's talk that the Working Class Union is planning to make trouble in Muskogee when they draw the numbers for the draft lottery."

"I don't concern myself with those things, Martha."

"You might want to start, Mama. Streeter heard a rumor from one of his clients in Muskogee that the I.W.W. sent someone here to Oklahoma especially to help the anti-draft faction start a rebellion. You know, give them advice and guidance."

Martha's warning gave Alafair a frisson of alarm. "What do you mean by a rebellion?"

"The word is that a passel of W.C.U. tenant farmers and such aim to resist the draft any way they can. Vandalism, sabotage, kidnapping, ambushing lawmen and landowners, anything they can do to create civil unrest." She paused and looked away for an instant before continuing. "I was thinking that it's quite a coincidence that Uncle Robin has shown up just now."

The hair on Alafair's arms stood up, but she leaped to Rob's defense. "Martha, folks shouldn't listen to such claptrap, and neither should you. My brother assures me that he is only here to visit his kin for a short while, and not on any union business. Robin might be a professional rabble-rouser, but he is no advocate for civil war. Besides, he would never do anything to call trouble down on his family."

"That's what I told Streeter." Martha's dark eyes narrowed. "He doesn't know what to believe. Streeter doesn't know Robin, not like we do. Right now I don't think that most in-town folks are even aware that Uncle Robin is here, and even fewer know that he's a union organizer. Streeter thinks that as long as Robin keeps his opinions to himself while he's here, the mayor and the rest of the board won't be inclined to bother him."

Alafair was insulted by the implication. "How big of them!"

Martha bit her lip. "Ma, maybe you'd better have a talk with Uncle Robin. I know he's your brother and you don't want to believe anything bad about him. I'd feel the same way if it was Gee Dub or Charlie. But you don't really know what Robin is like anymore. Maybe it's as you say. I expect that it is. But if he's here for some secret anti-war reason, he's like to bring suffering down on all of us."

"I will. I swear I don't know about folks anymore!"

Martha started to say something, but hesitated. Her expression made Alafair put down her mallet. "What's the matter, honey? Don't feel bad that you told me that. Robin has always been a gadfly. I'm used to hearing wild rumors about him."

"It's not…" Martha began, before her face crumpled. She pulled a handkerchief out of her pocket and wiped her eyes. "It's not just that, Mama. It's this Red Cross thing. I just got a letter from the state office saying that no one with a German last name can serve. I'm supposed to tell my own sister that she can't come to the meetings anymore."

For a moment, Alafair was speechless. Then she was overcome by a blaze of fury. The rage on her face so alarmed Martha that she stood and grabbed her mother's arm before she could dash out of the house with her mallet in hand and stave in someone's head. "Ma! I'm going to fight this. That's why I called a special meeting for tonight. We can't let this stand. Why, Miz Schneberg will have to quit too, and Miz Schmidt from Wainright. I'm sure the other ladies in my chapter will be as outraged as I am. If the state office won't listen to reason, we'll resign and start a war relief group on our own."

Alafair began to untie her apron. "I'm going with you over to Mary's."

"No, Ma, I'll talk to her myself." Martha was firm. "She and I can make our plans. If she wants to talk to you about it later I'm sure she'll be over directly."

Alafair gave in with bad grace, sorry that she couldn't command her grown daughters like she used to. Alafair didn't have Martha's faith in the goodwill of the other women in the Red

Cross chapter. She watched Martha pedal off on her bicycle toward Mary's house, wondering how she was going to comfort both of them when their plans failed miserably.

Chapter Thirty-seven

*"[These days] you can't even collect your thoughts
without getting arrested for unlawful assemblage."*
—Max Eastman, July 1917

Before his cousin Shaw married Alafair, Scott had only a passing acquaintance with the Gunn family. Alafair and her siblings were quite a bit younger than Scott and his sister, so he only remembered Rob as one of the ragtag boys who ran around town in packs. Cheeky, that was the only impression Scott had of the boy. He didn't know the man at all. Rob had the same sharp "I know you" expression in his dark eyes as did his sister, but that didn't mean the siblings held to the same values.

He rode out to his cousin's farm, where Alafair met him at the front door. "What brings you by, Scott?"

Her greeting was so pleasant that he hated to tell her. "Morning, Alafair. Is your brother around? I need a word with him."

The smile fell off her face. "What about?"

"I just got a visit from the county sheriff. Seems word has gotten around that there is a Wobblie in the area. I just thought I'd come out and put a bug in Rob's ear."

"Oh, mercy! Martha was by here this morning and told me something of the like." She pushed the screen door open. "Well, I guess you'd better come in, then." She led him into the parlor and seated him in a corner armchair with a cup of coffee and a piece of molasses cake while Sophronia ran to the fields to fetch Rob. Scott spent fifteen minutes eating cake and playing cat's cradle with Grace before Rob came in. Scott could tell by his expression that Alafair had already filled him in.

Rob took his time hanging up his hat, pulling off his gauntlets, and wiping his sweaty face with a bandana before he sat down across from Scott. Aside from his greeting, he said nothing until Scott had told him everything Sheriff Barger had said.

Rob leaned forward. "Scott, I've hardly left the property these past few days. I don't know anybody around here but my kin. Why on earth would I have any interest in causing trouble for Alafair? There're plenty of other places I can go to get myself arrested."

"Rob, for Alafair's sake the family has tried to keep it a close secret what it is you do for a living. But there are just too many of us around here for it to be a secret for long. And I'm telling you that there are folks all over this county who once they hear you work for the I.W.W. will be very willing to believe that you murdered Win Avey because he's a Council of Defense representative. Or maybe just because he was a brickworker and you want to cause a work slowdown. If there is one thing people know about the Wobblies it is their practice of strikes and slowdowns."

Rob sank back his chair, torn between outrage and an all-too-familiar feeling of déjà-vu. "Well, I ain't been doing any murdering and anybody who thinks so is an idiot," he said. The words came out sharper than he intended and grimaced. "I'm sorry. But it's got so that if you're union, you better get used to being accused of every nefarious act within a hundred miles of you. I know you feel like you have to ask. So I swear to you, Scott, on my mother's head, that I don't have anything to do with whatever has been going on out at that brick plant."

"I doubt you did. Still, on top of everything else, the Muskogee County sheriff has been informed that there is a W.C.U. plot in the state to raise an army and march to Washington to take over the government. And he's also been told that an I.W.W.

agitator has been sent here with the express purpose of egging them on. Your name was mentioned."

Rob's heart fell with a thud. Those tenant farmers were doomed. Still, he brazened it out. No use to blow the game before he had a chance to try and help the poor downtrodden critters. "That's damn unlikely, don't you think?"

"Damn impossible," Scott agreed. "That don't mean a bunch of blockheads who don't have the least idea how far it is to Washington, or what they'd run into even if they did get there, aren't aiming to try. And whether there's some sort of plot going on or not, I've been told that if I get wind of any of these said agitators, especially the I.W.W. agent, I should clap him in irons and send him to the marshal's office in Muskogee."

"So do you intend to clap me in irons?"

"Are you advocating the overthrow of the government?"

Rob laughed. "No. Wouldn't mind to see some changes, though."

"What were you up to before you came out to visit with Alafair?"

"Why do you ask?"

Scott nodded. Rob's unwillingness to answer told him what he wanted to know. "You weren't in Arizona by any chance, were you? Maybe Bisbee?"

"So word's finally gotten around about what happened in Bisbee, has it? That was an illegal action, Scott, them deporting the miners without due course of law before they were even on strike."

"You think that matters? It might be a wise thing if you was to move on at your earliest opportunity. I'd hate to have to try and get between you and a lynch mob."

Rob was not surprised at the warning. He was grateful that Scott didn't throw him in jail on general principle. That was what usually happened. He'd come into some town and start organizing and end up in jail. Or get picked up in the middle of the night, hauled out into the country and left stranded by the side of the road. Or beaten up. This time, he thought about that delicious chicken-fried steak, the little children vying to sit on his lap, the clean, cool, fresh sheets on his bed, and felt very sorry to have to go. The expression of outrage faded from his face. "I'm inclined to agree with you, Scott."

Scott looked surprised that he had caved in so easily. "Well, good, then."

"I'd like to go with the family to the Liberty Sing before I light out, though. Alafair asked me to."

"I don't know about that, Rob. Not now that Clover knows your name. I don't want trouble if I can avoid it."

"I'll keep my head down." His tone conveyed his determination to attend the Liberty Sing whether Scott liked it or not.

Scott was tempted to arrest him and have done with it. But in the end, family loyalty won out. "All right, but you keep your distance from your draft-dodger unionist friends, Rob. Don't look at me like that. I know you've been talking to Dutch Leonard. I'll have my eye on you."

Rob stood up. "There won't be anything to see. Now, I'm going back to work before Shaw misses me. Don't worry about telling Alafair what we talked about. If I know my sister she's got her ear pressed to the kitchen door and heard every word."

Chapter Thirty-eight

"Sabotage is preached to and by the I.W.W at all times, and every member is fully aware of subtle methods of destroying property with a minimum risk to his liberties."
—*The New York Times*, August 19,1917

The family was just sitting for dinner when Charlie came in from work by the back door. He was not alone. A tall, blond young man with a tattered shirt, bandaged arms, and the remnants of a black eye walked in with him. Alafair came over to meet them.

"Mama, this is my friend from work, Henry Blackwood," Charlie said. "Henry, meet my ma. Henry had a mishap at work and Mr. Cooper let him have the rest of the day off. I figured I'd invite him for dinner, if that's all right. It's just him and his uncle in that little house of theirs. I reckon he'd admire a real meal."

Henry snatched off his hat, and Alafair took it from him and patted him on the shoulder. "Sure, sugar. There're plenty of eats to go around." She turned to Gee Dub, who was leaning back on the cabinet with his ankles crossed, looking intrigued. "Gee, pull up another chair."

Gee Dub fetched a chair off the porch and squeezed it in between Rob and Blanche while Charlie and Henry washed up. Alafair had covered the table with platters and bowls of fried okra, yellow squash, biscuits and milk gravy, grits, corn on the cob, brown beans, fried sweet potatoes, and mashed potatoes as well. As always in summer, there were fresh-sliced tomatoes, green onions, and radishes to garnish one's plate. It was a meatless meal, but no one noticed. Only the immediate family was at dinner today. Two parents, two sons, three young daughters, and the uncle. Henry knew he was not going to be able to keep everyone straight—except for the bearded man he was seated next to.

Rob slapped him on the back. He hadn't seen Henry since they had parted ways at the train station. "Well, I'll declare. Fancy meeting you here, sport."

Henry was equally surprised to see his sometime champion. "Howdy, Mister. I didn't know you were kin to Charlie, here."

Shaw reached across Rob to shake Henry's hand. "You two know each other?"

"Yessir. We traveled out on the train from Muskogee together last week. Mr. Gunn helped me…"

Rob interrupted. "That's a tale for another time. So you're working at the brick factory with Charlie. Looks like you've added to your collection of bruises since the last time I saw you, slick."

"It was the strangest thing, Uncle Robin," Charlie said. "Henry's lucky he didn't get killed." He paused in case Henry wanted to tell the story, but his friend seemed more interested in buttering the fluffy biscuit in his hand.

"What happened?" Sophronia urged.

Charlie was only too happy to carry on. "You see, after the clay gets dug out of the hill, it's put in this dump car that gets pushed up on top of these big old trap doors over a conveyor belt that takes the clay to the plant. That's what me and Henry were doing today, dumping the dirt out of the car onto the doors. When the car's empty we're supposed to push it down the ramp and then Dutch Leonard pulls a lever and the dirt drops down onto the belt. Well, today the lever let loose too soon and dumped poor old Henry, dump car, clay, and all into the pit. If the car hadn't jammed the jaw crushers, Henry would have been chewed up into little bits. As it was, it was lucky he didn't bust his legs in the fall."

Alafair's hand went to her throat. "Oh, honey, that's terrible!" Henry looked up from his biscuit. Her concern made him uncomfortable. "Well, I wasn't hurt bad, Miz Tucker. Just skint up a little. I'll be back at work tomorrow. I can't afford to lay off, anyway."

"It sure stopped work for most of the morning," Charlie said. "Dutch swears up and down he didn't pull the lever before time, and Mr. Cooper believes him because it looks like one of the bolts had come out and the lever failed. Mr. Cooper took Henry up to the office and bandaged him up. He put me to stacking bricks for a shipment that's supposed to go out next week. Mr. Cooper figures that it'll take a couple of days to fix the lever and test it out."

"Poor Henry," Blanche exclaimed.

"Yeah, if he had busted his leg he wouldn't be able to work for who knows how long. Mr. Cooper told us that there has been a spate of machinery breaking down lately. Last week there was a fire in the steam shovel boiler that held up digging for half a day. The other night, a wheel fell off one of the kiln cars and bricks spilled all over the middle of the oven. It took a whole shift to clean it up and get the cars moving through again. They turned off the furnace, but I'd have hated to be one of the fellows working in that tunnel on a July afternoon."

Henry's attention was riveted on his plate, his face flushed with embarrassment at the unwanted attention.

Charlie wasn't finished. "You know, Billy Claude Walker thinks somebody is trying to delay production. He said all the accidents started happening after ol' Win Avey got killed. This morning I was wondering to Henry if we've got us a saboteur."

He immediately wished he hadn't said it when he saw the look on Alafair's face. He'd die of humiliation if his mother forbade him to go back to the plant. His father saved him.

Shaw scoffed. "I doubt it, son. Machinery is always breaking down, especially when it's being put to extra use."

Gee Dub changed the subject by asking Henry where he was from, but Rob wasn't listening anymore. He was thinking that if the workers at the plant had a compensation plan, Henry wouldn't be facing ruin because of an on-the-job injury. The brick plant was a prime target for unionization. But he bit his lip and said nothing. He'd notify the regional I.W.W. office, but the workers of the Francis Vitric Brick Company would have to rely on someone else to help them organize. He had promised Alafair.

"Henry, wait a minute. I want a word with you before you get off home." Alafair caught Henry as he untied his horse from the post in front of the house. He doffed his hat as she walked down the front steps with a towel-covered wicker basket in her hand.

"What can I do for you, ma'am?"

"Are you sure you don't want to take some of these vittles home for your supper? I've got enough to feed you and your uncle for a couple of meals and still have plenty of leftovers for us."

Henry hadn't been fussed over so much since he left his mother's house. He quite enjoyed it. "Thank you, ma'am. That is right kind of you. Uncle Eric's cooking keeps us from starving, but that's about all I can say about it."

"I wish you'd let me have a look at them wounds on your arms. I don't have much faith in Mr. Cooper's doctoring skills."

"Oh, no, really, ma'am, that's not necessary. They don't even hurt anymore."

"All right, then." Alafair nodded, glanced away, then back again. Something was on her mind.

"What is it, Miz Tucker?"

"I'm fretted about what's been going on at the plant. Especially after you near to got killed today. Win Avey worked at the plant, too, and he did get killed. Do you think Charlie's right about a saboteur?"

Henry shrugged. "Well, things like that lever failing happen all the time when you're working with big machinery, like Mr. Tucker said. I worked at the shipyards at Port Isabel near Brownsville for a spell. Something was always breaking down or falling into the Gulf or crashing into something else. I wouldn't worry about it none."

"Still, I don't like the idea of him working there if there's a killer on the loose."

She looked so troubled that Henry barely stopped himself from patting her shoulder. "Oh, now, Miz Tucker, I'd bet money that Win Avey's death didn't have anything to do with the brick works. But I hate for you to be worrying about Charlie. I like him. He's a good ol' boy. He's full of vim and vigor. I'll keep an eye on him for you, ma'am. Y'all been so kind to me it's the least I can do."

Alafair let out a breath. She knew she ought to feel guilty for going behind her son's back, but she didn't. "Thank you, son. You come over any time you want. And don't tell Charlie I talked to you. He'd wouldn't be pleased."

Henry laughed at that. "No, ma'am, I reckon he wouldn't."

Old Nick took off his bowler hat and began fanning himself with it. It was a hot day, and all the windows were open at Mr. Ober's office at the Francis Vitric Brick Company. "Mr. Ober, I think you need my particular know-how to deal with your recent troubles. I've been keeping the peace at private companies since God was a boy. Union-breaking is my specialty."

Ober was unconvinced. "I've added on a whole new shift to try and get this blasted order out to Fort Bliss on time and I've put guards on all the machinery to keep another 'accident' from happening. Why should I need a professional head-buster?"

His question raised a hint of a smile on Nick's face. "Believe me, I've dealt with unionists enough to know that you ain't going to be able to persuade them with gentle reason."

"I don't need to be dealing with work slowdowns right now, nor sabotage, which is why I'm talking to you," Ober admitted. "I'm not adverse to a bit of strong-arm persuasion, but I don't hold with murdering strikers either."

"You're the boss," Nick said. "I'll do it however you want."

Ober leaned his elbows on his desk, folded his hands under his chin, and stared out the window to his left for a long moment. Nick fanned himself with his hat.

Finally the plant manager sat back and dropped his hands into his lap. "When can you start?"

Chapter Thirty-nine

"I Am Public Opinion
All Men Fear Me"
—World War I poster,
U.S. Office of Propaganda

The Boynton Post Office resided in the last building on the west side of Main Street, just at the junction of Main and Third, where downtown Boynton segued into residences, an odd business or two, and a couple of churches before petering out into farmland. The post office consisted of one twenty-by-twenty-foot room divided in two by a counter, behind which was a wall covered with wooden cubbyholes, each neatly labeled with a name. To the right of the front door, a long table sat beneath the window. A bulletin board to the left of the window was covered with wanted posters containing mug shots of some disreputable-looking fellows, along with physical descriptions and a list of their sins. There was no telling what color the walls were painted, for the rest of the available wall space was taken up by a display of war posters.

The propagandizing had begun modestly, with a single poster urging all citizens to be patriotic and not waste resources. But lately the postmistress had made it her mission in life to see that that every propaganda message the government issued found a place on the wall and remained there for the duration:

a poster of a slavering ape in a pointed German helmet with the body of a limp child clutched under its arm; exhortations to join the Army, the Navy, the Red Cross; to sign the Food Pledge and the Loyalty Oath; to save sugar, corn, wheat, dairy, meat. A declaration that wasting food was "the greatest crime in Christendom" (which Alafair seriously doubted). It all made for a colorful, rousing, and rather frightening wallpaper effect that gave the viewer a dizzying feeling of doom, and yet diluted each individual message.

Today Nadine had cleared a space over the counter for a new poster. Alafair walked over for a better look, curious, since Nadine had gone to such trouble to be sure the message stood out from the others. A tall, muscular, young woman in a filmy gown strode forward, her outstretched arm pointing at the viewer, her face taut with purpose. Stitched on the brim of the cap covering her blond curls were the words *I Am Public Opinion*. Underneath her feet, the caption read :

ALL MEN FEAR ME

Chase Kemp was fascinated by the cubbyholes behind the counter, but when Alafair and Grace walked over to study the new poster, he asked, "What's it say?"

Grace imitated the icon's stance and scowl. "All men fear me!" she intoned. Alafair looked down at her, surprised. All those endless hours that Grace and Sophronia played school were paying off. Grace danced away and back before she looked up at Alafair, black eyes wide. "Why do all men fear her, Ma?"

Alafair hesitated an instant, composing an answer that would satisfy a four-year-old. "Because she's a tattletale."

Grace clapped her hands on her hips, her expression disapproving. "That's not very nice."

"No, it isn't, punkin."

The door to the sorting room in the back opened and Postmistress Nadine Fluke appeared behind the counter. "Oh, howdy, Alafair. I'm sorry to keep you waiting. Hello, Miss Grace. Chase

Kemp! I see you eyeballing my mail slots. Come around here and pull out your auntie's mail."

Chase practically fell over his own feet running around the counter. While the boy retrieved the mail from the cubbyhole marked "Tucker, Shaw, West of town," Nadine leaned across the counter on her elbows, eager for news. "How's things, Alafair? Lots going on in town these days. Has Scott arrested any spies or black marketers lately?"

Alafair couldn't help but smile. Nadine was an incorrigible snoop, and never failed to ask her what inside information Scott Tucker might have spilled to his kin. Alafair had assured her many times that Scott was pretty tight-lipped, even with relatives, but Nadine never gave up hope. The likelihood was that Nadine knew more about what Scott was up to than Alafair did.

"If he has, Nadine, I haven't heard about it. I have heard, though, that the government is watching over foreign-born people more than the rest of us. And…and someone told me that back in California, folks with German names are getting beat up and burned out for no other reason! It's an awful thing, scaring people that haven't done anything."

"I expect folks' blood is just up," Nadine said, "so you can't really blame them. Only foreigners have had any trouble. You know some night riders trampled Miz Schneberg's truck garden the other night. Left a sign tacked to her front door saying she ought to go home."

"Poor old Miz Schneberg!"

Nadine shrugged. "Well, she does talk funny."

Alafair had always liked Nadine, and more than once had found her to be a valuable source of information that she couldn't have discovered any other way. But her attitude sent a shock of anger through Alafair. "I don't think just being born in some other country means you deserve to have your property destroyed and be scared half to death for no reason, Nadine."

"Most foreigners are probably innocent, you're right." Nadine was either unaware of or unaffected by Alafair's sharp tone. "But they say that the Germans have been planting spies here in the

U.S. since 1914, 'cause they knew we'd eventually get drawn into it. Now, you just know there's somebody, even here in little old Boynton, sending secret messages back to Hindenburg. Maybe the vigilantes are pointing out the enemy for us. Maybe they know something that we don't know."

Alafair gaped at her. Nadine knew perfectly well that Alafair had a German-born son-in-law, yet she either hadn't made the connection, or she didn't care what effect her words were having.

Grace piped up, eager to join in the conversation. "I don't have to fear her, Miz Fluke!" She pointed at the poster.

Nadine leaned over the counter for a better view of the little girl. "And why is that, young lady?"

"Because only men have to fear and I'm a girl!"

The comment gave Chase a moment's pause. His eyes appeared over the countertop. "Do I have to fear, Aunt Alafair?"

"You don't have to fear anything, honey. Now hand me the mail and let's get going."

"Ma!" Grace shrieked, just as Chase said, "I didn't do nothin'!"

Alafair jerked around in the buggy seat and withered the guilty party with a look. "Chase Kemp, sit down before I pinch your head off. Y'all be quiet."

The children shrank into their seats in chastened silence and Alafair turned back around to see that the buggy was just coming up on Kenetick Street. On an impulse that she couldn't explain to herself, she turned west.

Chase made a surprised noise, but was too recently quashed to ask where she was going.

Alafair couldn't have told him, anyway. A detour. Kenetick was a long street, with some businesses close to town, thinning out into residences and small farms. She drove the buggy nearly to the edge of town, where the dirt street turned back north before it could peter out into a weedy field.

She knew very well that unless she went out of her way, she would probably never run across Rose Lovelock again. They lived in different worlds. What she couldn't understand was why did she want to run across Rose Lovelock again? Sally's behavior toward the fallen woman had gotten under her skin. The fact that her mother-in-law wanted to interact with Rose as one human being to another was one thing, but Sally had said that she had no agenda for doing so. She wasn't trying to save Rose or change her. She was just trying to be kind.

Sally's attitude had brought Alafair up hard against her own shortcomings. Alafair did judge Rose and her girls. She was afraid to have anything to do with the women, even for charity's sake. She did very much care about what other people thought of her and her family. That was the wise and practical way to look at it, wasn't it?

Then why did she feel vaguely ashamed of herself?

The big house at the end of the street looked deserted. The front door and all the windows were open on such a warm day, but no one was in the yard or on the porch. Alafair slowed Missy to a walk as she drove by, but there was nothing to see. Rose and the girls were probably still asleep.

"Hey, Miz Tucker!"

Alafair nearly leaped off the seat when she heard her name. She jerked her head around to see Henry Blackwood standing at the gate of the cottage directly across the lane from the bawdy house. She hadn't even realized there was a house there. She felt her cheeks burning. "Henry! You live here?"

He sauntered up to the side of the buggy, his face alight with a grin, and ruffled Grace's hair. "Howdy, children. Yes, ma'am. That is, my uncle Eric lives here and I'm bunking with him for a spell. What are you doing in town, Miz Tucker?"

Alafair pointedly did not look back at the bordello. Henry's little cottage behind the fence seemed like a pleasant place, homey and neat. But because the relationship between the late Mrs. Bent and the working girls, Henry's uncle, and probably Henry, certainly knew what kind of an establishment was operating ten yards from their front door. Of course, Henry probably didn't suspect that Alafair had the slightest inkling, and she wasn't going to tell him otherwise. "A friend of mine lives on this street up near town," she said. That was true. "I figured I'd go home this way just for a change of scenery." That was not quite as true, but it satisfied Henry.

He chuckled. "Well, yonder dried up field of buffalo grass and cockleburs isn't much of a view, but I hope you enjoy it. And now, if you'll excuse me, I'm running late, so I better be off to work. My regards to your family. Goodbye, children." He tipped his hat and headed down the road.

Alafair breathed a relieved sigh and felt a bit ridiculous about it. There was no reason to act like she had been caught doing something unsavory. She had every right to drive down this particular lane. She snapped the reins and turned Missy around the corner.

She nearly ran the buggy off the road when she saw the woman sitting on a stump by the side of the house, dressed in a plain shirtwaist, her face shaded by a straw bonnet. Her head was down and she was clutching her middle, rocking back and forth. Rose—the object of Alafair's fascination.

Alafair jerked the reins and Missy halted with a snort of disapproval and a head shake that jingled the harness.

Rose looked up, startled. Her face was ashen. For an instant their eyes locked, the virtuous woman and the whore. She had been pretty once, Alafair could tell. But her expression was hard as obsidian.

"Are you all right?" Alafair said.

Rose shrank from Alafair's gentle inquiry. "What do you want?"

Alafair was startled by her unfriendly tone. "You look like you're feeling poorly and I wondered if I could help."

"I ain't sick," Rose said. Alafair didn't take the hint and leave. Rose's brows knit, as though she were trying to figure out what strange foreign language Alafair was speaking.

It was such an odd expression that Alafair couldn't decide whether to be insulted or laugh. "I'm Miz Shaw Tucker," Alafair said. "I came by here the other day with my mother-in-law, Miz McBride."

"I remember. Miz Sally has taken to recruiting missionaries from the bosom of her family." Her tone was filled with sarcasm. "What did y'all think you we're doing, coming by and bearing gifts? Trying to make Christians of us with a couple jars of jam?"

Alafair straightened. "No, I'm just trying to make a good Christian of myself." Sally's reason was better than her own.

Rose hesitated at this unexpected response. She regrouped quickly and raised a hand to her hip. "I'll tell you what I keep telling her, lady. Leave me and my girls alone. I guarantee you ain't going to save a one of us."

"Look, Miz Lovelock, I don't reckon either of us is going to convert the other. Now, what is the matter?"

"Nothing that concerns you. Your kin the sheriff come by to ask me questions about the night Win Avey died. I didn't much enjoy the experience."

"Mr. Avey, the Secret Service man that got murdered? Was he a friend of yours?"

The idea caused Rose to laugh. "A friend? I hated him. He was the bouncer for Star Karsten when I worked there, and he was cruel to us girls just for the fun of it. The world is well shet of him."

"But…"

Rose didn't give her a chance to continue. "You better get on before somebody sees you talking to me or my evil influence infects them children."

Almost against her will, Alafair cast a look at the Bent house. Rose was right. It would do her no good to be seen in conversation with a madam. "All right then. Good day."

There was no reply, just a hard stare. Alafair flicked the reins and moved on. They were a quarter-mile down the road when Chase leaned over the seat back. "Who was that lady, Aunt Alafair?"

"Just somebody I know, sugar. We don't need to tell anybody that we stopped by to talk to her, all right? Now sit down."

Chapter Forty

"Are you doing all you can?"
—World War I propaganda poster

Rising at four in the morning, even before his early-rising parents, getting himself the two miles into town, working a shift at the plant, and then coming home and working just as hard on the farm for the rest of the day was beginning to wear Charlie down. Considering the fact that he was sixteen years old and as energetic as a squirrel, that was saying something. Not that he would ever tell his mother and father that. After the fuss he made in the first place, he would just as soon fall over from exhaustion as admit defeat.

By the time he rose from his bed, ate a leftover biscuit, grabbed the lunch pail his mother had packed the night before, saddled his horse and got to work, the sky was light and the sun was just beginning to peek over the horizon.

The white-maned roan never gave him trouble in the mornings. It enjoyed the pre-dawn ride as much as Charlie did, just the two of them on the road in the relative cool before the July heat kicked in. Charlie came up on the brick plant from the south, and could see the buildings from quite a distance, peeking over the fence that surrounded the yard. He usually exchanged greetings with members of the early morning crew straggling up the road on their way to work, preening when someone inevitably complimented him on his fine mount.

He was running a little behind his normal time this morning, and the road was deserted. He urged the roan to a trot and was just passing the outer fence when a movement in the gray light caught his eye. Something almost out of his line of sight. Someone was slipping through an opening in the fence, far at the back of the property where it backed up to the brushy clay hills.

Charlie reined in and squinted into the distance. Had he really seen what he thought he had? It looked like a skinny man in a tan Stetson with a high, uncreased crown. For a moment, he sat on horseback in the middle of the road, wondering if the viscous light of dawn was playing tricks on him. He didn't have time to ponder long. The steam whistle blew, signaling the start of the shift, startling him and causing the horse to sidle. Charlie dug his heels into the roan's side and headed for the gate. I'm getting too chary, he thought. It was probably only a deer.

Work was somewhat frantic that day, and between hauling and loading and packing rail cars, Charlie didn't have time to form any theories about nefarious fifth-columnists sneaking around the plant.

Still, the image of the skinny man preyed on him throughout the shift. When the noon whistle blew, ending his half-day, he found himself watching the men clocking out and retrieving their gear from the hooks in the changing room. But he saw no tan Stetson with an unshaped crown.

The roan was settled in the stable along with the other workers' horses, and wasn't eager to leave his friends and head back to the farm in the heat and dust. Charlie spent a good quarter-hour wrestling on the bridle and bit and getting the horse saddled for the twenty-minute trip home. By the time he arrived, the family had started eating without him.

He threw the horse's reins over the picket fence and left him standing unsaddled until after dinner, feeling resentful that the horse had made him late for dinner and that the family had not waited for him.

He washed up on the back porch before he went into the kitchen. Alafair stood up as soon as she saw him and filled a glass with sweet tea as he took his place at the table.

"You're late today, son," Shaw said. "Did the shift run long?"

Charlie reached for a piece of cornbread. "Nossir. Old Lightning Bolt just wasn't of a mind to hurry home today."

Sophronia chortled. Charlie changed the subject before she could comment. "There's a carload of bricks for Fort Bliss going out soon, and Mr. Cooper nearly run us all off our feet getting the order stacked and loaded so it'll be ready when the train comes through. I feel like I've been pulled through a knothole backwards. I'm mighty hungry, too, Mama. I could eat a boot."

The idea of a boot meal struck Grace as hilarious and Shaw had to raise his voice to be heard over peals of childish laughter. "You'd better save that knothole for bedtime, son," he said. "Fort Reno is expecting fifteen harness-broke mules by the end of the month, so there's a lot of work to be done to get them ready."

"Sounds like the U.S. Army has reason to appreciate your hard work and diligence, Charlie Boy," Gee Dub said.

Charlie spoke around a mouthful of rice and gravy. "I hope somebody does."

The Liberty Sing

Chapter Forty-one

"I recognize the danger that arises from the slacker who opposes the country. I realize that every breeder of sedition is as great a menace to our homes and our freedom as are our armed enemies across the sea. I therefore pledge myself to report to the chairman of my school district council of defense or to my county defense chairman any disloyal act or utterance that I may at any time know of. I will stamp out the enemies at home whose every act or word means more American graves in France."

— Oklahoma Loyalty Pledge, 1917

The special Friday Liberty Sing started out with a potluck picnic spread out over long tables that stretched along one side of the hall. The afternoon was hot and muggy, and everyone was milling about the grounds of the Masonic Hall, fanning themselves and talking too loudly.

There were a lot of people there that day whom Alafair didn't know. Including a young fellow who came in with one of her least-favorite neighbors, Dutch Leonard. They parked their buckboard and got out, but they stuck together, eyeing the crowd, like they were looking for somebody. Alafair saw Trenton Calder go over to talk to them, but he told her later that they didn't have much to say. Considering that it was Dutch, he expected the stranger had leftist tendencies and he meant to keep an eye on them. When he told her that, she cast an eye around for her brother. She was relieved to see that he was with Shaw and the boys. He took no notice of Dutch and his friends, and they didn't seem to pay any attention to him.

On this particular day, eight of the twelve men Scott had deputized were named Tucker, including Shaw, Gee Dub, and Scott's own son Slim. Gee Dub got a kick out of being a law man, teasing all the little children that he was going to arrest them. Trent told him that a real criminal with any brains would be out burgling houses, since there wasn't a solitary soul left at home.

Before the singing began, Scott instructed Gee Dub and Shaw to stand by the door and make sure nobody came in with a weapon. They were told to watch over any attendee with a German name. Scott wouldn't have put it past some of the local hotheads to decide not to wait until they got to Europe to begin killing Germans.

Blanche and Sophronia had decided to stay home with Phoebe's family. Kurt wanted to come and show his neighbors he was a loyal American, but Mary had talked him into staying away until the draft lottery was over. Mary herself refused to stay home, and had ridden in with her parents. Alafair was sorry that Kurt felt unwelcome, but she was glad he had decided to skip this particular gathering.

For an hour, enthusiasm reigned as the crowd belted out patriotic songs, and Alafair's voice rose as lustily as anyone's. No matter how much she was against getting into it in the first place, she did want America to win the war now. And besides, the singing was fun. Even Rob was enjoying himself and singing along. Grace joined several small children at the front of the hall to skip and dance to the music, and young men and women hovered about the buffet in gender-specific groups, eyeing each other and passing flirtatious remarks across the table. Younger folks like Charlie flitted in and out of the hall, sometimes joining in the singing and sometimes heading outside to look for mischief. Shaw spent half the hour at Alafair's side, singing loudly, if not always exactly on key, and the other half chatting with his brothers and other farmers about the effect the war was having on the price of cotton.

Just as everyone was growing hoarse, the singing wrapped up with "America the Beautiful," and there was a five-minute lull while the participants wet their whistles with lemonade and sweet tea.

Mary left her daughter Judy dancing with the other tots under Alafair's watchful eye, while she made her way through the crowd to retrieve a couple of glasses of lemonade. She was encouraged that several of her neighbors spoke to her, mostly to assure her that they harbored nothing but goodwill for her and her fine patriotic husband. So when Billy Claude Walker approached her as she began to walk back toward her mother, she was feeling secure enough to give him a friendly smile.

He did not smile back. "Where's your Bosch husband?"

Mary's mouth dropped open. She was so taken aback that she didn't reply.

Billy Claude had plenty more to say. "Smart of him to lay low. You better warn him to stay out of sight if he knows what's good for him. That family of your'n is full of traitors. All I have to do is say the word and the whole bunch of y'all will end up in Leavenworth." He paused long enough to draw a breath before continuing his harangue. "Just think how lonely it will be, you and your brat out there in your pretty white house when your Kraut husband goes to prison. We know that there's a Wobblie out to your folks' place, too. Maybe we won't go to the trouble of writing to the Justice Department about your traitor kin. The patriots around here might decide to save the state the cost of a trial and do a little hanging and burning ourselves."

Mary was just about to dash a glass of lemonade into Billy Claude's face, when a voice behind her said, "Mary, honey, we've been waiting for you!" Her heart lifted when she turned around and recognized Grandfather Khouri, gazing at her with concern.

"Yes, Mr. Khouri, I was just coming!"

Billy Claude grinned at the old man. "Well, if it isn't the town Jew shopkeeper!"

The look Grandfather Khouri gave him would have frozen flames into orange icicles. He put his arm around Mary and guided her away into the crowd without wasting a word on the likes of Billy Claude Walker.

"Thank you, Mr. Khouri."

He patted her shoulder. "Sometimes we all need a friend to help us escape, dear heart."

"That man scares the liver out of me and makes me afraid for my family."

Grandfather Khouri's expression hardened. "I knew many men like him when I was a boy in Turkey. Unless he is stopped he will cause misery wherever he can. Mark my words."

Chapter Forty-two

*"… red-blooded Oklahomans, Americans all,
rose to their feet as if one, and cheered and sobbed
and yelled at…the name of President Wilson."*
—*The Daily Oklahoman,* 1917

Mayor Jehu H. Ogle stepped up to the podium and banged his gavel until the crowd fell quiet. He called on Mr. Lacy, pastor of the First Christian Church of Boynton, to deliver the benediction. Then Lee Perkins harangued the crowd for exactly four minutes on the duty of patriots to buy Liberty Bonds and do everything possible to support the war effort.

Mr. Ogle returned to the podium and consulted his notes. "As y'all know, according to the Draft Act, every healthy, unmarried man between the ages of twenty-one and thirty-one had to register for service on June fifth. We are gathered here because today, at the county seat in Muskogee, the numbers are being drawn to determine who will have the privilege of serving his country. Mr. Kirby, editor of the *Boynton Index,* will be receiving the list by wire as soon as possible after the last number is drawn this evening. He will thereupon get himself over here to the hall and our senior Council of Defense officer, Mr. Emmanuel Clover, will read out the numbers, after which we'll post them on the wall."

An ugly murmur arose from the corner where the Dutch Leonard and his friends had stationed themselves. Out of the corner of her eye, Alafair saw Rob glance back at them over his shoulder.

Mr. Ogle plowed on. "Most of y'all may be wondering what will happen next. Within a few days or weeks, the boys whose numbers have come up will receive a notification from the War Department which will tell them when and where to report. If any man needs help arranging his affairs before he leaves, let me or Mr. Clover know and we will see that you get taken care of. Also, the Town Council will pay for transportation into Muskogee for any recruit who needs it. Come see me after the meeting if you want to know more."

Ogle looked up. "Ya'll know Miz Streeter McCoy, wife of our city treasurer." He gestured toward the right side of the room, and Martha waved. "Miz McCoy has taken on the task of organizing our local Red Cross chapter. She'd like to hear from every woman who can spare a minute to roll bandages, knit socks, pack supplies for the troops, and she hopes that includes every woman in town…" He squinted down at his notes. "…and she don't care what your name is.

"Also, we need more men to volunteer as Four Minute Men to talk before every public gathering, like at church or the moving pictures. The three we've got are going to have to figure out how to be in two places at once, otherwise. If some of you pastors know somebody in your church who likes to hold forth, put a bug in Emmanuel's ear about it." Ogle fell silent and assumed a benign expression as he waited for the crowd to stop murmuring. "Now. Mr. Clover has asked me if he could have a minute to speak, so I'll turn the meeting over to him. Emmanuel?"

Mr. Clover positioned himself behind the podium. His gaze swept the group, and his eyes narrowed when he caught sight of the Khouri family sitting together against the wall under the windows. Aram Khouri slumped down just a tad. But his father sat up straight and glared at Clover, his normally pleasant face as dark as an impending storm.

Clover straightened his tie, removed his glasses from his breast pocket, and positioned them on his nose before he began. "So happy to see y'all here today in this great demonstration of American solidarity. I wanted to mention that we've just been issued a new list of Food Administration restrictions for stores and shops. I already asked Isaiah Kirby to print the rules, and we'll be getting you shop owners your own copies to post directly. As you know, these restrictions are voluntary, but as your Council of Defense representative, I will be reminding y'all to comply." Mr. Clover ripped his spectacles off and jabbed the air with them. "We've got to stick together and we'll get through this, friends. I know many of you have already sent your sons and brothers to take up arms. I expect every healthy young fellow to join up if he isn't drafted. I expect everyone in this town to support the war effort as best they can. No hoarding. No profiteering or raising prices."

Emmanuel straightened and cleared his throat, and when he spoke, his voice rang against the rafters like a revival preacher's. "I am sure you all have heard of the death of my fellow CD representative, Win Avey, under suspicious circumstances. Why did he die? Was he killed by anti-war activists? By German sympathizers? Fifth columnists? The enemy is at the gates, my friends. I do not countenance vigilante justice. But every true American has to do everything he can to support our boys who will be putting their lives on the line for the one-hundred-percent American way of life. We must be ever vigilant against subversion and dissension. If I find a disloyal person in our midst, I intend to give his name to the Department of Justice in Washington and tell them where to find him. And it is y'all's duty to report to me if you hear anybody talk against the war, even if it's your friend or your brother…"

"Oh, shut up, Clover!"

The crowd gasped, everyone craning this way and that to see from where the comment had come. A tide of noise arose, like a moan, crescendoed, then receded. Rob was standing to Alafair's right, next to Shaw, with his arms crossed tightly over his chest. Alafair couldn't read his expression, but his cheeks sported hectic spots of red.

Shaw leaned in to whisper in her ear. "Get the children." It was time to get out of there.

Alafair took Mary's arm and the two of them began to make their way forward through the sea of neighbors, intent on finding Grace, Judy, and Chase.

Mr. Clover jerked with shock and glanced wildly around the room. "Who said that?"

"I did, you idiot!"

Mary seized Chase Kemp and Judy and made her way out. Alafair spied Grace at the front of the hall, elbows up, leaning against the stage. She reached under a man's arm, seized the tail of the little girl's frock, and drew her back into the crowd. She recognized the voice. People drew back, repelled.

The crowd parted to reveal Dutch Leonard standing alone in the middle of the space, one hand on his hip. He didn't appear to be worried about the consequences of his outburst. In fact, he was just getting started. He raised his voice to be heard over the shocked commentary going on around him. "I'm not joining up to fight the German Army. Let them Europeans tend to their own house. I ain't shedding blood for the damn capitalists! Leave us real Americans alone. And you, Billy Claude Walker, you pile of shit, you and your pinhead 'Knights of Liberty'!"

Alafair hoisted Grace into her arms, but momentarily forgot about leaving. She had a good view of Leonard, standing in the clear spot. She had always thought of the Leonard brothers as sneaks and cowards, and certainly did not consider Dutch a man who would stand in the middle of a hostile crowd loudly espousing an opinion that was likely to get him beaten up or worse. She waved at Martha and Alice and gestured for them to head out. On her way to the door, Alafair passed Shaw, going in the opposite direction. "Get the children out of here," he said again, as though she needed reminding.

Scott was elbowing his way through the milling crowd, desperate to get to Leonard and shut him up.

Charlie was standing at the food table with Henry Blackwood when Dutch made his move. Charlie gasped and gripped Henry's arm. "That's him!"

"What are you talking about?

"I recognize that hat! It was Dutch I saw sneaking into the plant..."

Henry wasn't paying attention. Things were getting ugly. "Come on, young'un, let's get out of here."

Emmanuel Clover was leaning over the edge of the stage, gesticulating at the crowd and yelling. "There are spies among us! Spies! We've got to be vigilant, for there are spies amongst us and we've got to root them out. Anybody who talks against the war might as well be fighting for the Germans!"

He pointed directly at Dutch Leonard, who launched himself forward like he had been shot out of a cannon.

Trenton Calder had never seen a riot before, but he figured he was about to. He could see Billy Claude Walker and two or three of his cronies standing at the back of the hall, waving their fists in the air, and over on the other side of the room, the Khouris and a couple of the Schmidts were looking like they could eat nails. Trent could see Scott with Shaw Tucker next to the stage. They looked as apprehensive as he felt. Women and children were flooding out of the hall.

Trent craned his neck to see where Ruth Tucker was, and was relieved to catch sight of her going out the door with her mentor Beckie McKenzie in tow.

Dutch Leonard went after Emmanuel Clover, but he never made it, because that's when everything went to hell. Trent didn't see who threw the first punch, but next thing he knew the whole world was nothing but fists and elbows, knees and boots. The rest of Clover's rant was lost in the hubbub. The mayor was pounding his gavel on the podium, but nobody paid any attention. Somehow Trent ended up on the floor, looking up at two men in overalls trying to strangle each other. He had to taste blood before he realized that someone had socked him in the mouth.

He saw red, then, and forgot all about keeping the peace and restoring civic order. He was on his feet in a trice and throwing punches with the best of them.

Trent was just hitting his stride when the blast of a gunshot roared through the hall, and the brawlers froze in place like they'd been hexed.

Scott had pulled his sidearm and blown a hole in the ceiling. For a minute, the only sounds in the hall were the panting of combatants and chunks of plaster hitting the floor.

"Anybody who ain't out of this hall in five minutes is going to jail." Scott's voice boomed like the trump at the Second Coming. "And if me or my deputies find anybody on the street tonight, he'll spend the night in irons!"

It was unclear how many heard the last bit, since Scott had hollered it over a stampede of men heading for any exit they could find, door or window, as long as it was convenient.

"Not you, Billy Claude!" Scott grabbed Billy Claude Walker by the collar as he passed and jerked him back. Only a few people were left in the hall by this time. Scott was surrounded by his deputies Shaw, Gee Dub, and Slim, and Mayor Ogle. The rest of the Knights of Liberty made a feeble attempt to back up their leader, but Scott gave them a heated glare and they slunk out, muttering. The .45 in his hand helped persuade them. Trent made his way over, wiping the blood off of his lip and counting his teeth.

"Billy Claude, dad blast it!" Scott was too furious not to blaspheme. "What in the name of Saint Peter and his eleven sidekicks do you think you're up to? I ought to fling you behind bars for inciting a riot."

"Me?" Billy Claude protested. "What about that clown Dutch Leonard? What about them Red rabble rousers that have come to town? You know as well as I do that anyone who utters any scurrilous language about the government should to be sent to prison."

"Yes, I've read the Espionage Act, too, Billy Claude, you don't need to educate me. And I'll take care of Dutch. You stick to watching the bridges for saboteurs and invaders and leave the law-enforcing to me." He let go of Billy Claude's collar like it was something nasty. "Now go home, and stay there for a few days, if you know what's good for you."

Billy Claude straightened his shirt with as much dignity as he could muster. "Mark my words, Sheriff. You'll be sorry about this." He looked around at the rest of the group. "You'll all be sorry."

After Billy Claude was gone, Gee Dub turned to Trent and shook his head. "I'll bet he doesn't have any idea what 'scurrilous' means."

"Well, neither do I, Gee Dub," Trent admitted. "But I can tell it's nothing good."

Chapter Forty-three

"We need more loyal and less 'thinking' Americans…
Are you an American?"
—Appeal to buy Liberty Bonds,
Tulsa Daily World, 1917

By the time Alafair escaped the hall and accounted for all her children, Rob was already standing outside, leaning against the building, lighting a newly rolled cigarette. Two men were standing with him, but when Alafair started toward them, they faded away into the dark. Alafair handed Grace to Martha and walked over to him. Rob shook out his match and turned his head to look at her as she approached. The noise of a brouhaha was still spilling out of the hall, along with a straggle of rioters who had acquired some sense along with a bloody nose and finally decided to get out of there.

Alafair broke the silence. "Mercy!"

Rob smiled, but hardly seemed amused. "Now you know what's in store, anyway."

"Robin, who are those fellows you were talking to? Just what are you up to?"

"I'm not up to anything that ought to bother you, Sis, so don't get fretted. All this to-do wasn't none of my doing, as you could see. Even so, I'm thinking that it's time I was leaving."

"Where will you go?" Shaw asked. Alafair started. She hadn't realized that Shaw had finally come outside and was standing behind her.

Rob's gaze shifted to look over Alafair's shoulder. "I planned to head to Arkansas before going up to Illinois. I suppose I'll just get there sooner than I expected."

"Will you be back?"

"I don't think I better, Shaw. I told you early on that I don't intend for y'all to suffer on my account, and you just heard in what regard your neighbors hold the I.W.W."

"Now wait a minute. It's not up to you to protect us. We can speak for ourselves." Shaw moved up beside Alafair and readjusted his hat to give himself time to consider how he was going to put this. "I admire your intentions, Robin, but I think you're wrong about this war."

Rob raised an eyebrow. This was no news to him.

Shaw continued. "I'm afraid that you're in for trouble, too, if you don't rein in while this war is going on. I hope that the consequences of your wooly thinking don't spill over on us, too. But even so, you got a right to your opinion and you ought not to be punished for it. And I won't be forced to turn out my own kin for fear of what folks think of him."

Rob's skeptical expression had changed to one of admiration. "You're a brave man, Shaw. A man has to take a stand for his principles, and I aim to. But you'll have enough to worry about without me in your hair right about now. I'll head out in a couple of days, if y'all can put up with me that long."

Alafair seized his arm, on the verge of tears. "Robin..."

He patted her hand. "It's all right, Sis. It's all right. It's better this way. I see Martha and Alice standing yonder. I'll go take my leave of them now and meet you at the wagon directly."

He crushed the butt under his heel and ambled away, leaving Alafair and Shaw standing alone at the corner of the building. Shaw looked down at her. "Are the children accounted for?"

"Yes, Ruth left with Miz Beckie in her rig. Streeter and Martha are going to drive Alice and Linda home so they don't have to walk. Mary's already at the wagon with the little ones. Is everything under control inside? Where are the boys?"

"Gee Dub is still in the hall. I saw Charlie and his friend Henry take off like a couple of scalded cats after Scott shot up the ceiling. He'll either turn up at home later or spend the night with Alice or my sister, I reckon."

Alafair nodded. In such a small town, with half of the population related to one another, there were plenty of surrogate parents around to keep an eye on your children.

"How are you, honey?" Shaw asked her. "You feeling bad about Robin leaving?"

She looked away. "I wish he didn't have to. But maybe it's for the best. He's up to something, Shaw."

"Ain't he always? Listen, sugar, I've got to stay in town. Scott's hunting for Dutch and wants us to scout the town for a spell and make sure everybody is off the streets and home like they ought to be. You and the children take the buckboard and head on home."

Chapter Forty-four

"We are less concerned with autocracy that is abroad and remote than that which is immediate, imminent, and at home."
—Socialist Bruce Rogers, 1917

Old Nick hadn't had such a good time since the miners' strike in Arizona. He took up a place across the road from the Masonic Hall, in the shadow of a large tree, where he could get a good view of the brawl and of the crowd running for their lives. For a long time he watched with interest as the bearded traveler who had brought him to Boynton in the first place stood behind the building talking to a man and a woman whom Nick didn't know. Eventually the traveler made his way toward the field where the wagons were parked, alone.

There had been so much interesting activity in town over the past week that Nick had almost forgotten about the traveler, a true believer whose single-minded dedication to his cause promised so much in the way of trouble and strife. Nick slipped out of the shadows to follow the man as he walked toward the two who had started the trouble in the hall.

Nick sidled up in the shadows, unnoticed, just close enough to overhear what the men were talking about. Plans were afoot, which made Nick happy.

Nick headed back across the road, but he was distracted by a solitary figure walking quickly away from the hall and toward town. A stink of fear and the heat of determination emanated from the figure, and Nick turned in his tracks to follow.

He waited until the object of his interest was well away from the hall and walking alone down a residential street before he approached from behind. The person heard footsteps and halted in the middle of the road, but didn't turn around.

Nick leaned in, close enough to whisper in an ear. "I know what you want," he said.

The figure stiffened, but said nothing.

Nick paused long enough to be sure his mark would not run away. "Give me a name," he whispered, "and I will take care of it."

It was nearly nine o'clock by the time Isaiah Kirby, editor of the *Boynton Index*, received the wire from Muskogee with the complete list of draft numbers drawn for the county. Kirby folded the list, put it in his breast pocket, donned his hat, and locked the door to the newspaper office before making his way at a trot toward the Masonic hall.

He expected to be greeted by a waiting crowd, but he slowed to a walk when he got close enough to see that the hall was dark. He stopped in the middle of the road, trying to figure out what had happened, until he saw a lanky figure holding a kerosene lantern come around the corner.

"Trent," he called. "What in the world is going on?"

"Mr. Kirby! I'll be danged. In all the excitement I plumb forgot what everybody was here for in the first place." He ambled over. "Sorry we didn't send somebody over to the paper so's to save you the trip. The Liberty Sing didn't go well. The pro-drafters and the anti-drafters butted heads and we had us a regular riot. Scott busted up the proceedings and sent everybody home. I reckon you'll just have to print the list in the paper tomorrow."

"Well, I'll be!" Kirby was annoyed that he had wasted the evening waiting for a list of draft numbers when he could have been covering a riot. He pulled out the little notebook that he carried everywhere. "Tell me what happened."

Trent held the lantern high. "You got the list of draft numbers with you?"

A knowing look crossed Kirby's face as he patted his breast pocket. "I do. I reckon you registered, didn't you?"

"How about if you let me have a peek? Then I'll give you a story that'll knock your readers on their butts."

Kirby reached into his pocket. "Son, I'd appreciate if you would, but you can look to see if your number came up for nothing."

◇◇◇

When Billy Claude Walker called a secret meeting of the Knights of Liberty at the pool hall after the riot, Nick almost rubbed his hands together with glee.

The group gathered around their usual table. Nick took a chair in the corner, just behind Billy Claude. They looked pretty beat up, Nick noted. Several black eyes and a split lip or two. Rather than serving as a cautionary example, the injuries had stiffened the combatants' resolve. "We can't let this stand, fellows," Billy Claude said. "Sheriff Tucker won't do nothing about it, but it's pretty obvious that we've got us a nest of traitors in town. And what about all them incidents at the brick plant? Somebody is trying to make sure that the bricks to build that Army installation don't get where they're supposed to go. Even if it takes murder. Look at what happened to Win. Who of us is going to be next, I ask you?"

One of Billy Claude's henchmen piped up. "We ought to write to the Justice Department, tell them we know who the culprits are. You're on the Council of Defense, Billy Claude. They'll listen to you."

A new man at the end of the table said, "Get Emmanuel Clover to back you up. Two CD men are better than one."

Billy Claude sniffed. "Clover is useless. So is Sheriff Tucker. Neither one of them is going to do what needs to be done. Let them write all the letters they want. I say we need to take action now."

"What kind of action, Billy Claude?"

Billy Claude leaned back in his chair and hooked his thumbs through his suspenders. "Let me think on it, Victor. We need to make sure to let everybody in town know that treason will not go unpunished."

Nick leaned forward and gently placed his root beer bottle on the table beside Billy Claude. "I have a suggestion," he said.

Chapter Forty-five

"The test of loyalty in war times is whether a man is wholeheartedly for the war and subordinates everything else to its successful prosecution."
—Minnesota Commission of Public Safety

Considering the excitement of the evening, the night was turning out to be exceptionally quiet, Alafair thought. Rob had gone into the kitchen to have a bowl of sweetened rice before turning in. Charlie had turned up an hour or so after everyone else. Alafair expected him to be excited and full of chatter, but he was unusually subdued.

After putting the children to bed, Alafair came out of the bedroom to find Shaw sitting in an armchair, reading the latest edition of the *Muskogee Phoenix*. On the other side of the lamp table, sharing his father's light, Charlie was engrossed in a book with pictures of soldiers in it. Charlie Dog lay snoring softly under the boy's feet. Gee Dub had already gone out to the shed. She passed into the kitchen and found her brother sitting at the kitchen table, a kerosene lamp before him, perusing a yellow piece of paper that looked suspiciously like a telegram.

He looked up at her and smiled. "Finally got the little ones settled?"

She sat down on the other side of the table. "It took a while. They were too excited to sleep."

Rob leaned his elbows on the table. "Well, I was glad to see how the law handled the situation without taking sides. That don't always happen, I'm afraid, especially if your family is full of subversives and foreign-born, like yours is."

"It helps if the sheriff is kin and his deputy is sweet on one of your daughters."

"Is that so?" Rob grinned. "That carrot-topped youngster fancies one of yours? Ruth, I'm guessing."

"That's right. If I'm any judge of these things they'll be wed before long. And even if it weren't so, that boy is like family."

"Well, that's good. That's all good! In time of trouble, you can't rely on anybody to stand with you like your own kinfolks. Who belongs to this Knights of Liberty group, Alafair? Gee Dub thinks it's the same bunch that jumped Dutch Leonard at the Liberty Sing tonight."

Alafair shrugged. "The Knights like to keep their faces covered, so it can't yet be proved who they are. The word has got around, though, that Billy Claude Walker and the rest of the late Win Avey's pals are involved. They all hold to a rigid standard for what it means to be American."

Rob looked thoughtful. "Huh. I'd like to have a word with this Walker fellow."

"Now, Robin, you'd better just keep your distance from his kind. Billy Claude is the new Secret Service man in town since Win died. I think him and his crew are just itching for an excuse to run somebody just like you out of town on a rail, or at least get you thrown in prison." Her voice was heavy with dread.

"I can handle myself, Alafair. Most of these puffed up rubes are nothing but a case of big behavior. They love to push you around, until you push back." He began to drum absently on the piece of paper that lay on the table beneath his fingers.

"What are you reading?" Alafair said.

"Nothing to worry about, Sis." He casually folded the paper and slipped it into his breast pocket. "Got a telegram from I.W.W. headquarters this morning. They got a little assignment for me before I leave Oklahoma."

That piece of news did not please Alafair at all. "What do they want you to do?"

"Oh, nothing much. Just stop an uprising."

Alafair didn't laugh at his joke. "I thought you were getting ready to leave Oklahoma because you're worried folks will think me and Shaw approve of your politics."

Rob felt a stab of annoyance. "Don't worry. My business is too far away from here to bring the wrath of public opinion down on you."

"Don't get all tied in a knot, now. I didn't mean it that way. I fret when I know you're about to roil the waters. Especially now that everybody's nerves are so frazzled."

"Alafair, you been trying to mother me for as long as I can remember. Quit it, now. You've got enough kids to be fussing over. I've been at this for a long time. I know what I'm doing."

"I'm sorry, Robin. I guess mothering is what I do without thinking about it. I know you're good at your business. But I've never seen a time like this one before. It's like everyone has gone barking mad. I can't help but fear."

As he listened, Rob's expression softened. Alafair put her hand on his shoulder and gave it a shake. "Robin, don't be messing with Billy Claude. And don't go traipsing off and get yourself in trouble again. I got a bad feeling about all this."

He puffed. She would never change. "I do, too, Alafair. That's why I've got to try to stop a bunch of fellows from doing something really stupid. Don't fret over me. I know how to walk the razor's edge, if anybody does. I've been in a lot worse situations than this will be. I ain't looking for trouble."

"Trouble just finds you, Robin, whether you're looking for it or not."

Chapter Forty-six

"We are surrounded on all sides by enemies."
—V. Lenin, 1901

The whole town of Boynton was in quite a state after the Liberty Sing. Alafair had no idea what was going to happen now. Only weeks earlier much of the county had been dead set against getting involved in a European war. Then one little riot and suddenly the whole community was wild with patriotism and looking for spies and traitors under every bush.

At first, someone who said that he didn't look forward to America being in a shooting war, or someone who skipped buying a war stamp one week, might have his front door egged in the middle of the night. Or a lady who said she wished her boy hadn't joined up so quickly may have found a fresh cow pat on her doorstep. When Mrs. Schneberg's victory garden was ripped up yet again, she caught the miscreants in the act. She was a feisty old dame, so she grabbed up a broomstick and went after them, but it was too late. She couldn't identify any of them.

People were afraid to say what was on their minds. And not just because their neighbors might look at them askance. One could end up in Federal prison for talking against the war. Or lose his livelihood, or at the very least expect all his friends to shun him and his family, either out of conviction or fear.

Mr. Eichelberger's corn crib was burned down. Mr. Kritchel north of town found a dead cat down his well. The only things the victims had in common was a German-sounding name. Eichelberger hadn't seen the ruffians. Kritchel got a glimpse but the night was dark. There had been five or six of them on horseback, but he couldn't tell who they were because they were all wearing black robes and hoods.

Scott had a pretty good idea who was behind all the mischief, but at the moment he did not have enough evidence to arrest anyone. After inspecting the damage at Eichelberger's place, he paced the office floor, his face so red that Trent feared he might have a stroke right then and there. "It's bad enough that we have to fight the Huns, Trent. Why do these idiots think we need to fight little old ladies and old men with feebleminded sons who never bothered anybody? I want to catch them vandals so bad I can taste it."

Chapter Forty-seven

"There is no fear in love; but perfect love casteth out fear."
—1 John 4:18

Trenton Calder paused at the door and adjusted his collar, though it didn't need adjusting. He was feeling as nervous as a maiden in a mining camp. Shaw Tucker was sitting at the kitchen table, and Alafair was bustling around from stove to cabinet to table, serving her husband cornbread and butter and refilling his coffee mug. Shaw smiled when he saw who had come in, but the smile dropped away when he gauged the look on Trent's face. His eyes narrowed and he put his cup on the table.

"Sit yourself down, Trent," he said. "Mama, get this boy something to wet his whistle."

Trent sat down opposite him and thanked Alafair when she brought him a glass of something. He wasn't paying much attention to anything but the look on Shaw's face. Amused.

Shaw had been through this with four daughters before Ruth. He could smell the flop sweat on a prospective son-in-law from a mile away.

Trent decided to jump right in with both feet. "Mr. Tucker, I'd like your permission to ask Ruth to marry me."

Alafair made a little noise and Shaw turned to look at her. They stared at one another for about an hour, by Trent's reckoning, before she walked over to stand behind Shaw's chair.

"I suppose you think that surprises me, son," Shaw said. "I assume Ruth is open to the notion."

"Yes, sir, she is."

Shaw leaned forward and placed his elbows on the table. "What are your plans?"

He didn't have to explain to Trent what plans he meant. There was a war going on. "Well, sir, my number came up, all right, but I'll be joining the Navy, if they'll have me. I know Ruth and me can't be married until I come back for good. I'd never ask her to saddle herself with a cripple or end up a widow before she's twenty."

"You and Ruth have talked about this, about what it really means for you to be going off to war?"

"Yes, sir. She says she don't mind waiting for me."

Alafair had placed her hand on her husband's shoulder. Trent couldn't tell if she was kindly disposed toward the idea or not. His mouth was so dry that he feared he would never be able to spit again.

Shaw wasn't finished with his interrogation. "What do you intend to do after the war, if you manage to come back all in one piece?"

"I'm thinking I might stay in law enforcement, sir. Maybe get on at the Muskogee Police Department. Might even study to be a lawyer eventually. It all depends on how things are after we win the war."

Shaw's mouth twitched at this show of bravado. "Well, Trent, Miz Tucker informed me some months ago that this was going to happen, so I've had time to gird my loins. We've pondered the idea at some length and come to the conclusion that having you in the family wouldn't be the worst thing that ever happened."

Trent flung himself across the table to grab his hand, and Shaw laughed. "No need to pump my arm off. Now go find Ruth and start making your arrangements, because I expect she's out there on the porch about to bust."

Alafair hadn't said a word during the entire conversation, but she couldn't keep quiet one more second. "Trenton Calder, it's about time, is all I can say! I was afraid I was going to run out of daughters before one of them fell for you."

Trent leaped to his feet and reached for her hand as well, but she pulled him in for a hug before he ran to find Ruth.

"Well, Shaw," she said, "looks like we're going to have some redheaded grandchildren."

"I kind of wish they had waited a while longer, though, honey. I'd hate to see Ruth get a broken heart if something happens to him."

"It's too late to worry about that. Whether they're betrothed or not, she's already in love with him."

"I notice that you're mighty pleased about it."

"Well, I am. I've had a soft spot for that boy since he was knee-high. Only problem is, now I have one more boy to worry about getting killed in the war."

Chapter Forty-eight

*"Tidal Wave of Patriotism Arouses City's
Business Men to Action."*
—*The Daily Oklahoman*, June 8, 1917

Eric Bent caught Dutch Leonard before he was able to punch the time clock on Monday morning. "Mr. Ober wants a word with you, Dutch. He asked me to send you over as soon as you got in."

Dutch sighed. He had been expecting something like this. "Is this because of what I said at the Liberty Sing on Friday? He planning to dock me?"

Bent shook his head. "I really don't know, Dutch. He just asked me to send you up before you punched in."

Dutch wasn't encouraged by the look of sympathy on Bent's face. "Well, this don't sound good."

Bent didn't disagree with him. "Go on up, then. I'll hold on to your lunch pail if you want. You can put it in your locker after you clock in."

Mr. Ober's office was located over the machine shop, up a long flight of stairs on the outside of the building. As he climbed, he couldn't keep the image of a scaffold out of his head. He knocked and entered without waiting for an invitation.

Mr. Ober stood when he recognized who had come in. "Dutch Leonard," he said, "are you the one who has been undermining the machinery here at the plant and causing work stoppages?"

Dutch drew back like he had been slapped. "Well, don't beat around the bush, Mr. Ober. I ain't no sneak nor killer, either."

Ober was not convinced. "Are you or are you not with the I.W.W. or the Working Class Union?"

"Is this because of what I said to Mr. Clover the other night? Now you've decided I'm a Wobblie? What if I was?"

"I won't have unionists stirring up trouble here at the brick works, Leonard. You're not a bad worker, but there are plenty of men looking for war work who aren't eligible for the military. I'll let you stay on the job if you'll swear to me right now that you renounce all ties to unionism and renew your loyalty oath."

Dutch said nothing for a long minute. Frank Ober was generally a fair man who treated his employees well. But he was a businessman and a capitalist. He probably treated his dogs well, too.

"Mr. Ober, I ain't a member of the W.C.U. I am a wage earner. I am a card-carrying member of the Industrial Workers of the World, and I won't renounce the right of workers to bargain collectively."

Ober's face flushed. "Who else at this plant is a unionist?"

Dutch wasn't about to get his fellow workers fired. "If they want to make themselves known to you, that's up to them."

Ober came around his desk so fast that Dutch was alarmed, but the manager simply opened the door. "You can collect your pay from the paymaster. Don't ever set foot on this property again. If I find out that you're trying to recruit my workers into the I.W.W. or any other damn socialist organization I'll see that you're arrested and thrown in Leavenworth for twenty years."

◇◇◇

Old Nick was sitting under a tree outside the main gate to the brick plant when Dutch Leonard came out.

Nick tipped his derby and gave the man a smile. "Howdy. You're Dutch Leonard, ain't you? Call me Nick. I was impressed by what you did the other night at the Masonic Hall, when everybody went to whaling on each other."

Dutch's forehead wrinkled. There was something familiar about the man. Had he seen the stranger at the Liberty Sing? Somehow Dutch thought so, though he couldn't say why. Nor could he bring to mind which side of the brouhaha the man had been on. Nick stood up and walked toward him. He seemed friendly enough, but Dutch took a step back, just in case.

Nick smiled. "That was some shindy, wasn't it? My punching hand is pretty sore today, though."

Dutch snorted and resumed walking. Nick fell in beside him. "It took a heap of guts to call that pinhead out, to my way of thinking. I don't know if I'd have had the brass to do it."

"Yeah, well, fat lot of good it did me. I spent two days in the hoosegow for it, and I just got fired for my convictions."

"You're joshing me. You mean to say that things have got so bad that a man can lose his livelihood for speaking his mind at a public meeting?"

"Reckon so. Ober has got it in his head that I had something to do with the machinery breakdowns just because I'm agin' the draft."

"He thinks you're the saboteur everybody's been talking about lately?"

"Well, I told him I ain't. But it don't matter. He'll be sorry. They'll all be sorry."

"There's plenty anti-war folks around here that are against conscription. I figure that the socialists will be taking matters into their own hands directly."

"You got that right."

"So you ain't the one who's been throwing wrenches into the works back at the plant?

"Whoever is slowing down the work has got my vote, though I don't hold with throat-slitting."

Nick shrugged. "Could be that Avey fellow just hung around with the wrong sort. Hung around. Get it?" Nick laughed at his own joke. "Anyway, I wouldn't mind teaching Ober a lesson myself, you know. A man shouldn't be able to tell his workers what to think."

Dutch shot Nick a suspicious glance. "What do you have against Ober?"

"Same thing I have against all capitalists."

Dutch stopped walking. "Are you a socialist?"

Nick hung an arm over Dutch's shoulder. "Listen, brother, I know which way the wind is blowing. You can bet that Ober is aiming to turn you over to the sheriff for sedition. You know the layout of the plant and the best way to delay that brick shipment from going out. How'd you like to get back at Ober and help me advance the socialist cause all at once? You might as well be hanged for a sheep as a lamb."

"They ain't nothing I'd like better, and I do know a way to get onto the property without being seen. But it'd be hard to get away with. Ober has guards all over the place nowadays."

Nick made a dismissive noise. "I don't care how many guards he's got. They can't be everywhere at once. I got a couple of ideas for mischief, and nobody would ever know it was us."

Who is this man, Dutch thought? Is he trying to trap me? Still, revenging himself on Ober and Cooper and the rest of that pack of capitalist overlords appealed to him greatly. "Tell you what, you buy me a beer and we'll talk about it."

Chapter Forty-nine

```
DEPARTMENT OF JUSTICE
WASHINGTON, D.C.

                               APRIL 6, 1917

    TO ALL UNITED STATES ATTORNEYS AND MARSHALS:
    DEAR SIR:
        YOU ARE HEREBY DIRECTED TO GIVE FULL PUBLIC-
    ITY TO THE FOLLOWING STATEMENT:
        NO GERMAN ALIEN ENEMY IN THIS COUNTRY, WHO
    HAS NOT HITHERTO BEEN IMPLICATED IN PLOTS
    AGAINST THE INTERESTS OF THE UNITED STATES,
    NEED HAVE ANY FEAR OF ACTION BY THE DEPART-
    MENT OF JUSTICE SO LONG AS HE OBSERVES THE
    FOLLOWING WARNINGS:
        OBEY THE LAW; KEEP YOUR MOUTH SHUT.
                               RESPECTFULLY,
                               T.W. GREGORY
                            ATTORNEY GENERAL.
```

Life was good for Mary and Kurt Lukenbach. They were in love, they had adopted a beautiful daughter, and they were making money hand over fist, what with Kurt's new business of raising and butchering hogs and selling the meat to the U.S. Army as well as to local markets.

Until the war broke out, the only shadow on their happiness had been that after almost two years of marriage, no more children had blessed their union, and if anybody was made for motherhood, it was Mary. But her mother had told her that babies came along on their own time and it was no use to worry. And so she didn't. She had her darling Judy, and loved having her cousin Chase constantly running in and out of the house and tailing Kurt like a faithful dog. Worry didn't suit Mary's sunny ways, in any event.

She ladled pancake batter into the skillet and watched with pleasure as it spread out to cover the bottom. Not for Mary were skimpy little cakes that would fit two or three to a pan. If it wasn't as big as the bottom of the skillet, it wasn't worth bothering with. She eyed the cake as bubbles began to form in the batter, and started counting. Her father insisted that a pancake was not ready to flip until exactly twenty bubbles had formed over the top. Not one more or one less. It was a pretty good rule of thumb, Mary had discovered, and besides, she enjoyed the game of counting bubbles. As she was growing up it had been a source of hilarity for the kids to huddle over the skillet, turner at the ready, trying desperately to flip the pancake at exactly twenty bubbles.

The memory made her smile. They never made it in time.

A pair of long arms slid around her middle, causing her to start. She laughed and leaned back on Kurt's shoulder. "You made me lose count!"

"It's okay," he said into her ear. "Me and Chase will be happy to eat pancakes even with twenty-five bubbles." Chase appeared around the side of Kurt's leg, grinning with pleasure at having surprised Mary.

"Well, sit down, then, boys, and pour yourselves a glass of milk. These flapjacks will be ready in a few minutes, and you want to eat them while they're hot. How are the sows this morning?" Two of their breeding sows had recently given birth to big litters of piglets.

Kurt released her reluctantly. Her soft form was warm and sweet on a cool morning. "Little babies are eating greedy like swines. The Hampshire sow was upset, walking up and down her sty, complaining. All the piglets were squealing like mad, wanting to nurse." He surveyed the breakfast table before he sat down. "There is no bacon this morning?"

"No, it's Meatless Tuesday, honey. I'll fry you up a couple of eggs if you want something savory to go with your hotcakes."

"All right, that's good." He tickled Judy's nose before he sat down next to her highchair, and was rewarded with a silvery giggle. He picked up the crockery pitcher of fresh milk from the table and poured a tall glass for himself and one for Chase. "It is silly, though, this meatless day, for us. Meat we have plenty of."

Mary set a tall stack of wheel-sized pancakes in front of him. "Those are the rules. We got to save as much of your meat as we can for the troops, now." She retrieved a bottle of sorghum from the cabinet and handed it to Kurt, who set it aside while he slathered butter over the top of each cake, starting from the bottom of the pile and going up.

Mary watched in satisfaction as he finished by pouring half the sorghum over his cakes and the other half over Chase's. She took a couple of eggs from the bowl on the windowsill and poured a quarter inch of fat from her grease jar into the skillet for frying. Kurt was six feet and three inches tall, and he only weighed one hundred and seventy-five pounds on days when he carried rocks in his pockets. As far as his wife was concerned, the more fat and calories he consumed, the better.

"You lads going into town today?" she asked, as the eggs sizzled.

Kurt swallowed a syrupy mouthful before he answered. "I'm needing hog feed. I will take the wagon in later, after morning chores. Carlon Welsh and couple other boys will help me load up pigs for the train to the hog auction in Muskogee tomorrow."

"Can I go feed the chickens?" Chase interrupted.

Mary gave the boy a half-serious glare. "Chase Kemp, I do declare! What did you do? Dump them pancakes on the floor?"

Chase was indignant. "Of course not! I ate them up."

"You'll give yourself the belly ache," Kurt warned.

"I'm sorry," Chase said, not sorry at all. "But they were real good, Cousin Mary. I couldn't stop eating them up! Now can I go?"

He was laying it on a bit thick, but Mary knew that feeding the chickens was Chase's favorite chore, so she was inclined to forgive his overly enthusiastic praise of her cooking. She made a shooing motion with the pancake turner. "All right, off with you, then. Go out the front and leave the door open. It's going to be hot today."

Kurt and Mary's bedroom had two doors, one directly into the kitchen and the other into the parlor. Normally, they came straight into the kitchen without passing through the parlor when they got up, and Kurt left out the back door to feed the animals while Mary made breakfast. Neither had used the front door that morning.

Chase sped off and Mary bent over to wipe syrup off of Judy's face. She was about to make some comment to Kurt when a horrified shriek from Chase caused her to jerk upright and Judy to emit a startled wail.

Kurt stood so quickly that his chair clattered over onto the floor. "Chase! *Was ist los?*"

Chase streaked back into the kitchen as quickly as he had streaked out. He made a flying leap into Kurt's arms and waved at the front door.

Mary lifted Judy out of the highchair. "What is it, Chase?"

"Show me," Kurt said. But Chase dug his face into Kurt's shoulder and made incoherent whimpering noises.

Kurt frowned and put the boy down before walking into the parlor to investigate. The front door was about half-way open into the room. He had only taken a few steps into the room before he could tell that something definitely was not right. There was a smear of something dark across the white face of the door.

Mary stood where she was in the kitchen for half a minute, patting a trembling Chase on the back and waiting for Kurt to come back in and tell her it was nothing.

When he didn't, she placed Chase firmly in a chair and ordered him to watch Judy. Then she took a breath and went to see for herself.

Kurt was standing on the porch with his hands on his hips staring at the front of the house. His face was so red that she rushed toward him in fear that he had taken ill.

He seized her wrist and drew her under his arm, and as her body turned toward the house, she saw what had turned his normally placid expression so thunderous.

One of the newborn piglets had been skewered to the wall with one of Kurt's own trimming knives. Its throat was cut, and written in its blood across the door were the words DIE HEINE. TRATORS GIT HUNG. KNITES OF LIBERTY was scrawled in coal on the porch floor, beneath her feet.

Mary's hands flew up to press her temples. Neither spoke for a long time. This was an occurrence so foreign to Mary's experience that she was finding it hard to believe her own eyes. When she finally made a move toward the poor crucified piglet, Kurt stopped her.

"No, leave it." His voice was low when he spoke. "Honey, damp your stove and get the children, now. We are going to see Sheriff Tucker."

"But Carlon will be here directly. He'll see this and wonder where we are and think something has happened to us. We'll leave him a note on the back screen. Yes, he always goes around back when he first gets here." Even as she said it, Mary realized she sounded ridiculously fussy.

Kurt looked down at her. His tone was surprisingly gentle. "Get your coat, *Leibling*."

Mary picked her way through the gore to follow him back into the house, still feeling dazed. She knew Kurt was exactly right to go to the sheriff, but all she could think was that she wished her mother and father were here.

Chapter Fifty

"Germany has filled our unsuspecting communities with vicious spies and conspirators and sought to corrupt the opinion of our people in their own behalf."
—Woodrow Wilson, Flag Day Speech, 1917

Trenton Calder generally arrived at the jailhouse at five or six in the morning, unless there was a prisoner. In that case he slept on a cot in the office, or sometimes in the other cell. Truth be told, he slept at the jailhouse more often than there were evil-doers in jail, just to get out of his too-quiet room in the American Hotel.

He had just risen and was tucking in his shirttail when he looked out the front window and saw Kurt and Mary Lukenbach's wagon pull up.

Even before they dismounted, he could tell that something was very wrong. He sat down behind his desk, unlocked the top drawer, and put his hand on his gun belt while he waited for them to come in. He had no good reason to do so, but it made him feel better to be ready for anything.

Trent could hardly believe his ears when he heard what had happened. This was the first vicious act of vandalism against somebody he knew well.

Mary was pale and shaky when she told the story. Chase stood next to her chair, silent and white-faced. Judy was in Mary's lap, quiet, sensing the mood. Kurt had plenty to say as well, but he was so spitting mad that Trent figured he had forgotten how to speak English, for he couldn't understand a word.

Trent telephoned Scott, who walked over from home in less than five minutes. Scott made them repeat the whole tale.

When Scott finally spoke, his voice was quiet, which usually meant somebody was in for trouble. "Is there anybody out to your farm right now, Kurt?"

Mary answered for him. "Carlon Welsh was supposed to be there any minute when we left. I put a note on the back door for him so he'd know what happened and where we'd gone. I told him not to clean anything up until we got back."

Scott nodded. "That's good. I want y'all to go home, now, and stay there. Trent, you go with them. Take a look at the scene and make sure there's no other damage to the property. I'm paying a visit to Billy Claude."

Trent stood up and strapped on his gun belt.

"What should we do?" Mary asked.

Scott directed his answer to Kurt. "I think y'all should post some guards at the house for a while. Talk to Carlon. Him and his brother could probably use the extra money. Talk it over with Shaw, too. I don't want y'all coming back into town until I give you the all-clear…"

Kurt started to protest, but Scott cut him off. "I know you've got your business to tend to. Send Carlon to do your deliveries. Streeter and Martha are right here in town to take your orders, or the Kelleys. You've got plenty of family who'll be happy to help you out."

"I am not going to hide," Kurt said. "I am sending out a load of hogs on the train in a few days." He made himself very well understood that time.

Scott shook his head. "I want you to do what I say, now. It ain't fair, but you're German-born and folks are all stirred up. Send me a message when your stock is ready to ship. Until then, you stay out of town until I tell you otherwise. You get some men to keep a good lookout." He turned to Mary. "And as for you, honey, try not to worry. I'm going to do my very best to try and find out who did it and clap them in jail."

Chapter Fifty-one

*"Our allegiance must be purely to the United States.
We must unsparingly condemn any man who holds
any other allegiance. But if he is heartily and singly
loyal to this Republic, then no matter where he was
born, he is just as good an American as anyone else."*
—Theodore Roosevelt, October 12, 1915

Trent rode behind the Lukenbachs' wagon on his big standard bay, Brownie. Brownie was a tall, fumble-footed thing and riding him was like riding a bicycle over a washboard, but Trent had never owned a sweeter-natured horse.

As they neared the Lukenbach farm, Trent could see people milling around in the front yard. Word spread fast, even if it seemed there was no one to spread it. Mary's parents were there, along with Gee Dub, who was leaning against a tree, his cowboy hat pushed back on his head. Kurt's sometime hand, Carlon Welsh was there with his wife, Georgie, and Carlon's brother, Coleman. Rob Gunn was not there.

People started walking toward them as they came up the drive, and by the time Kurt pulled up in front, the wagon was surrounded and everyone was talking at once. Mary stepped down and flung herself and Judy into her mother's arms.

The Welsh brothers were pressing Kurt to tell them what happened, and Alafair and Shaw were concerned with Mary and the children. Gee Dub walked up to Trent.

"How'd y'all know to come?" Trent asked Gee Dub, after he stepped out of the saddle.

"Carlon came up to the house and told us what happened. He showed us Mary's note. We've been here a spell."

Trent figured he'd better take hold of the situation. "Everybody calm down!" he hollered, and much to his surprise, they did. "Scott asked me to have a look at the situation. Did y'all leave everything like you found it?"

"We did, son," Shaw said. "Coleman has a good fist with a pencil and drew you a picture to take away."

Trent nodded, wishing he had thought of that. "Well, I guess I'd better give the scene the once-over my own self." He wasn't eager to do it. He could see the piglet skewered to the front door from where he stood. The knife was stuck right through its body, and blood had run down the door in a broad streak that was already dried to a blackish red color. He walked up the steps to get a better look at the writing smeared on the wall—DIE HEINE, and TRATORS GIT HUNG. Trent wasn't sure what a 'heine' was, but he did know that whoever wrote it didn't mean it as a compliment.

He pushed his hat back. "Knites of Liberty. Too bad they didn't sign their names…"

Gee Dub was standing at the bottom of the steps and heard him, even though Trent was more or less talking to myself. "Everybody knows who they are, Trent."

Trent twisted around. Shaw and Kurt were standing behind Gee Dub, and the way they were looking up at Trent gave him a bad feeling. "Now, let's nobody go off half-cocked. We may think we know, but we need proof that'll stand up in court. Scott said the best thing Kurt can do right now is to post a lookout for a while and stay home until he says otherwise."

It was Shaw who answered. "Don't worry, Trent. We'll look after our kin."

Kurt asked Carlon Welsh if he knew of anyone in the colored community who was looking to pick up some extra money doing guard duty. Carlon said he reckoned he could come up with some men. Between the Tuckers and the Welshes, Kurt and Mary would have an Army guarding their place. Trent didn't know if that made him feel better or worse.

While the men inspected the damage to her house and her peace of mind, Mary sat on the open tailgate of the buckboard with her legs dangling over the edge. Judy was toddling around the yard after a barn kitten, unconcerned with the excitement going on around her. Mary watched the baby's innocent play and wished she could regain her equilibrium so easily. Chase was huddled in a corner of the buckboard, behind her. He had no desire to look at the ghastly sight again. He'll probably have nightmares for a month, Mary thought. Her mother sat close on one side of her, and Georgie Welsh sat on the other, their very presence a comfort.

"Kurt and me were talking all the way back home." Mary was staring at her lap as she spoke. "He's fit to be tied, and I can't get him calmed down. I've never seen him like this."

"Well, it ain't no wonder," Georgie said.

Mary glanced at her and shook her head. "Y'all know how he is. Folks tease him all the time, and he just takes it with a smile. But this affects his family. I'm afraid he's going to haul off and knock somebody rear-end over teakettle one of these days, and end up run out of town, or worse. I wish he would just lay low, like Scott told him to, but he won't do it. He says it took him ten years to work his way all the way here to Oklahoma from Germany, and he'll be jiggered if he's going let a bunch of yahoos scare him any."

She took Alafair's hand. "Oh, Ma, even folks who have known Kurt for years are looking funny at him. And some who I thought were my friends have said things to me that made we want to pin their ears back." Her blue eyes suddenly filled with tears. "On the way into town, Kurt told me he wants to join up, Ma. Says he'd make a perfect spy for the United States, or at least he could translate German newspapers and captured documents or interrogate prisoners. I'm afraid he'll try to enlist and get thrown in prison just for being born in Germany. What can I do? What if he goes to war? What will I do?"

Alafair threw her arms around Mary, but said nothing. All she could feel was a burning fury at the idiots who had done this.

Georgie was patting Mary on the back. "I know just how you feel, Miz Lukenbach. Men just don't listen to reason! My Carlon is already gone and enlisted up in the Army."

Alafair squeezed Mary's head to her shoulder, as if she didn't want Mary to hear such shocking news. "Oh, Georgie, I had no idea! When did this happen?"

Georgie's mouth bent up in a bitter little smile. "He signed up last week. Said to me, 'Girl, they'll be needed ever man they can get for this fracas and I expect they'll be as happy to take a colored man as a white one.' Fool thinks that if he volunteers to get shot that white folks will..." She suddenly remembered who she was talking to and changed the subject in the middle of her sentence. "He said he'll send home his Army pay, but I don't know what he thinks me and the babies are going to do without him."

Alafair tried to think of something to say, but every comment that occurred to her seemed pitifully inadequate.

Mary extricated herself from her mother's grasp and impatiently wiped her eyes with the back of her hand. "Well, Georgie, looks like you and me may be in the same boat."

"I think that after all this, y'all better come spend tonight at home," Alafair said to Mary.

"Oh, Mama, don't be fussing. Kurt and I don't need to be moving home to the folks' at the first sign of trouble."

"I don't mean that. Just for tonight. Y'all have had a shock. Let the menfolks make their plans to set a guard. We'll come back tomorrow and scrub the place up from top to bottom."

"Me and my kin Marva and Sugar would be proud to scrub floors with you," Georgie said.

Mary was touched in spite of herself at all the concern directed toward her. She turned her head to look at Kurt. The other men were still at the bottom of the steps with their heads together, hashing out their plan of action. But Kurt had gone up onto the porch. He was standing with his hands balled into fists, staring at the crucified piglet. Mary was glad she couldn't see his face. His stiff posture was alarming enough.

Mary started when he reached out and jerked the knife out of the door in one violent motion, catching the pig carcass before it hit the floor. Absorbed in conversation, none of the men noticed when Kurt lay the little body on the porch, wiped the bloody knife on his trouser leg, and disappeared with it into the house.

Alafair was watching, too, and the evidence of Kurt's rage disturbed her as much as it did Mary. She resolved to have a word about Kurt with Shaw later. Shaw had a way about him when it came to calming animals, and people, too.

Trent came toward the wagon and removed his hat. His redhead's complexion was flushed and blotchy.

"Mary," he opened, "your daddy has suggested that you and Kurt and the children stay over to your folks' place for a few days, but Kurt don't want to. He says you and the younguns ought, though. I think it's a good idea."

Mary shook her head. "No, thanks, Trent. I aim to stay with my husband. I imagine Chase will want to, though. And I'll let Mama take Judy for the night."

Trent nodded. "Betwixt the Welshes and all your kinfolks, you'll have a watch outside your door every night from now until doomsday if you want. So I expect y'all will be safe enough until we can catch these goobers. Carlon told me he'll be gone after next week…" Trent glanced at Georgie and his face flushed even redder. "…but Coleman is game to help, and Carlon is going to talk to their kinfolks about seeing who else might take a turn at guard duty."

"Thank you, Trent," Mary said.

Alafair seized Trent's sleeve and gave his arm a shake. "I'm going home to make dinner. You want something to eat, son?"

"No, thank you, ma'am. I got my rounds to do."

Mary looked ill. "I couldn't eat a thing, Mama!"

"You can help me in the kitchen, then. Kurt'll be hungry. Nothing bothers a working man's appetite. Trent, are you sure?"

He looked thoughtful, but shook his head. "I better not stay, Miz Tucker. Scott will be wanting a report."

Alafair slid down off the tailgate and straightened her skirt. "Well, all right then. By the way, you needn't tell the girls in town about this until tomorrow. There's not a thing they can do."

Chapter Fifty-two

"College Boys…Don't Read American History. Make It!"
—U.S. Navy recruiting poster, 1917

Shaw and the boys spent much of the day at Kurt's farm, helping with the cleanup and making plans for a twenty-four-hour guard on the property. The shadows were long when they finally got home, and the comforting smells of supper greeted them as they approached the house. When they reached the back porch, Charlie bounded up the steps and disappeared into the kitchen. Before Shaw could follow, Gee Dub put a hand on his arm.

"I want to talk to you for a minute, Dad."

"All right, son. Let's go inside and wash up."

Gee Dub's voice dropped. "What I got to say, I'd rather not bring up in front of Mama just yet."

A jolt took Shaw in the chest like one of his mules had kicked him. He had been expecting this moment for weeks.

Gee Dub's dark eyes examined Shaw's face for a silent moment. His expression was almost curious, as though he was expecting to find some sign of how his father was going to take this. Shaw didn't press. There was always plenty of time for bad news.

Gee Dub's gaze skittered off toward the children playing in the yard before he began. "Did y'all know that since the war was declared, all us boys up at A&M who are over eighteen were required to join the National Guard?"

Shaw swallowed. "We hadn't heard that."

"The government is requiring National Guard service of all college boys now. I was training a couple times a week and on weekends before the term was over. I've already had a physical for the Army and passed."

"What does that mean, Gee? Will you have to go into the Army when you graduate?"

Gee Dub was silent for an uncomfortable moment. "I won't be going back to A&M in the fall. My unit has been activated, Daddy. I have to report over to Muskogee in the middle of September. After I've turned twenty-one. I'll probably go to Fort Riley, Kansas, for training. Most of the fellows in my class are gone already. I just wanted to come home for the summer, spend some time with y'all before I go." He hesitated. "I didn't want to ask for y'all to sign a permission paper so I could join up before I came of age. Maybe make it a little easier on Mama."

Gee Dub couldn't see his father's face well in the gathering darkness, but he was well aware of Shaw's stoic way of receiving unwelcome news.

When he did speak, Shaw's voice was full of forced good humor. "Your mama will as soon dig out her own liver with a spoon than hear this, but you know that she'll stand behind you, son, just like I do."

"I know it, Daddy. I hate for her to be scared for me, is all." He sighed audibly. "Soon as I turn twenty-one they'd draft me anyway. But I'll be danged if I'm going to wait for them to come and get me. Besides, after what happened to Kurt and Mary, I'm going to do whatever I can to get this war over and done with." His gaze slid across his shoulder to look at his father. "Tell you the truth, I'm scared, too, Dad."

"I'm scared for you, son."

"No, well, I'm not so much scared of getting killed. I'm afraid I might not be able to do it."

"Kill someone?"

"No. I expect that if somebody tries to gut me with a bayonet,

I won't be too delicate to blow his brains out. It's just that…"
He paused, unable to articulate what was on his mind.

Shaw didn't have to be told. "You wonder if you'll be able to
do your duty like a man."

Gee Dub grimaced. "Yes. I'm afraid that when that first bullet
whizzes by my ear, I'll run clean to the Atlantic Ocean before I
even realize what I've done. Or end up groveling around in the
mud trying to hunt myself up a backbone."

What a remarkable feeling, Shaw thought. I don't know
whether to laugh or bawl. But he said, "Gee Dub, every man
wonders the same thing when he knows he's going into a scrape.
There's nothing shameful about being scared. Even if you wet your
drawers when the bombs start to fall, you won't be the only one."

Gee Dub cocked an eyebrow. "I'll think of it as something
me and my pals can do together."

Now Shaw did laugh. "Son, I mean only a fool wouldn't
be scared in the middle of a war. You're no fool. And you're no
coward, either. I know you. You've got a heart like a lodestone.
It never fails to find the right direction. You'll do what needs to
be done. Do you believe me?"

Gee Dub shrugged. "I believe you believe it, Dad, and I'm
glad. I hope you're right. I hope I know how to die standing up."

The look on Shaw's face caused Gee Dub to regret that he had
put it that way. He grasped his father's shoulder. "Don't worry,
Daddy. I don't aim to die any which way."

Alafair said nothing at all when Gee Dub told her the news. Charlie and Sophronia cheered and clapped their brother on the back,
and Grace and Judy danced around, caught up in the general
merriment. Blanche looked worried. Mary murmured something
encouraging, but she shot her mother a look of concern. When
the family discussed Gee Dub's plans over supper, Alafair didn't
contribute to the conversation. Shaw didn't press her.

He didn't say anything to her until later in the night, when
they were lying together in bed. "You know there wasn't hardly
anything else the boy could do."

He heard her sniff. "If it was up to me, he'd run and hide." She sounded bitter. "But it ain't, so I'll make the best of it. I won't be making it any harder on him than it already is. At least he's not like most of these knothead boys around here, all bloodthirsty and bragging that they'll bring home the Kaiser's head in a sack. I hope he has enough sense to keep his head down."

"You know Gee Dub. It's hard to tell how he really feels about it. I think his blood is up more than he's letting on, but he don't want us to know he's excited."

"You think he's afraid?"

"He wouldn't have much sense if he wasn't. Of course, he's twenty. I don't know how much sense he can have."

"Well, I'm afraid enough for both of us, Shaw."

"I know, honey."

"I fear for all the children. For Charlie and Ruth. For poor Mary. I fear for you, and for Robin. The world has gone mad, Shaw, and there isn't anything I can do about it."

Chapter Fifty-three

"There are citizens of the United States, I blush to admit, born under other flags...who have poured the poison of disloyalty into the very arteries of our national life."
—Woodrow Wilson, Address to Congress, 1915

Trenton Calder came across the damage at Khouri's market while making his early morning rounds. It was so early that objects were just dark shapes against a lighter sky, so he was carrying a lantern. The first thing he noticed was that the front door to the market was open. It occurred to him that perhaps Mr. Khouri was attending to something in the shop, but there was no light coming through the windows. He drew his sidearm and slipped inside.

A foul smell nearly knocked him over. He held the lantern up high, but it took a moment for his eyes to adjust. The place was a wreck. Every single piece of merchandise had been taken from every counter and cabinet and piled in the middle of the room, and a load of manure had been dumped on top of everything. The miscreants had smeared manure all over the walls, the shelves, the counters. Trent couldn't stand the stench and stepped back out onto the sidewalk, eyes watering. The sky was just lightening, and he could finally see that the vandals had taken a handful of dung and written JEW, and ONLY AMERICANS WLCOM HERE on the front window.

He stood there a while, stunned. The Khouris lived in an apartment over the store. Why had they not heard the ruckus? It struck him that perhaps the culprits hadn't stopped at vandalism, and he ran up the stairs at the side of the building like his feet were on fire and pounded on their door, yelling at the top of his lungs.

Trent nearly fainted with relief when Mr. Khouri threw the door open, a look on his face that was half terror and half like he could skin whoever had roused him. Mrs. Khouri and all the little ones were pressed up against his back. Trent could barely see old Grandfather Khouri standing in a bedroom door at the back, holding a wicked, curved knife in his hand, as though he intended to skewer the knocker if he turned out to be a threat.

Five minutes later, Trent, Aram Khouri, and his father were all downstairs inspecting the damage. The Khouris were still in their nightshirts.

"But why, Trent?" The younger Mr. Khouri had a handkerchief pressed to his nose and tears in his eyes as he took in the ruination of his business. "We're not Germans, or Turks, or anarchists! We're all natural-born Americans, except for Papa, here, and he's been a citizen for forty years! We're not foreigners."

Trent had no answer to that. The Khouris had a funny name. Grandfather Khouri spoke with an accent. Whoever was doing these ugly things didn't seem to care about what was true, only how things looked.

Grandfather Khouri shook his fist at the writing on the window. "We are not even Jews! We are Syrian Orthodox Christians."

This did surprise Trent. Because they came from the Middle East and didn't go to church in Boynton, everybody in town thought the Khouris were Jews. Not that anyone had ever asked. Of course, now that Trent thought about it, they did close the market every Sunday and drive off in their buggy. He had never heard of Syrian Orthodox. He wondered if there was such a church in Muskogee, or anywhere else in Oklahoma?

The sun was coming up. People were beginning to stir. One man wandered over to see what the rumpus was, then another. Trent sent a passerby to rouse Scott.

A crowd began to gather and Trent had Khouri lock the door. He sent Mrs. Khouri back upstairs to wait, then asked all the gawkers if anyone had heard anything during the night. If anyone had, he wouldn't admit to it. Trent caught sight of Billy Claude Walker standing across the street with Victor Hayes. And behind them a man in a bowler hat with a little scar beside his eye, watching the action. When Billy Claude saw Trent give him the once-over, he smiled and nudged Victor in the ribs. The man in the bowler hat melted into the shadows. Trent was sorely tempted to go over there and knock that smirk off of Billy Claude's face, but he mastered the urge and posted himself in front of the doors of the market to wait for Scott.

He hadn't seen it the first time, but written on the boardwalk with coal were the words KNITES OF LIBTERY.

Trent forgot his intention to remain at his post. He stomped across the street and grabbed a startled Billy Claude by the collar. Victor Hayes decided he had business elsewhere and disappeared.

Trent nearly lifted Billy Claude off the ground by his collar. "What do you know about the nighttime activities of the Knights of Liberty around here?"

A sneaky look came over Billy Claude's face. "I don't know what you're talking about, Deputy. And besides, it's a good thing there're some patriots around here to keep the enemy in his place."

"If I ever find out who's dressing up like a bunch of haints and scaring the tar out of good honest folks, I'm going to see they go to jail for destruction of property, malicious mischief, disturbing the peace, threatening bodily harm, and anything else I can think of, right after I kick their asses clean to Montana." He gave Billy Claude an angry shake. "So if by any stretch you have an idea who's causing all this folderol, you'd better let them know that they'd do a heap better by joining the Army and fighting the real enemy."

Nick had slipped into the alley when Trent crossed the street, but he watched the exchange between Billy Claude and the red-haired deputy with interest. The local law knew very well who their troublemakers were, but as long as Billy Claude and his cronies didn't do something as blatant as sign their names to their handiwork, Nick knew it was going to be hard to prove that they were the vandals.

A good-sized crowd had gathered on the street by now. Half the citizens of Boynton were gawking at the mess in Khouri's market or expressing their outrage to Mr. Khouri himself. The other half was eagerly watching Trenton Calder read the riot act to Billy Claude, hoping that fists would fly.

Nick watched the chaos for a good long time before he noticed someone standing silently amidst the mobs of people in front of the market, emanating waves of fury. Nick sensed something else besides simple anger, too. Murderous intent.

He cocked his bowler with his thumb, touched his scar for luck, and made his way quietly across the road. He was able to slide in behind his quarry without being seen. He leaned in close. "I can help you," he whispered.

Chapter Fifty-four

*"Patriotic ardor must not be allowed
to become a license for lawlessness."*
—Oklahoma Governor Robert L. Williams

Billy Claude Walker had lived at Mrs. Worley's boardinghouse for going on three years. His room was small and cramped, but the food was good and he liked the fact that his room was located at the back corner of the first floor. He liked his privacy.

Billy Claude kept his space neat, for a bachelor. He didn't own much. A couple of personal items, a few pieces of clothing, and one black robe with matching hood. His life revolved around work and the pool hall, so he never had occasion to entertain visitors. He only used the room for sleeping.

He had left the window open when he went to work that morning, since it was hot and he hated coming home to a stuffy room. Besides, he had been staying out a lot later than usual over the past weeks, and found it more convenient to slip into the room through the window rather than rousing Mrs. Worley or one of the other boarders by coming in the front door after ten.

It had been a long day at the brick plant, and a longer evening with his compadres at the pool hall, planning a few more patriotic nocturnal adventures. Billy Claude was tired and half-drunk when he raised the sash on his window and slung a leg over the sill to crawl inside. Otherwise he would have seen that someone was waiting for him.

His friends were worried when he didn't show up for work the next morning. When the noon whistle blew, Victor Hayes took it upon himself to go by the boardinghouse to check on Billy Claude.

Mrs. Worley had not seen him. No, not since yesterday's breakfast. Victor was welcome to knock on Billy Claude's door but she doubted he was there. He never missed meals.

There was no response, which gave Victor a very bad feeling. He tried the door handle.

Even before he saw Billy Claude's body lying on the floor in a pool of blood, Victor knew something very bad had happened. He recognized the smell of a violent death when it hit him in the face.

Chapter Fifty-five

*"Organization to resist draft law thought
to exist in several counties in Oklahoma."*
—*Ada Weekly News*, August 2, 1917

Now Scott had two murders on his hands. Both were Council of
Defense officers and both had had their throats slit from ear to
ear. It made illogical sense to Scott that someone had such strong
anti-war convictions that he would kill in the name of peace.

He was receiving daily bulletins from Sheriff Barger about
gatherings of slackers and unionists in several rural areas between
Muskogee and Oklahoma City. Infiltrators were reporting
that there were a thousand or more Working Class Union and
I.W.W. agitators camped in the Seminole hills. They had taken
to destroying bridges, telephone wires, and pipelines in an armed
protest against the Draft Act, trying to incite young men to resist
the call to arms. With violence, if necessary.

It was bad enough that the United States was at war with
Germany. Scott feared he was going to have to deal with a civil
war right in his own town. He met with the mayor and town
council to determine a course of action. Until now, Scott had
not gone out of his way to enforce the Espionage Act. Like it
or not, forbearance wasn't possible anymore.

The council resolved to issue a statement declaring that
anyone espousing anti-government sentiment would be arrested

and clapped in jail. Things being what they were, no one had a better idea.

After the meeting broke up, Scott buttonholed Emmanuel Clover on his way down the stairs.

"Emmanuel, if I was you, I'd get out of town for a while, at least until we find out who's doing in CD men."

Clover seemed grateful for Scott's concern. "Mr. Tucker, don't think I haven't considered it. I'd hate for Forsythia Lily to be an orphan. But I have sent her and her grandmother to stay with my wife's sister in Krebs until I think it's safe for them to come back."

"Wise move. But I'd feel better if you'd go with them."

"I know you don't need the bother of watching over me while you're trying to find a killer and keep the peace at the same time," Clover said. "But don't worry about me." He pulled back his suit coat to reveal the handle of a brand-new .45 caliber M1911 semi-automatic pistol protruding from the waistband of his trousers.

Scott gave a low whistle. "That'll sure put a hole in anybody who gets in your way. Just don't blow your foot off with it."

Clover was mildly affronted. "I've been practicing, Mr. Tucker. I know how to defend myself if I have to."

"All right, then. If you aim to stay in town, watch your back. In fact, why don't you take up residence in my wife's hotel until I arrest the culprit? There's a vacant room right next to the one where my deputy lives. You can stay for free."

"Thank you, sir, I appreciate it." Clover was touched. He leaned in confidentially. "You know as well as I do who is behind all this trouble, Sheriff. It's that loudmouthed traitor Dutch Leonard, as sure as I'm standing here. He's had it in for our CD representatives ever since you arrested his friend after that altercation with Mr. Avey at the house of ill-repute. And you saw for yourself how he behaved at the Liberty Sing. You know it was him who killed Win and Billy Claude."

"I know no such thing, Emmanuel. The fool may be after a change in government, but until that happens, a man is still innocent until proven guilty in this country. You stay away from Dutch and his kind. Do your job and let me do mine."

Mr. Clover took Scott's warning to heart. "You are absolutely right, Sheriff. I won't go looking for trouble. But I guarantee that if Dutch or anyone tries to hurt me or mine, well, he'd just better watch out, is all I can say."

"I appreciate your grit, Emmanuel," Scott said. "But keep your head down just the same."

Chapter Fifty-six

*"Be sober, be vigilant; because your adversary
the devil, as a roaring lion, walketh about,
seeking whom he may devour."*

—1 Peter 5:8

So many of her friends and neighbors had been suffering in one
form or another lately that Alafair packed a straw-lined crate
full of food to take to town to parcel out to the wounded and
bereaved. After leaving a stew with her neighbor Mr. Eichelberger, she dropped off two loaves of bread and a poke of greens
to Win Avey's mother. She might not have recognized Mrs. Avey
on the street, but she had lost children herself and understood
a mother's grief better than some.

She drove into town and headed up Kennetick Street with a
chicken pot pie for Henry Blackwood and his uncle. She came
up to the house from the back, along the dirt road at the edge
of town. As she neared the turn, she could see activity in the
backyard of the bawdy house. A wagon was parked at the back
door, piled high with furniture and trunks. Rose stood beside
the tailgate, directing Dave as he arranged boxes in the back of
the wagon. She was dressed for travel.

Dave trudged back up to the house and Rose turned to see
Alafair pull her buggy into the back drive and dismount.

Rose did not seem happy to see her. "What do you want?"

"Where are you going?" Alafair countered.

"You and your busybody mother-in-law can breathe easy. We're being shut down. Emmanuel Clover got a writ."

"Oh! I didn't hear that. When do you have to be out? Is there anything I can bring you to help ease the move? Do your girls need some traveling clothes or some food for the trip?"

"You never give up, do you?" Rose's tone was ironic, but not bitter. "Scott give us a week to be out, but I sold the house yesterday to Meriwether's law firm, so I don't see no need to hang around. And we don't need your cast-offs. I got plenty of money and the girls have already took their cut and gone their separate ways."

Alafair could barely see one very young-looking girl peeking out from behind the screen door at the back of the house. Rose followed her gaze. "Oh, that's Lucy. She ain't a working girl. Not quite right in the head. She's coming with me. Maybe she can get some schooling in Denver."

"So you're going to Denver? Are you going to…?" Alafair hesitated. Never in her life had she imagined she'd be standing in a driveway asking another woman if she was going to open a bordello in Denver. But Rose got the gist.

"The political climate is a mite hot for sporting houses these days. Reckon I'll have to find myself another line of work. Maybe I'll open a dress shop." Rose paused, a sarcastic twinkle in her eye. "Or maybe a bar. I'd make a hell of a lot more money that way."

Alafair expected that she was right about the bar. Vice was always more profitable than virtue, money-wise. "Miz Lovelock, I want to ask you something."

Rose looked wary.

"Don't worry, I ain't going to ask about your customers. I don't want to know."

Rose scoffed. "You worried that your man ain't getting what he needs at home? Need some tips?"

The uncalled-for snipe annoyed Alafair but she tamped down her irritation and ignored the comment. No use to expect Rose to change her nature. A whipped dog was likely to bite. "I figure you must hear many an indiscreet comment over the course of an evening, once men are in their cups."

That made Rose laugh. "Don't hardly hear any other kind."

"I'm wondering if anybody has let slip something that would give you an idea about who's committing the awful crimes around here lately."

"I wouldn't tell you if I had. Besides, what does that sordid business have to do with you?"

"A lot of the trouble of the last few weeks has had some connection to the brick plant." Alafair said. "My youngest boy has taken on work there. He's but sixteen years old. I can't get him to quit and I don't want him to get caught up in whatever this evil is. I want to know who's been damaging the equipment and causing men to get hurt. I want to know who killed Mr. Avey, and if they are one and the same." Alafair did not voice her suspicion that at least some of the night riders who had terrorized her daughter Mary worked at the plant as well.

As Alafair spoke, Rose's expression softened into something that resembled compassion. "You'd better get him out of there, Alafair."

Alafair was so surprised that Rose had called her by name that she almost didn't register what the woman had said to her. "You know something." It wasn't a question.

Rose heaved a sigh. "I'm telling you for your child's sake that something real bad is abroad in this town. You get that boy away from that place and keep him near home."

Rose's tone made Alafair's skin crawl. "You know who the killer is?"

Rose fell quiet. Dave came out of the house carrying a trunk and loaded it onto the back of the wagon. He did not look at the two women standing in the yard, staring at one another in silence. Once the trunk was tied down, Dave went back into the house.

Alafair did not break eye contact and neither did Rose. Finally Rose must have seen something in Alafair's gaze that she trusted, for she said, "I do. I know who killed Avey, at least. It was me."

Alafair blinked. Her face grew hot. "You…"

Rose shrugged. "Well, I didn't actually do the deed. You know, when Scott come out here to question me about Avey, I figured he suspected me because Avey's throat was cut. It was me who stabbed Star Karsten when she sold my girl. I did my best to take care of my baby girl but Karsten sold her off to a rich man when she was twelve and I ain't seen her since. And Avey is the one who pulled her out of my arms and locked me in my room while a stranger drove away with her. I didn't kill him, but he got killed because I said his name to the one who did. I wanted him dead and dead he is."

"Why haven't you told Scott who killed him?"

"Because he'd never believe me and there's nothing he could do about it if he did. Most people don't believe a true thing even when they see it with their own eyes. But I recognized the evil one right off. He found me on the street in Dallas, after my daddy tossed me out when I got in the family way. He kept me until my baby was born, then sold us to Karsten. That's the last time I saw him until the other night."

Alafair restrained herself from grabbing the woman by the shoulders and shaking her. "Well, who is it, for the love of Jesus?"

Rose's cheeks reddened and she leaned forward. "He's changed a hell of a lot. But I when I first saw standing out in front of the house, looking at me, I recognized the eyes. He come by here that night, but never did come in the house. After I closed, he sneaked up behind me in the yard. 'Give me a name,' he said. And I did. I figured he owed me my vengeance. When Scott told me what happened to Avey, I knew it was because of me."

Alafair was listening to this with her hand pressed to her forehead, torn between disbelief and horror. "Are you saying that you asked somebody to kill Win Avey and he did it?"

"Not somebody. Old Nick."

"Who?" Alafair said, just before the penny dropped. "The devil? You're saying that the devil is loose in Boynton and is hurting folks because you asked him to?"

"I don't have nothing to do with the whatever is going on over to the brick plant. But I sicced him on Avey, for sure. I wasn't headed for heaven anyway, but now there's a special room for me in the other place."

Alafair had no idea what to say. She scrambled for an intelligent response and decided that direct was best. "You're right, Miz Lovelock. No one will believe that the devil killed Win Avey because you wished it on him. So I reckon that even if it is true, you'd better make the best peace with it you can and get out of town while the gettin' is good."

"I aim to take that advice." Rose gestured toward the back door for the young peeper to come out. The girl was very pretty and very young. She glanced shyly at Alafair as Dave followed her out and handed her up onto the wagon seat, then climbed up beside her. The girl's eyes were so innocent. Alafair couldn't help but wonder who she was and how she had ended up sweeping floors in a bawdy house. She drew a breath to speak but Rose cut her off.

"Goodbye forever, Miz Tucker."

Alafair clapped her mouth shut and turned to walk back to her buggy when it occurred to her that she hadn't asked the most obvious question. "Miz Lovelock, what does the devil look like?"

Rose stepped up onto the wagon and settled herself beside the silent Lucy before she answered. "Not such a much. You'd hardly notice him, but for his thousand-yard stare and his bowler hat."

No one was home at Eric Bent's place, so Alafair left the stew in the straw-lined crate on the porch. After that, she sat in the buggy for a long time, thinking about what Rose Lovelock had said to her and trying to decide whether to tell Scott about it. Could Rose have actually spoken to the killer? Or was it all an hallucination brought on by her own grief and rage? Considering that Rose had named Satan himself as the murderer, Alafair was inclined to believe the latter. Besides, she wasn't sure she wanted to Scott to know she was acquainted with Rose Lovelock. She determined to stop by Sally's on the way home as ask her advice.

She still had food to deliver before she could think of anything else. She took a bushel basket of produce to Mrs. Schneberg, who had lost most of her garden to the vandals, and then headed downtown to deliver a pail of fried chicken to the Khouris, The market was closed, so she climbed the stairs and knocked on the door to their apartment. Aram Khouri opened the door and gave her a slightly relieved smile when he recognized her.

There was a lot of activity going on in the parlor, behind him. Ana and the children were packing up.

"Oh, no," Alafair said, instead of a greeting. "Not you, too! Y'all ain't leaving, are you?"

Khouri invited her in. "No, just sending Ana and the children back to Chicago for a while. My father and I will stay on and get the store reopened when we can." Ana took Alafair's offering, then ushered her to the one seat in the parlor that wasn't covered with clothing. Grandfather Khouri greeted her with a giant grin and cleared an armchair so he could take a seat next to her. Ana served glasses of a delicious, minty, hot tea and plates stacked high with treats from the huge collection of cakes and sweets the family had been showered with over the past few days. Alafair was glad to see that at least some people in the community had responded to the Khouris' troubles with kindness.

After Ana had served everyone and shooed the children out of the parlor to finish their packing, she joined Alafair on the settee.

"I'm so sorry you feel you must leave," Alafair said to her. "I'll miss you, and I'm sure my girls with miss their playmates."

"I hope we won't be gone long," Ana replied. "Boynton is our home now."

"I think my son is too cautious," Grandfather said. "There will be no more trouble now, I think."

Before Alafair could ask why he thought so, Aram Khouri said, "Did you hear that Billy Claude Walker was found murdered this morning?"

Alafair nearly choked on her tea. "No! Gracious me. What happened?."

"He died the same way as Win Avey. Throat cut. His friend found him in his room at Mrs. Worley's boardinghouse."

"Oh, this is terrible."

Grandfather Khouri gave a derisive "Hah!" He didn't look at all sorry about Billy Claude Walker's demise. Ana was embarrassed. "Papa thinks Mr. Walker was behind the damage to the store."

"He was," Grandfather assured her. "And I am not sorry. I curse him. I prayed for vengeance and vengeance was done."

Khouri and his wife admonished the old man, but Alafair's skin began to prickle. She put her tea glass on the table and sat back. "I heard the strangest thing this very morning about what happened to Win Avey. I was talking to…someone…who said that the devil came to her and she wished aloud to him that Mr. Avey would die. And then he did. She's convinced that her evil wish caused his death."

Ana crossed herself, horrified. "My mother told me that there are dark forces on the earth. She saw curses come to pass many times in the old country."

"I believe there are things that can't be explained," Alafair admitted. "But I have my doubts that this woman conjured the devil. She said that her devil had on a bowler hat, which last I heard was not part of Satan's wardrobe."

Ana shook her head. "The devil comes in many guises…" she began, but Grandfather Khouri burst into laughter and she swallowed her sentence.

Khouri gaped at his father. "Papa, two men are dead. Why do you laugh?"

The old man wiped his eyes and tamped his mustache with his napkin. "I know this man. This bowler hat man. After the store is wrecked, he comes to me on the sidewalk. 'I can help you,' he says. I will not let happen to my children such things as I endured in Turkey. And now all my people there are being killed and made to lose everything. Find who did this, I say to the man. Do not let such a thing happen here. And Walker has been punished. Righteous punishment is from God. No, this man in the hat is not the devil, my children. He is a man."

Chapter Fifty-seven

"Watch your neighbor. If he is not doing everything in his power to help the nation in this crisis, see that he is reported to the authorities."
—*Tulsa Daily World*

After he punched his time card and hung up his hat in the changing room, Henry flopped down on the bench next to Charlie. "How you doing, young'un?"

"All right, I reckon."

"I hear your sister had some trouble out at her place. I'm sorry to hear it."

Charlie couldn't meet his eyes. "I'm sorry too. Mary don't deserve it, that's for sure."

Henry flung an arm over Charlie's shoulder. "Well, I sure don't hold it against your brother-in-law that he was born in Germany, and anybody that does is a dang jackass."

The way that Henry spat out the word "jackass" made Charlie smile. "I agree with you. Kurt can't help where he was born."

"Nor can any of us," Henry agreed. "Well, anyhow, I just want you to know that not everybody thinks like Billy Claude Walker and his gang."

"I appreciate that." Charlie studied Henry out of the corner of his eye for a moment as they chewed their sandwiches. Henry might be a decade older than Charlie, but he had always treated

Charlie like a friend. "Say, Henry, I've been mulling over the what has been going on here at the plant over the past weeks."

Henry didn't look at him. "Have you, now?"

"Somebody is trying to sabotage production."

"Some folks think so."

"I'm one of them. Mr. Ober thinks so, too, considering how he's added armed men to the night watch."

"Do you have some notion of who might be behind it all?"

Charlie bit his lip. He trusted Henry, but did he dare? "Promise you won't tell a soul?"

The blue eyes widened. "Well, now, I don't know about that, especially if you're about to tell me it's you. I don't want to be thrown in the clink as an accessory to treason."

It took Charlie a moment to realize he was being teased. "No, it ain't me." He hesitated, and took a breath. "Have you heard about my uncle who is visiting out to our farm?"

The corners of Henry's mouth lifted. "The rabble-rousing Wobblie? Yeah, I heard."

So much for keeping Robin's socialist leanings a secret. Charlie cast a glance around. "Listen, I'd appreciate it if you'd keep that to yourself, in case there's somebody in all of Boynton who ain't heard it. Anyway, my uncle just came to Boynton to visit with my ma for a spell, and he's swore on a stack of Bibles that he's not here to cause trouble."

"Don't worry, young'un. I don't care what your uncle's philosophy is and don't intend to spread the word. Every man to his own affairs, I say."

"Good. Thanks. I don't agree with my uncle, but I like him a lot. The thing is I saw him talking to old Dutch Leonard who got let go from the plant for getting into it with Billy Claude Walker at the Liberty Sing. If Dutch is an anti-war unionist, he might be the type to engage in sabotage. Maybe killing, too."

Charlie's reasoning intrigued Henry. "You suspect your uncle is involved?

"No, no. Lord, I hope not. But Robin might have given old Dutch some ideas without knowing how far he'd go."

"Have you asked your uncle what him and Leonard were talking about? Have you told anybody what you saw?"

Charlie shook his head. "No, I haven't. Uncle Robin is getting ready to leave, anyway. But what if it is Dutch Leonard? And what if somebody saw him and Robin talking and figured they're in it together? I don't want anybody to go off half-cocked and decide my whole family is involved."

"Why are you telling me this, Charlie? What do you want me to do about it? I'm not confronting Dutch Leonard, that's for sure."

"I ain't asking you to. No, I'm thinking that if I could get a handle on who the saboteur is, then my uncle and my whole family would be off the hook. And I got a strong feeling it's Dutch Leonard."

Henry huffed and leaned back on the bench. "You know, Charlie, even if Dutch was the one who was messing with the machinery, he could have been doing it while he was on the job. And if it is him, how are we going to know when and where he'll strike next? This is a big area to keep an eye on."

"I don't know for sure. But listen, you know how there's a couple carloads of bricks sitting on the side rail, ready to ship out to Fort Bliss day after tomorrow? Well, I'm thinking that it would be a fine opportunity for an outlaw to do something to keep that shipment from leaving out."

Henry thought it over for a moment. "Sounds like you'd make a good saboteur yourself, if you ever decide to change professions. So what are we going to do to stop this from happening? When we see Dutch sidling up to the rail car with a stick of dynamite, shall we jump out and throttle him?"

"I ain't got that far yet. There are two of us and one of him, though."

"What if he's armed? Besides, I'm not much of a brawler."

"Well, maybe it's enough if we catch him in the act. If we holler loud enough, a few of them armed guards will come a'running before Dutch can do any damage."

"You think he's going to sneak back in the dead of night now that Mr. Ober has hired all these bulls to patrol around at night? How can you can catch him if the law and all the king's men can't?"

Henry had more counter-arguments than Charlie had arguments, but the boy was not dissuaded. "I've got to try. I got a Red in the family and a German, too. If I can help catch this traitor then nobody is going to question where the Tuckers' loyalties lie."

An expression of surprised sympathy passed over Henry's face and was gone. He leaned forward and draped his forearms over his knees. "I suspect you have a plan."

The fact that Henry hadn't laughed at him or dismissed his fears out of hand gave Charlie a surge of confidence. "Well, I been thinking about it, Henry. Dutch is not going to try and walk right in the front gate. But he worked here a long time. He knows how to get around without being seen. And I've seen him, real early in the morning, creeping around the clay hill behind the plant and entering at a place where a section of the fence has fallen down. I went and had a look at it myself the other day."

Henry considered this for a moment. "All right, say you're right. What do you propose we do about it?"

"Let's set a watch on that gap in the fence tonight. With all the guards wandering around, Dutch will have to sneak into the plant. And he knows to use that gap to slip in unseen."

Henry smiled and looked away, but didn't try to come up with another objection. He could see that Charlie was going to attempt this clandestine surveillance, no matter what he said. He shook his head. "All right, young'un. I don't know whether you're smarter than everybody in town or just love to chase wild geese, but I'd hate to see you get your head stove in. I'll watch with you."

Charlie bit his lip. "We may have to keep an eye on that gap for more than one night."

"Well, I don't know how long I'll be up for nighttime skull-duggery, Charlie. My delicate constitution flags without a good night's sleep."

Charlie's face fell, and Henry chuckled. "I'll tell you what. I'll give you until the shipment for Bliss goes out. That's two nights. If nothing happens, will you give this up?"

"It's a deal!"

Chapter Fifty-eight

*"One Thousand Possemen Prepare to Round Up
Four Hundred Heavily Armed Rioters Near Sasakwa"*
—*Tulsa Daily World*, August 4, 1917

Nick snatched his bowler off his head as he stood in front of the deputy's desk. "Good afternoon," he said. "Is the constable about?"

Trent cocked his head, curious. The nondescript man with the little white scar was a stranger to him, but he could swear there was something familiar about the eyes. "No, Mr. Tucker isn't here right now. Is there something I can do to help you?"

Nick sat down. "I contemplated for days whether or not to come in and tell you about this, Deputy. I'm just passing through town and I don't like getting mixed up in things that are none of my business. But I been thinking about it and I figure it's my duty to let y'all know that I heard something the other night that you'll want to look into. It sounded like treason to me."

Trent blinked at him. "Well, then you'd better tell me what you heard."

"It was at the Liberty Sing on Friday. That was quite the event, I must say. I applaud your sheriff for his peacekeeping abilities. Nothing gets rioters' attention like blasting a hole in the ceiling. Anyway, I didn't want to get caught up in the brawling, so I was heading back for my room when I passed by three fellows standing in the shadows at the back of the building with their heads together. I heard one of them say something about the Industrial Workers of the World, so I strolled by real casual and hid myself behind a bush around the corner so I could hear what they were talking about."

Nick gave a self-depreciating smile. "I know it's unseemly to eavesdrop, but I recognized one of them as the man who started the fracas. He had on this tall hat. You know, the one who told your CD man to shut up?"

Trent was interested, now. "Yes, I know who you mean."

"I could hear them pretty well. The tall-hat one and his friend were making arrangements with the third man to go with them to meet with a bunch of draft-resisters. Seems that a mob of them are getting together to form an army and start an uprising. The young one plans to meet the third guy tomorrow morning out behind the Masonic Hall and lead him to the place where the rebels are camped. Someplace called Sasakwa."

So it was true. Trent could hardly keep from dashing out the door to find Scott. "Did they say what time they're meeting?"

"Early. I heard them say around dawn."

"Is Dutch going, too?"

"Dutch?"

"The one in the tall hat." Trent sounded impatient.

"He didn't say so. Just the young one, the Indian."

"Can you describe the third one?"

"Wiry little fellow with a beard. Had on an U.S. Army uniform hat. They said he was a Wobblie."

Scott didn't bother to say hello to his deputy when he strode into the jailhouse with a piece of paper in his hand. "I just got a wire from Sheriff Duncan over in Pontotoc County. He's asking for volunteers to ride on a large gathering of W.C.U. agitators who have gathered near Little River with a mind to start a rebellion."

Trent stood up so quickly that his chair nearly tipped over. "Scott, there was man in here not five minutes ago who told me that he overheard three fellows planning to leave out tomorrow to join up with an army of draft resisters not far from Sasakwa. Said one of them was the man with the tall hat who started the riot—Dutch Leonard."

Scott's eyebrows knit. "Who was this helpful eavesdropper?"

"I didn't know him. Called himself Nick Smith. Said he hasn't been in town but a little while and didn't fancy getting mixed up in doings that were none of his business, but he had been thinking about it and he couldn't conscience treason. He told me he's staying at Miz Worley's, in case you want to talk to him."

"Did he describe the other two conspirators?"

"Said there was a young one who looked like an Indian." Trent hesitated and bit his lip. "He said the other one was a wiry little fellow with a beard and a U.S. Army uniform hat."

Scott lowered himself into one of the chairs under the window.

Trent plowed on. "Mr. Smith said the young one made plans to meet the bearded fellow at dawn tomorrow, out behind the Masonic Hall, and lead him to the place where the rebels are camped."

Scott unlocked his desk drawer and retrieved his gun belt. "Let's go talk to this Nick Smith."

◇◇◇

Mrs. Worley had never heard of Nick Smith. Scott and Trent stood together in the middle of the road in front of the boarding-house for a few minutes to consider their options.

"Well, Trent, what did Smith look like?"

"Not much of anything. Ordinary as dirt. He had a little scar next to his right eye. Oh, and he did have on one of them hats that look like an upside-down pot."

"He don't sound familiar to me," Scott admitted. "Do you reckon he was trying to send us on a wild goose chase?"

"Listen, I hate to, but got to say it…" Trent's face flushed as only a redhead's can.

"So say it."

"All this trouble started after Ruth's uncle Rob Gunn came to town."

Scott was not surprised at Trent's suspicion. "You think Rob Gunn is behind all this trouble?"

"I don't know. I only met him a couple times and he seemed all right. But Ruthie told me right off that he's a Wobblie organizer. And she also told me that he's leaving Boynton tomorrow." Trent had formed an opinion about Rob Gunn which wasn't all that complimentary. Still. "I hope to heaven he ain't involved. I'd hate to have to look Ruth in the eye if we have to arrest her mother's brother for sedition."

"I'll tell you what, son, let's you and me try to follow these two rebels after they meet up at the Masonic Hall in the morning. Maybe we can nip this uprising in the bud and save Ruth's kin to boot."

Chapter Fifty-nine

"There is a wrong organization in Pontotoc,
Seminole, Pottawatomie…counties, the purpose
of which is to resist the draft law."
—*Ada Weekly News*, August 2, 1917

Following Rob Gunn and Dick Miller from Boynton to the rebel
headquarters outside of Sasakwa wasn't easy for Scott and Trent.
Scott wished mightily that Rob had just left town on his own
never to be heard from again. But as it was, he felt he had no
choice but to see for himself what was Rob was up to and stop
him if he could. If Rob was planning to join the insurgents just
as Sheriff Duncan and his posse converged on the slacker army
with guns blazing, there wouldn't be anything Scott could do
to keep the situation from going to hell. Rob would either end
up dead or in Leavenworth.

Trent met up with Scott at the jailhouse before dawn with
two saddled horses in tow, and were well hidden by the time
Rob rendezvoused with his contact. Miller picked Rob up in
an automobile, which caused the men on horseback some con-
sternation at first. But the roads were so bad that Miller and
Rob spent about as much time pushing the auto out of ruts and
changing flat tires as they did driving in a forward direction.
Sometimes the lawmen had to spend half an hour at a time
sitting in the saddle, watching them from the woods off to the

side of the road. It was late in the afternoon by the time they got where they were going.

Scott and his deputy dismounted and followed along on foot as the straining auto headed deeper into the trees. It wasn't long until they began to hear voices ahead. A lot of voices. Scott motioned to Trent and they stopped as Miller's auto ground to a halt twenty feet ahead of them.

Trent followed Scott's lead and tied Brownie's reins to a skinny blackjack before the two of them crept forward. They were at the bottom of a craggy hill. A red flag flapped from a pole at the crest, near a broad, flat tree trunk. Trent drew a breath. There were at least a couple hundred people gathered in the clearing.

Scott surveyed the situation for some minutes. By following Rob he had found the rebel army. Yet he was disappointed that he was not going to be able to do anything for his shirttail kin. It was too late. Rob was in the middle of the enemy camp. "I think we'd better withdraw," Scott whispered. "Let's ride south and see if we can meet up with Duncan and his posse before they get here."

The two men scooted backwards on their bellies until they were far enough into the woods not to be seen, then crept back to where the horses were tied.

Someone was there ahead of them. Standing at Brownie's shoulder was a rough-looking old man in overalls and bare feet. He greeted them with the barrel of a shotgun.

"We've come to join the revolution," Scott said, without missing a beat.

"Your tin badge says otherwise," the man replied. "But I ain't one to judge. What's the password?"

Scott knew they were sunk. "Don't know. But I finally had enough. I want to join up."

The old man wasn't buying it. "Reckon you can join after I tie you up to yonder persimmon tree. Go ahead on, then, and don't make any quick moves or I'll send you both to hell."

Chapter Sixty

"A wise son maketh a glad father,
but a foolish son is the heaviness of his mother."
—Proverbs 10:1

Since Charlie slept by himself on a cot in the parlor, he thought that it would be easy for him to sneak out of the house after everyone went to bed. He and Henry had arranged to meet near the plant as soon as Charlie could get away after it became full dark. Which since it was late summer, full dark didn't happen until nearly nine o'clock. Henry lived in town and didn't have to account for himself to his uncle, so he volunteered to begin the stakeout earlier. If all went as planned, Charlie could expect everyone in the house to be asleep in time for him to get away by nine-thirty or so. If he had the roan saddled and ready when he snuck out, he could join Henry at the stakeout by ten.

Things did not go as planned.

Charlie got home from the brick plant a little after two in the afternoon, ate a mashed bean sandwich, caught a twenty-minute nap, and reported to his father in the corral for his afternoon work assignment.

One of Shaw's hands, Tommy Cloud, was working with a newly saddle-broken mule and Shaw was standing outside the fence, watching, when Charlie walked up.

"Ah, there you are, son. I've been waiting for you. Kurt has a load of finisher hogs ready to ship out to the co-op in Tulsa. He's made arrangements to put them on the eleven-fifteen to Muskogee tonight and travel with them all the way to Tulsa. After their troubles, we figured it'd be better for Kurt to start the trip from Boynton late while nobody much is around. Mary and Judy are staying here with Mama until he gets back. Coleman Welsh is going to watch over their place for a spell."

Charlie's heart fell into his boots. Under any other circumstance he'd be champing at the bit to take a train trip, even if it was only to look after a stock car full of pigs. As it was, he envisioned Henry Blackwood sitting outside the brick plant at midnight, wondering where he was. Or worse, Henry catching Dutch Leonard in the act of sabotage and becoming the town hero—without Charlie. He schooled his face to remain impassive. He'd have to figure out some way to get to Henry and call it off. "What do you need me to do, Daddy?"

"Well, right now we need to get over there to Kurt's and help him separate out the hogs and get them fed and watered and loaded on the wagons. Me and Gee Dub are going to Tulsa with Kurt. We won't be leaving for town until maybe eight o'clock, but as soon as it gets dark, I want you to come back here and stay with Mama and them. I reckon you can go on in to work at the plant tomorrow, but stay around close otherwise."

Charlie didn't say anything, but his face must have registered surprise, for Shaw said, "Now, I know you want to go with us, but you're the one who wanted a war job and you can't just take the day off when there's something else you'd rather be doing. Besides, I'm going to feel better about the gals if you're here to keep an eye out for trouble."

Charlie breathed a sigh of relief. He didn't have to abandon his plans after all. He just had to get around his mother, which was always going to be a task. She had ears like a bat.

◇◇◇

Readying two wagonloads of hogs for transport was hard work. The men had to convince the animals to go through the makeshift chutes, up the ramps, and into the wagons, and if a two-hundred-fifty-pound animal had other plans, then a great deal of persuasion was called for. The sun had already sunk below the horizon before Shaw released Charlie to go home.

Rather than put the white-maned roan into his stall when he got home, Charlie tied him to a post in the barn, fed and watered him and rubbed him down. When he put the saddle back on, the horse was not happy.

"Don't give me no trouble, now, Hero," Charlie admonished. "You and me got important spy work to do tonight."

The roan laid his ears back and blew snot all over Charlie's shoulder. Undeterred by the horse's reluctance, the boy walked back up to the house, changed his shirt, and had a light supper with his family as though this night were the same as all the nights that had come before in his unexciting life.

Chapter Sixty-one

"Men are as clay in the hands of the consummate leader."
—*Leaders of Men* by Woodrow Wilson, 1890

Sasakwa was about sixty miles southwest of Boynton, as the crow flies. But a crow would have gotten thoroughly lost if he took the circuitous route that Miller followed as he drove Rob Gunn to the rebel camp. At first the roads were wide enough, but dusty and pitted from the long dry spell, so the going was slow from the beginning. But when they turned off the main thoroughfare onto the farm trails and wagon ruts that led into the interior of Seminole County, Rob found himself profoundly wishing that they had just travelled on horseback in the first place. As they drew nearer their destination, they were stopped a couple of times and questioned at roadblocks that had been set up by the resistance faction. What would normally have been a three-hour trip took twice that, and by the time they reached a bluff on a hill near a remote farm, it was late in the day.

Rob was surprised at the size of the crowd that awaited them. Tents lined the edge of the woods and a red flag had been hoisted up a makeshift flag pole in the center of the camp. How long had this rebellion been brewing, he wondered? A haunch of beef was roasting on a spit, and a group of women sitting near the fire, shucked ears of corn. Children chased each other through the crowd, their shrill laughter adding to the general chaos. It reminded Rob of a camp meeting, an old-fashioned revival like the ones his father had conducted. He could even feel the fervor of the holy spirit of socialism upon the crowd. He stepped out of the automobile and followed Miller as he walked toward the group. People were turning to look at them, moving toward them, colored and white and Indian, all happy to see him.

So many hands slapped his back as Miller led him through the crowd that he figured he would be bruised in the morning. He mounted a planed-off stump that doubled as a podium and surveyed the eager faces in front of him as Miller made the introductions, judging his audience before deciding the approach he was going to take.

He had seen them all before. They were the same impoverished, uneducated, ill-used working men and women he had come to know all over the United States. These were mostly tenant farmers and sharecroppers, so far in debt to banks and landlords that they had no hope of ever being free of it. His heart swelled with compassion. Rob turned his attention back to Miller when he heard his name spoken.

Miller was looking at him. "Mr. Gunn," he said, "this here is our army, and we intend to march on Washington, gathering up the thousands of citizens who oppose this banker's war on the way. We will live off the land, and if anybody can, it's us folks who turn the soil with our own hands. Mr. Gunn, we aim to sustain ourselves on the crops of this green land all the way to Washington."

He moved aside to allow Rob to step forward, and the audience erupted into applause and excited whoops. He stood eyeing the crowd for a long minute after silence fell, until he could feel every eye on him.

"I hope y'all will call me Rob, and not 'Mr. Gunn,' because I'm just a plain working man, just like every one of you." His voice was pitched high and loud enough to be heard at the farthest reaches of the clearing. "Dick told me your plan. I consulted the governing board of the International Workers of the World about it, and they put their heads together with the leaders of the American Socialist Party. I'm telling y'all this so you'll know that I ain't just blowing hot air." He waited while the crowd cheered it's approval. Miller slapped Rob on the back so hard that he staggered.

As he readjusted his hat, his eye fell on an old man escorting two figures into the clearing at the point of a shotgun. He tried not to fall off the stump when he recognized the prisoners. He recovered himself quickly. "Yes, well. Both them organizations had a thing or two they want me to relay to y'all before you get your revolution to going. The leadership of the Industrial Workers of the World have conveyed to me that the union cannot back your plan. They advocate resistance, but not open rebellion during time of war. Y'all are on your own."

A strange surge of noise rose on the air, like a moan, that seemed to have no source. Rob was suddenly reminded of a lynching. The hair stood up on the back of his neck. He glanced toward Trent and Scott, now both tied to the bole of a persimmon tree at the edge of his line of sight. They had both fixed him with a grim stare. He took a breath and sternly returned his thoughts to the matter at hand. "I've been recruiting and organizing for the I.W.W. for a decade. I'm a union man to my bones, and I'll not change my stripes now. But I'm telling you that hanging by your principals is not going to be easy. In fact it will be downright dangerous. Your march will not succeed. Most Americans are not on your side. Don't think for a minute that the powers-that-be don't know your plans. There are spies in your midst right now." He glanced toward the prisoners again. "We may lose the fight this time. We may lose the fight next time, and the next. They will try to beat us down again and again. But if we persevere in the right, we cannot help but win over the powers of evil."

Scott Tucker figured that he and Trent would be lucky if they didn't get shot in the melee that would break out when Duncan and his band finally showed up. Until that happened there wasn't much either of them could do, trussed up hand and foot as they were, so Scott tried to find a comfortable seat against the tree trunk and set himself to listen to what Rob was saying to the insurgents.

Scott had attended many of Elder Robert Gunn's tent revivals when he was boy, and though the Elder Gunn's son did not physically resemble him in the least, Scott was overcome with an eerie feeling of being transported back in time as he listened to Rob speak. The voice was the same; the tone, the pitch, the passion. The pure and untainted belief in the truth of his words.

The crowd had sunken into silence when Rob delivered the I.W.W.'s decision, but enthusiasm was building again as he continued. "This war was started by the capitalists and industrialists as a way to line their pockets. If you want to win you've got to hit them where it hurts. In the pocketbook. They live by your toil, so quit working for the bankers and the landlords. Work for each other. Form a commune. As for the draft, no force on earth can make a man fight if he don't want to. If they come for you, refuse to fight. If they throw your brother into prison for resisting, spread the word. See that the world knows how a real man stands up for his principles."

Scott could tell that Trent was outraged by the speech. The young man's face was beet red. But almost against his will, Scott was fascinated. Rob was transported, lit from within. "Violence begets violence, brothers and sisters. If you return blow for blow, you're no better than them who would crush you. There ain't nothing stronger than the power of folded arms.

"It was you who plowed this prairie, dug mines, laid the railroad. You build their buildings and grow the crops that feed them. You are not helpless. They can't do without you. But you can't do it alone, neither. Stand together." He raised a fist into the air. "Solidarity! Unite! Unite! Unite!"

The crowd was electrified. They began chanting with him, "Unite! Unite! Unite!"

It took a minute for Scott to realize that the chant was turning to screams. Gunfire punctuated the yelling, and all at once there was chaos, people running for their lives, scattered by dozens of armed men on horseback, charging up the hill.

Trent tried to struggle to his feet. "We're rescued!"

"Sit down, boy," Scott hissed, "before a stray bullet gets you."

The prisoners huddled close under the tree, trying not to get trampled or shot in the confusion, yelling to be released at any likely looking posse member who dashed by, but nobody cast a glance in their direction. It occurred to Scott that the two of them would make good hostages for the rebels. He was getting nervous. It didn't help when he felt someone sawing at the rope that bound them to the tree.

A ferocious whisper cautioned them to be still.

"Robin?" Scott said.

"Dang it, I said hold still." Rob was just out of Scott's line of sight, behind Trent, whose hands had been miraculously freed from their bonds. Trent scrambled up and Rob appeared around the tree trunk in a crouch, a wicked-looking buck knife in his hand, and went to work on Scott's fetters. "We've got to get out of here," he said, as he sawed, "before some yahoo figures out y'all would be good bargaining chips."

Trent and Rob helped Scott to stand and the three of them made for the woods as anarchy reigned around them. Rob led them to the area where the horses were picketed. They were lucky to find their own horses still there. Fugitives were mounting up and fleeing right and left.

"Looks like the cowards cut and run," Trent crowed. Rob didn't respond. The unnatural glow was gone from his face. He looked diminished.

Scott grabbed the reins of Rob's mule as he mounted. "I thank you for rescuing us, Robin, but I'm going to have to arrest you on suspicion of sabotage and maybe the murder of Win Avey and Billy Claude Walker."

Rob's eyes widened. "I didn't kill nobody…"

Scott spoke over him. "I ain't got time to argue with you. Let's get out of here before Duncan and his gang decide to haul you in for inciting a riot and being a traitor."

"Our firearms," Trent attempted.

Scott ignored him. "Let's go, boys. No time to debate the finer points of the law."

Chapter Sixty-two

"Fools rush in where angels fear to tread."
—Alexander Pope

It took forever for Alafair and Mary to put the children to bed. On top of everything, Chase wanted to sleep in the parlor with Charlie, so Alafair fixed up a pallet beside Charlie's cot before she even began to get ready for bed herself. Mary and Judy bunked in one of the two double beds in the girls' room, and Grace happily went to sleep with her mother.

Charlie lay in the dark, staring at the ceiling, for what seemed to him to be hours and hours, trying to wait long enough for everyone to be well asleep before he made his move. Chase fell asleep instantly and deeply, in the way of seven-year-old boys, so Charlie slipped out of bed and stepped over him without worry. He retrieved his shirt and trousers from the end of his bed and went into the kitchen to pull on his boots and creep out the back door. The screen creaked when he opened it, giving him pause, but he didn't hear anyone stir and made his way carefully down the steps before running for the barn.

He was horrified to see the roan in the barnyard, still saddled, his reins dragging the ground as he grazed. The horse had gotten loose, untied himself somehow from the post in the barn. The animal raised his head when he saw Charlie approaching, and began to trot off toward the grassy field behind the tool shed.

Apparently the roan was not convinced that this trip was necessary, for Charlie chased him, begged him, pleaded with him, for a quarter of an hour. The roan never let him get within arm's length.

Charlie was nearly in tears and had exhausted his supply of profanity when he gave up and ran back to the barn to saddle Pork Chop, a much more obliging horse even if he was built like a barrel. If he had had the time, Charlie would have picked out a likelier mount, but the stables were a far piece from the barn, and he was desperate not to keep Henry waiting any longer than he had to. Since he had to pass the house before he reached the road to town, he headed out at a walk. His plan to slip silently past the house didn't pan out.

His mother was standing on the front porch in her nightgown. He couldn't see her expression in the dark, but it didn't matter. The tone of her voice told him all he needed to know.

"Charlie, where are you going?"

He was caught, but it was too late. He wasn't about to come this far with his plan only to be thwarted by his mother. He reined in by the picket fence. "Me and Henry Blackwood got it figured out who the brick plant saboteur is, Ma. We think he's going to try to pull something tonight, and we're going to hide and catch him in the act. We made our plans before I knew Daddy and Gee Dub would be gone, but it's got to be tonight. Y'all will be all right."

His reasoning didn't sway Alafair. "Charlie, get back in the house, now. You can't go gallivanting off in the middle of the night on some harebrained scheme and leave us all on our own out here."

It was hard for Charlie to concentrate on what Alafair was saying. Pork Chop was eager to get on with his nighttime ride, and so was the boy. "Faugh, Mama, they ain't a helpless female among you. Nobody is going to bother y'all and even if they do, Mary's twice as better a shot than me."

"Charlie, your daddy said…"

Charlie cut her off. "You don't understand, Ma! You don't go to town enough to hear how folks are talking about us. You don't know what it's like to have everybody look at you funny because your sister's husband is a German and your uncle is a socialist. I got to prove we're one hundred percent with the president, and then maybe they'll leave us alone." He dug heels into Pork Chop's flanks and took off.

"Charlie Boy!" He was halfway down the drive when she cried his name.

She barely heard his reply when he called back over his shoulder. "I ain't a child, Ma."

Alafair watched openmouthed as he galloped off. She was not used to outright mutiny from her children. She could feel the blood pumping in her temples.

Gee Dub was going off to war, as was her soon-to-be son-in-law Trent. Kurt and Mary were being threatened and harassed. Robin had been accused of fomenting revolution and maybe of murder. Innocent people were being hounded and run out of town. And there was nothing she could do about any of it. And now her wild-hearted boy was rushing headlong to confront the devil.

She was not going to have it.

Sophronia, Grace, Mary, and Chase were standing at the screen in their nightclothes, watching aghast as Charlie staged his getaway. Sophronia crashed out the door and down the steps as Charlie rode away. "Charlie, come back! Come back before you can't come back no more!"

Alafair strode back up the porch steps. "Mary, do you figure you and the children will be all right for a spell while I go to fetch him back?"

Mary was generally a cheerful woman, but the times had blunted her sense of humor. Her expression was grim as she nodded at Alafair. "Don't worry about us, Ma. I'm just in the mood to shoot somebody. Maybe you should stop by Martha's and take Streeter with you, or maybe Walter."

Mary was following her mother through the house as Alafair threw on a dress, retrieved a key from the top shelf of the armoire in her bedroom, and unlocked the gun cabinet in the corner of the parlor. She took down a rifle and a box of shells before heading for the back door. "I'm too far behind the lunkheaded youngster as it is, honey. No, Grace, I ain't going to shoot Charlie, howsoever much I feel like it. I have to saddle up Missy and that'll take me a fair spell to get out to the stable and all. No, Fronie, you can't help and you can't come. You neither, Chase. Y'all stay in the house. I mean it, now. Blanche, you help Mary with Judy. I'll be back as soon as I can."

And with that she was out the back door and striding toward the barn, shaking with anger and outrage and fear that her hot-headed boy was riding into far more trouble than he knew. She stopped in her tracks when she saw a large, dark shape in the barnyard. A saddled horse, judging by the jingle of its tack. She slowed and walked toward it carefully, trying not to spook it. The animal stood where it was, its head turned in her direction, until she was close enough to see that it was Charlie's beloved white-maned roan gelding.

"Well, I'll be," she said aloud. She knew that Charlie and the horse had their differences, so she sized up the situation quickly. "So you decided not to go along with this idiot scheme."

The horse snorted an acknowledgement.

Alafair could have passed by the obstreperous horse and gone to the stable to saddle her own mare as she had planned. But here before her stood a fast beast all ready to go. She made up her mind in an instant and strode toward him. He shied and backed away.

"Hold still, Sweet Honey Baby," she barked.

The roan knew better than to argue.

Alafair was too far behind Charlie to follow him by sight, and it was too dark to track him. All she knew was what he had told her. He and Henry Blackwood intended to catch the saboteur in the act, which meant he was headed for the brick plant. The plant covered eighty acres, and she had no idea where the boys planned to set up surveillance. The best she could hope for was to be able to get there before they went into hiding, or perhaps she could rouse the night watchman and alert him to what the boys were up to. If all else failed, she'd wake up Mr. Ober at his house and have Charlie and Henry arrested for trespassing.

Chapter Sixty-three

"Treachery and sedition must be combatted. Unworthy and sordid motives must be ferreted out and their authors deprived of all power for wrong doing."
—Tulsa County Council of Defense Report

As he neared the brick plant, Charlie could see an armed man standing at the front entrance. He halted Pork Chop well back from the gate and studied the situation for a moment. Even from his vantage point on the main road, he could see two or three ghostly lights floating around the yard. The lanterns of the night watchmen.

He had known that Mr. Ober had hired extra security, but it had not occurred to him until this moment that the guards wandering around the grounds were likely to interfere with his plans to catch Dutch Leonard in the commission of his crime. Yet Charlie knew about the gap in the fence. All Dutch had to do was get onto the grounds without being seen, and then if he were careful, he would be able to move around while avoiding detection.

His mother's voice in his head interrupted his rationalization. *Why don't you just tell Mr. Ober what you know? He's better equipped to confront a traitor than you are.*

Charlie firmly ignored the voice of reason and turned his horse onto the field that led to the clay hills at the rear of the plant.

He found Henry waiting for him in the copse of trees that backed up to the hills, as they had arranged. Charlie dismounted and led his horse into the trees. "Seen anything?" Charlie kept his voice low.

"Not a thing. Where you been, young'un? I was about to decide you weren't coming."

"It's a long story. My ma saw me leave, though. I'm going to catch hell tomorrow. If Dutch don't come tonight, I don't reckon I'm going to be able to do this again. Not unless I leave home for good, that is."

Henry sighed. He had only gone along with Charlie's wild idea because he liked the boy and he had told Alafair he'd look after him. Looking after Charlie was turning out to be a harder job than Henry had anticipated. "Well, maybe that's just as well. I don't know how long I could keep up this twenty-four-hour-a-day schedule."

"I'll bet you money that tonight is all we'll need."

"Keep your money. I'll tell you what. If Dutch don't show up tonight, I'll go with you to Mr. Ober tomorrow and we'll tell him everything you saw…" He swallowed his sentence and squinted into the dark. "I'll be damned," he whispered. "There's somebody out there."

◇◇◇

The guard stationed at the entrance to the brick plant held up his lantern in order to get a good look at whoever was approaching in the dead of night. A middle-sized woman on horseback, brandishing a rifle, was the last person on earth he expected to see. He walked forward to meet her as she reined at the gate.

Alafair didn't recognize the man, but he had the bean-pole, beaky-nosed look of the Tyler family who raised cotton out south of town. "Howdy," she said. "Have you seen a couple of young fellows come by tonight? One of them would be on a pinto."

"Nobody's been down this road since the last shift finished, ma'am, except for you."

"Are you acquainted with Charlie Tucker or Henry Black-wood?"

"Can't say I am."

"Well, keep an eye out for them, anyway. Both tall boys with fair hair. I fear they aim to sneak onto the grounds. My son and his friend have got it into their heads that somebody is going to slip in here tonight and do some damage, and they think it's up to them to stop it."

Her warning amused the guard no end. "Ma'am, Mr. Ober has so many men guarding this plant that a rat couldn't slip onto the premises without us knowing. I guarantee that nobody is going to tamper with any machinery tonight or any other night."

"Well, that's good to hear. But I hope you'll pass the word that they're around. If they try to sneak into the plant, I'd appreciate it if you wouldn't shoot them. My boy is sixteen and I'm hoping he'll live to see seventeen."

"I'll let my boss know, ma'am. We'll keep a watch for them. I've got a fifteen-year-old son myself, and he's always looking for ways to get his head busted."

Alafair guided the roan back out to the main road at a walk and started back the way she had come. She didn't know what to do, now. She wasn't as panicky as she had been when Charlie rode off into the dark, determined to accost a killer. There were plenty of guards around to arrest anyone who wasn't supposed to be there. She was disappointed in Henry for going along with this scheme, though. Or perhaps Henry thought he was keeping Charlie from doing anything stupider than lying in wait all night. She hoped so. Henry had seemed like a level-headed young man.

Should she go back and wait for Charlie to come home with his tail between his legs in the morning? The girls were probably worried, and she didn't like the thought of Mary out there alone with a bunch of little children. Maybe she'd just take one turn around the perimeter of the plant, and see if she could catch a glimpse of the boys or old Pork Chop.

Chapter Sixty-four

*"The necessities arising from a great emergency
furnished sufficient authority for the herculean efforts
of...determined, virile, loyal and fearless men..."*
—Tulsa County Council of Defense Report

"I'll be danged all to hell, Charlie, look yonder." Henry spoke in an exited undertone. "I do believe that you may get your chance to be a hero yet."

Henry and Charlie both hit the dirt and crawled to the edge of the copse in order to get a better view of the dark figure skulking toward them along the fence. It was impossible to see the man's face, but the figure of the skinny man in a tan Stetson with a high, uncreased crown was unmistakable.

Henry reached over and slapped Charlie's shoulder. "Dutch Leonard," he whispered.

"I reckon," Charlie whispered back. He could hardly believe his eyes. Could it be that he was actually right? He bit his lip to keep from cheering.

They watched in silence as Dutch approached the gap in the fence. He had come too close for the boys to take a chance on speaking to each other, so Charlie wasn't quite sure what action they were going to take now. He expected the best thing to do was wait until Dutch slipped into the yard and then sneak after him. He was going to try signing his intentions to Henry when something else caught his eye. "Who's that?" he said, too surprised to keep quiet.

Someone else had appeared at the gap and was signaling for Dutch to come on.

"I can't tell," Henry whispered. "I don't recognize him."

Dutch and the mystery man disappeared together through the fence.

"It's an inside job!" Charlie started forward on his hands and knees. "Come on, Henry."

Henry reached for him, but Charlie was already halfway across the open space to the fence, running in a crouch. "Dang," he murmured, and started after him.

Alafair was about to give up when she spotted a glint of moonlight off of something just inside the copse by the back corner of the fence. The roan huffed, and a whinny answered him from the trees. Pork Chop.

Alafair sighed with relief and urged the roan forward. Pork Chop was tethered to a pin oak a few feet within the copse, along with a mule that she assumed belonged to Henry. But the boys were gone. "Charlie, where are you?" she called. Her voice echoed in the silence. She scanned the fence, but didn't see the gap until she had practically ridden into it. She let out a breath, relieved, irritated, and worried all at once. She guided the roan through the gap.

Chapter Sixty-five

"No Mercy for Slackers."
—*Tulsa Daily World*, August 5, 1917

Dutch and the shadowy stranger were nowhere to be seen when Henry and Charlie made it through the fence.

"Let's alert the guards," Henry suggested. "There's two of them, and I fear you and I are not equipped to take on a couple of subversives bent on mayhem."

Charlie was not about to capitulate now. "No, not yet. Let's find them first. I think they must be headed for the rail siding."

"All right, but whether they're there or not, I'm calling in reinforcements once we reach the siding."

Charlie gritted his teeth, sorry now that he had asked Henry to come along, but he said nothing. He could see a globe of light in the distance, a guard walking the perimeter. He was coming in their direction.

"Come on," he whispered, and slunk off toward one of the tall brick piles without checking to see if Henry was behind him. They hunkered down behind the stacks until the guard had ambled by. The boys sat in silence for ten minutes to make sure he was gone before dashing across an open space to skirt along the long covered kiln and head toward the rail siding.

They were approaching the tracks when Charlie noticed something hanging from the steel scaffolding at the end of the kiln. A man. No, a body, hanging by its heels.

Charlie gasped and turned toward Henry, but Henry was no longer standing behind him. He was splayed out in the dirt at Charlie's feet, out cold. A dark figure in a bowler hat was standing over him with a wooden baton in one bloody hand and a knife in the other.

The voice that spoke out of the dark sounded downright cheerful. "Why, what have we here?"

Charlie intended to scream for help, but the shadow man swung the baton at his head before he could make a sound.

Alafair saw the roving guard's lantern and halted the roan behind a stack of bricks, waiting for him to pass. She sat on the horse's back for a couple of minutes, unable to see much of anything in the dark, listening for movement. The brick stack she was hiding behind was situated close to the entrance of one of the two thirty-foot-long continuous kilns, where carloads of green bricks rolled slowly through the heated tunnels and emerged dry and ready to stack at the other end. She was not familiar with the layout of the brick plant, but she could see the hulking shapes of boxcars in the distance, at the end of the kilns, and a raised shape nearby that she assumed was a loading dock.

She could see something else, too, hanging from the iron scaffolding near the rail spur. Her first thought was that someone had hoisted up a side of beef. But then a side of beef didn't have arms dangling toward the ground.

Had her heart not leaped into her throat at the thought that the dangling body might be Charlie, she would have ridden off to find the guard. As it was, she unholstered her rifle and dug her heels into the roan's sides.

Alafair saw the movement on the ground under the hanging man before she quite got close enough to make out what was happening. She reined hard when she realized that the figure on his knees, trying to get to his feet, was her son. She recognized the man in the bowler standing over him, as well. The devil.

"You!" she cried.

Nick barely had time to turn toward her before she raised the rifle and fired. She winged him and he staggered, but he recovered quickly and drew his sidearm. The roan was dancing around, raising dust, making it hard for Alafair to aim again. Before she could draw a bead, Nick pulled Charlie to his feet and pressed the pistol against the boy's temple.

"Ma?" Charlie mumbled.

Lights were coming toward them now, and men shouting in the dark. Three or four guards, alerted by the gunfire.

"Don't shoot! Don't shoot!" Alafair's voice halted the men in their tracks. All were armed, and the rifle barrels waved back and forth as the guards tried to decide who to aim at.

"Is that Miz Tucker?" One of the guards had recognized her, though she didn't have time to call his name to mind.

"Yes, don't shoot! He's got my boy. Look yonder, he's killed someone."

The gun barrels swiveled as one in Nick's direction. "Everybody stand back, now," Nick said. He sounded calm. "Lady, drop that rifle and get down off that horse. I'm going to ride out of here easy as you please and take this boy with me. If nobody follows me, I'll drop him off down the road. Otherwise I'll blast a hole in his skull."

For an instant, nobody moved. Charlie was woozy, unsteady on his feet. In the yellow light of the guards' lanterns, Nick's hostage looked even younger than he was, for which Alafair was grateful. None of the watchmen was willing to take a chance on shooting a child.

Alafair dropped her rifle. "Don't hurt him," she said, as she dismounted. Keeping the boy in front of him, Nick sidled around so that the roan was between them and the guards. The graze on his shoulder hurt, but he could move his arm without difficulty. His plan was to hoist the boy up front of the saddle horn and mount behind him, keeping the pistol pressed against Charlie's head.

But that was easier said than done.

As Alafair backed off, Nick grabbed at the reins, but the white-maned roan tossed his head and shied. Charlie was reeling. If he passed out before Nick could get him tossed over the horse's withers, he figured he'd be shot full of holes before the boy hit the ground. He growled and reached again. He managed to get hold of a handful of leather and gave the reins a vicious jerk.

The horse went crazy. He shrieked and leaped straight up in the air, all four hooves off the ground, and began to buck like the ground was on fire. Nick let go of Charlie and fired at the roan. The shot went wild and Nick didn't get a chance to fire another. The roan came down right on top of him, rearing and kicking.

Alafair dashed in and hauled Charlie out of the way, dragging him through the dirt by both arms. The guards were hollering and trying to get a clear shot, but the light was too dim to see who was whom and what was happening. A demon was loose, it looked like, or the jaws of hell had opened.

It was all over in a couple of minutes. The roan hopped several times and ran off a few yards. He calmed down on his own, then trotted back as though nothing unusual had occurred. Charlie was lying on the ground half-conscious, his head cradled in his mother's lap, when the horse walked up and nosed him.

One of the guards was bending over Henry, who was still alive but out cold.

Nick did not move. There wasn't much left of him.

Chapter Sixty-six

"Once lead [the American] people into war and they will forget there ever was such a thing as tolerance."
—Woodrow Wilson, April 1917

Since Scott and Trent were both gone, Scott's eldest son and sometime-deputy, Slim Tucker, responded to the call from the brick plant. Slim hadn't been able to make sense of the tale the excited watchman had told him, so he was unprepared for the chaotic scene in the yard when he arrived.

Slim couldn't identify the trampled corpse on the ground near the rail spur, but the body still hanging from the scaffolding with a surprised expression on its face and its throat cut was definitely the earthly remains of Dutch Leonard.

Slim examined the scene as best he could in the dim lantern light, made some drawings and took some notes, then gave permission to cut down Leonard and send for the undertaker. The boss watchman offered a desk and chair in the machine shop so Slim could interview everyone who had been involved—the three roving guards, a woman, and two young fellows with head wounds.

Slim blinked in the bright electric light when he first entered the machine shop and caught sight of his first cousin by marriage, once removed, tending to a couple of wounded young men seated in chairs in the corner. He didn't know the blond youth with the damp rag pressed to the side of his head, but the boy getting his scalp bandaged was Charlie.

"Alafair?" His tone indicated that he didn't quite believe his own eyes.

She straightened when Slim called her name, a bandage roll in her hand. Her eyes were sunken with fatigue and worry. She also looked exasperated beyond endurance. "Where's your daddy, Slim?"

Slim wasn't about to tell her that his daddy was on a mission to stop her brother from committing treason. He sat down behind the desk. "He'll be back directly. Now, you'd better tell me what the sam hill is going on."

The horizon had lightened and the town was stirring by the time Scott and his deputy finally arrived in Boynton with their prisoner in tow on the mule they had commandeered in the confusion. Scott was looking forward to heading for home and a hot meal as soon as he got Rob Gunn locked in a cell.

He could tell by the expression on Slim's face that it was not to be.

He left Trent at the jailhouse and followed Slim to the brick plant. By the time he found himself standing with Slim, Mr. Ober, and couple of night watchmen, gazing down at the deceased, the sun was well up and the first shift had begun to arrive.

The bodies had been decently laid out on a tarp on the ground near where they had died. Mr. Lee, the undertaker, was standing off to one side, next to his hearse, patiently awaiting the go-ahead to remove the dead. Scott sighed. "Well, I recognize Dutch Leonard, all right, but I don't know this other one. You say he worked for you, Mr. Ober?"

Ober looked grim. "He did, I'm sorry to say. He said he could root out whoever was causing the troubles here at the plant. I told him I didn't cotton to violence, but I reckon he had his own agenda."

Scott gave Ober a mild glance. "Were you so afraid that your hands might get organized that you felt you had to hire a union buster?"

Ober had the good grace to look chagrined. "You don't know what kind of pressure I'm under to get this shipment out, Scott. I can't afford these slowdowns. Mr. Vitric is bound and determined that we don't lose the Army contract."

Mr. Francis Vitric was Frank Ober's father-in-law, so Scott could well imagine what kind of pressure he was under. Scott picked up the crushed bowler hat that someone had placed next to the remains and studied it thoughtfully. "What was his name?"

"He told me it was Nick Smith. Didn't say where he was from, just that he came in from New Mexico. I don't know if he had any family who need to be notified."

The men pondered this piece of information in silence for a moment before Scott said, "Well, I doubt if that was his real name. He sure killed Dutch Leonard, though. But was it Dutch who killed Avey and Walker? Or was it this old boy here? I didn't much cotton to Dutch, but I never thought of him as a murderer."

Ober's brows drew together. "Why would a union buster kill a couple of Council of Defense men? Surely it was Dutch, or one of his I.W.W. cronies. I'll bet money he was the one sabotaging my equipment, anyway."

Scott was thinking of the man he had locked up in his jailhouse, the I.W.W. agitator who owned a buck knife. "It was a stranger in a bowler hat by the name of Nick Smith who told Trent about an uprising over by Little River and sent us hightailing out of town tonight." He made the observation without drawing a conclusion. He turned to his son. "Slim, did you tell Alafair and the two youngsters that they could go home?"

"I took all three of them over to Doc Addison's house, Dad. I expect they're still there. Both the boys had pretty bad conks on the head."

◇ ◇ ◇

Alafair was sitting in Dr. Jasper Addison's parlor with a coffee mug in her hands when Emmanuel Clover came in. Alafair looked up at him with tired eyes, but didn't rise. He was dressed in his usual black suit and white shirt, but Alafair had never before seen him without a tie. "What are you doing here, Mr. Clover?"

"I saw the wagon carrying you and the lads from the hotel window when it came down Main Street."

"At this hour?"

"I don't sleep well lately, Mrs. Tucker. How are the boys?" His voice was full of concern.

"You heard what happened?"

"Just now. Mr. Tyler, the watchman who drove y'all over here, told me that Dutch Leonard and an accomplice were killed while attempting to perpetrate an act of sabotage at the brick plant. He said that your son and another young man caught them in the act and were badly injured."

"Doc says they'll both be all right." She smiled, relieved to be able to say it. "The man who killed Dutch swung a club at Charlie, but just grazed him. He has a pretty ugly cut on his scalp. Henry Blackwood got knocked cold, though, and has a big old dent in his skull. He's awake, but he wasn't making much sense last I heard. His uncle Mr. Bent is in there with him. Doc told me I can take Charlie home directly, but he wants to keep an eye on Henry for a day or so."

"I'm so sorry, Mrs. Tucker. I knew Dutch Leonard was a dangerous agitator, but I had no idea that he would be so low as to attack a boy as young as Charlie."

Alafair blinked at him. "He didn't. Mr. Tyler didn't tell you everything, did he? Dutch was murdered by the man he was with, the same man who tried to kill Charlie and his friend." She related the whole story to Clover, and when she was finished, he sat back in his chair, astounded.

"But who is this despicable murderer? Someone bent on revenge for the deaths of my fellow CD officers?"

Alafair was silent for a moment while she considered what to say. She glanced at Mrs. Doc Addison, who was standing in the hall door, listening eagerly. "I don't know who he was or why he killed Dutch, Mr. Clover. But just last evening I was talking to… Someone told me a thing that makes me believe the man I saw trampled to death tonight is the same man who killed Win and Billy Claude, too."

"Was he someone you knew?"

"No, sir. I never saw him before. He was a plain fellow with no memorable qualities except for a white scar beside his eye and a bowler hat."

The expression of horror that passed over Clover's face caused Mrs. Doc to rush to his side. "You look like you're fixing to faint, Mr. Clover."

Clover bent his head over his knees. "May I have a glass of water, Mrs. Addison?"

Alafair leaned toward him when Mrs. Doc was out of earshot. "Mr. Clover, when did you talk to the man in the bowler hat?"

He looked up at her from under his eyebrows, but said nothing.

"Did you tell him that you wished Dutch Leonard was dead?"

Clover gasped and paled, but didn't deny it. "He came to me after the riot at the Liberty Sing. What Dutch did was treason. I feared that if no one stopped him, Dutch would bring chaos down on us. I was walking home when someone in just such a hat came up behind me. It was like a dream, Mrs. Tucker. He said all I had to do was nod and he would take care of it. I didn't like to think what he meant. But I nodded."

"Why did you do it?"

"Dutch had just incited a riot. I was afraid, Mrs. Tucker. I am afraid."

Alafair put a comforting hand on Clover's arm. "Fear will sure make you do things you're sorry for later. I surely know it."

Mrs. Doc passed through and handed Clover a glass of water before answering a knock at the door. Scott followed her back into the parlor.

Scott Tucker was closer to sixty than to fifty, balding, with a comfortable belly and crinkly blue eyes. He was normally an unthreatening presence, but his manner when he came to a stop in front of Alafair's chair indicated that he was not in the mood for pleasantries. "Alafair, bodies are piling up like cordwood around here. The story that Slim told me about the goings-on tonight is pretty hard to believe. I think I'd better hear it from you." He noticed the man in the chair beside her. "Emmanuel? I hope you have a good reason for being here."

Mr. Ober was sorry that so many lives had been lost, but he couldn't help but be relieved that the saboteur was no more, and the Francis Vitric Brick Company could get back to business as usual. The two boxcar loads of building brick had been saved and were on the siding ready to go on the appointed morning. Fort Bliss would receive its shipment on time and Mr. Ober's father-in-law would have no cause for complaint.

He was standing on the loading dock bright and early, dressed in his serge suit, checking his pocket watch, when the messenger walked up the path beside the tracks and asked for him by name.

"I'm Frank Ober. We're expecting an engine any minute now, so I don't have much time. What can I do for you?"

The man was muscular, sweat-stained, and covered with coal dust. He removed the bandana from his neck and wiped his face. "My engineer sent me up here to tell you that he can't get up the spur. The trestle over that little creek yonder has collapsed. I had a gander at it and it sure weren't no accident. Somebody spent a goodly time digging and sawing those bridge supports. The track went down with it. Looks like the St. Louis-San Francisco line won't be hauling any bricks for you for a long spell."

Chapter Sixty-seven

"Backbone of Draft Rebellion Believed Broken"
—*Tulsa Daily World*, August 5, 1917

Scott looked up from the papers on his desk when Alafair and Shaw came into the office late the next morning. "Well, hey. Y'all here to visit Robin before I haul him off to Muskogee?"

Alafair heaved a great sigh in lieu of an answer.

"How's Charlie?"

"In trouble," Shaw answered. "But I reckon he'll live to tell the tale."

Scott lifted a wanted poster off the desk and handed it to Alafair. "Does this old cuss look familiar?"

Alafair peered at the poster. "Well, he isn't wearing a bowler hat, but I reckon that's the same fellow that tried to kill my boy. He's got them creepy eyes and that little scar."

Shaw took the paper from her and began to read. "Nicholas Zrska. That's an odd moniker. Says here he's wanted in California and in Colorado for murder."

Scott nodded. "Yesterday I wired the U.S. Marshal's office in Oklahoma City for more information on him. Zrska was involved in the killing of those five Wobblies who tried to organize the loggers up in Washington State last year. But that's not what got him in trouble. Seems he knifed the man who hired him to police the dockworkers in San Pedro, and is suspected of killing a supervisor at the steel mill in Pueblo, Colorado. He didn't play favorites when it came to murder."

"So he wasn't the devil after all," Alafair said, half to herself. Shaw glanced over the list of Nick's crimes. "I don't know if I'd say that, honey."

"Did you talk to Mr. Khouri's father?" Alafair asked Scott. "I hope he's not in hot water." She had told Scott about Nick's encounters with Grandfather Khouri and Emmanuel Clover had admitted his own. She hadn't mentioned her conversation with Rose Lovelock. Her mother-in-law Sally had pointed out that Rose was long gone. Besides, the woman had enough troubles.

"I did talk to him," Scott said. "I don't arrest folks for wishing harm to their enemies. But after what him and Emmanuel told me I'm convinced that it was Zrska who murdered Win and Billy Claude, not Dutch. Nor was Robin involved, either. Not in the killings, at least. Ober still thinks that Dutch was the saboteur at the plant, and it is true that he was I.W.W., same as Robin. Ober figures that Dutch and Zrska had undermined the train trestle together before they made their way into the plant bent on some other mischief."

"You don't really think Robin had anything to do with sabotage, do you?"

"I don't, Alafair. But that's not for me to judge."

Alafair didn't look happy, but she said, "I know it. Can I see him now?"

Scott nodded toward the door to the cells. "Go ahead on."

She disappeared and Shaw sat down in one of the chairs under the window. "You ain't going in?" Scott asked him.

"I'll give her a minute."

"It was good of you to bring her in to town to visit with him before I haul him off."

The corner of Shaw's mouth twisted up in an ironic smile. "I ain't letting her out of my sight again for a long spell, Scott. There is no telling what she might get up to."

Scott chuckled. "Good luck to you."

Shaw stood up, reconsidered, and sat back down. "Scott, Robin is a misguided pain in the neck, but he is not a traitor. Besides, he's family. Do you really have to turn him over to the marshal in the morning?"

"I'd just as soon not, but there must have been a hundred posse men who heard his anti-war rant. He was in cahoots with the draft rioters, there's no denying that. The insurgents are being rounded up all over the state, and for the moment the U.S. Marshal's Office is holding most of them in the federal jails in Holdenville and Muskogee. I don't have any choice but to take Robin in."

Shaw leaned forward in his chair, an earnest expression on his face. "I ain't a socialist, Scott. Far from it. It is not the business of government to take a man's property or skills that he worked hard to gain and give them to someone else without even asking. But there's many a man I respect who believes that party line, to one degree or another. There are so many socialists in Oklahoma they can't all be put in jail! The majority rules in this country, but don't the minority have rights, as well?"

Scott regarded his cousin for a moment before answering. "They used to. I guess we're about to see if they still do."

Chapter Sixty-eight

"I am opposed to every war but one; I am for that war with heart and soul, and that is the world-wide war of the social revolution."
—Eugene Debs, 1915

Rob stood up from his seat on the cot when Alafair came up to the bars. For a long moment they gazed at one another in silence.

"Reckon I won't be seeing Mama on this trip," Rob finally ventured.

Alafair didn't know whether to laugh or smack him. "Oh, Robin." Her voice was filled with vexation. She reached into her handbag and withdrew an envelope. "I just got another letter from Elizabeth." She waved it in his face. "She says that a while back you wired her from New Mexico to come bail you out of a tight spot." She began to read. "Seems Robin was being held along with several hundred other union men in a detention camp at Hermana, New Mexico. They were deported from Bisbee in cattle cars after all the miners in town went on strike…"

"Not all the miners." Rob gave a thin smile. "Most of them, though. After we got to Hermana the Army let me wire my sister in Tempe. I asked Elizabeth to contact the I.W.W. lawyer in San Francisco, and she did." His voice took on an incredulous tone. "Then her and Web got on the train and come all the way out to Hermana to spring me, even though neither one of them is licensed to practice in New Mexico. I wasn't going to leave my comrades stuck behind barbed wire. But the camp commander didn't give me a choice. I figure he was eager to get shet of me, because he didn't look too close at Web's credentials or Elizabeth's, either one. He told me to get out of the state. Elizabeth wanted me to go back to Arizona with her. I'll tell you, I was amazed that they'd take that chance, especially Web. I know Elizabeth has never given a good…a tinker's…a fig about what anybody thinks of her, but I always figured Web for a stooge of the…I mean, a solid citizen who was pretty interested in his reputation."

Alafair appreciated the fact that he had avoided strong language in favor of sparing her delicate sensibilities. "It shook Web up some when she near to left him last year," she said. "Any man who goes into law practice with his wife had better have no fear of the judgment of others."

Rob shook his head. "Whatever the reason, I surely have amended my opinion of Webster Kemp."

"So why didn't you go back with them?"

"I figured the law in Arizona wouldn't be pleased to see me." He shrugged. "Besides, they took a big chance for me. I didn't want to make life hard for them."

"So you decided to come out here and make life hard for me?"

Her sharp tone took him aback. "No, I…"

She interrupted him. "You lied to me, Robin." The bitter disappointment in her voice pierced Rob like a knife. "You said you had no idea of causing trouble for us while you were here, and then you turned right around and went out to talk to those mutineers."

For an instant, he couldn't speak. He swallowed the lump in his throat and said, "I didn't want you to know, Sister. You can't be held responsible for what you don't know."

She grasped the bars and leaned in. "I love you, Brother, but you break my heart."

He put a hand over one of hers. "I love you too, Alafair. And I'm beholden to y'all for your hospitality, even to such a rogue as I. I ain't et so good in years! You take my leave of the children for me. When this mess is over, I'll come back and see how y'all are doing. Until then, will you come and visit me in prison?"

Alafair pulled back and wiped her eyes with her fingers. "Of course I will."

Chapter Sixty-nine

*"Anti-draft rioters…this afternoon faced the U.S.
Commissioner to answer the charge of treason.
District Attorney McGinnis announced that where
evidence is sufficient he will ask for the death
penalty….Authorities are confident they have two
national organizers among the 250 prisoners."*
—*Ada Weekly News*, August 7, 1917

Scott pulled off the road at the crossroad and stopped the car.
Rob felt a thrill of alarm. He had known Scott Tucker since he
was a child, and trusted his honor. But he had been taken to a
secluded location by the law before, and it hadn't turned out
well for him.

He leaned forward toward the front seat, anxious. "Why are
we stopping?"

For a long moment Scott neither turned nor spoke, until Rob
began to consider making a break for it. He didn't expect he'd get
far, handcuffed as he was, but he was damned if he was going to
just sit and take it. Even from someone who was his almost-family.

"I knew I should have brought a deputy with me." When he
finally spoke, Scott seemed to be talking to himself.

"What?"

"That's the trouble with transporting a prisoner all the way to Muskogee by yourself," he said to the air. "You turn your back for a minute, and the son-of-a-gun gets clean away from you."

Rob's eyes widened, and he eased himself back into the upholstery. Scott turned around and stretched his right arm across the seat back. The keys to the handcuffs were dangling from his fingers. The two men eyed one another for a minute.

Rob finally broke the silence. "What is this?"

"Yonder is Texas." Scott pointed to the south with the keys. "Arkansas is closer, but I'd go south for a spell anyway, before you turn back east. Whichever way you go, stay off the main roads 'til you cross the Oklahoma line."

"You're letting me go?" Rob envisioned himself shot in the back while 'trying to escape.'

"Get them cuffs off, pick up that bindle, and get to hoofing. And don't come back here. Do you understand?"

"No," Rob confessed.

"I promised the citizens of Boynton that I'd keep the peace for them, and you're no peaceful creature, Robin Gunn. I'll remove you from their midst, but I'll be jiggered if I'm going to deliver a man up to prison for trying to help his fellow man and stop a civil war in the process."

"But how are you going to explain this?"

"Damned if I know. You want to argue about it?"

Rob did not want to argue about it. He took the keys without another word, unlocked the cuffs around his wrists, and scrambled out of the automobile. "I won't forget this."

"You'd better not, you dad-blasted Red."

"Tell my sister…"

"Get out of here," Scott interrupted, "before I change my mind."

Rob flashed a grin, hoisted the backpack onto his shoulder, and took off. He was ten yards down the road when he slipped his hands in his pockets and began whistling "Arkansas Traveler."

Scott sat in the front seat of his automobile for a long time, watching the jaunty figure grow smaller and smaller as it retreated down the narrow dirt road to the south. He was still sitting there when he heard the clop of hooves coming up the road from Muskogee. He turned his head enough to see Trent Calder rein in beside the car.

Trent pushed his hat back off his forehead. "Howdy, Scott. You having car trouble?"

Scott shrugged. "Just pondering the state of the world. So did you join up?"

"You're looking at a U.S. sailor."

"Good for you, son. Get in and I'll give you a lift back into Boynton."

Trent dismounted and tied his horse to the back of the Paige, and had just settled into the front seat next to Scott when he caught sight of the distant figure walking away from them, toward Texas.

"Who's that yonder?"

"Who knows? Some bindlestiff out of a job and on the road."

Trent's eyes narrowed as he peered into the distance. "Looks more like a boy."

Scott put the car in gear and pulled onto the road. "Naw. I reckon I know a man when I see one."

Chapter Seventy

*"The actual peril confronting the United States through
the perfidy of the Imperial Germany Government had
not been appreciated or realized by the general public
in the early stages of the World War."*
—Final Report of the Tulsa County
Council of Defense, 1919

Charlie's zeal was considerably subdued over the next few weeks.
He was forced to give up his job at the plant, suffered with a
headache and double vision for a while, and had the fear of God
put into him by his parents. In fact, he was so humiliated that he
barely spoke for days. But there was one thing he had to broach
with his mother, howsoever much he dreaded approaching her.

He waited until one early morning after breakfast, while she
was out in the woods behind the house, feeding the turkeys, as
was her habit.

The birds scattered when he walked up, and Alafair gave
him a curious glance. She was still torn between anger, relief,
and abiding affection for her wayward boy. She was also aware
of his chagrin and couldn't help but feel sorry for him. Even if
it was his own fault.

"What do you want, son?"

He was encouraged by her mild tone. "Mama, I know you and
everybody told Daddy what happened to that killer that night,

how my horse trampled him and all." He hesitated, and Alafair nodded to urge him on. "Well, back when Daddy first let me have the roan he told me that if it ever hurt anybody he'd put it down. I been scared to ask him why he hasn't shot the horse already. But Ma, couldn't you please, please ask him not to do it? That horse may be half-crazy, but he saved my life for sure."

Alafair tried not to smile and didn't quite succeed. "Honey, your daddy and I already discussed it. He figures that beast is just too smart and knew that awful man aimed to do you harm. You go and talk to him about it, son. The roan may still be on probation, but on this occasion he's been given a reprieve."

Charlie sagged. "Thank you, Ma. Oh, thank you. That old horse may be a pain, but I love him even if he loves Fronie more than me. In fact I'll let her name him Honey Pie or Sugar Darling Cuddle Baby or whatever. If he wants to be called by a baby-talk name, I reckon I owe it to him."

Henry Blackwood examined his head wound in the mirror over the dressing table in his bedroom. The bandage was finally off and the hair that Doc Addison had shaved was growing back. The stitches were out, but the wound was still scabby and ugly. Henry huffed his disappointment. He swung his arm back and forth a few times. At least the shoulder sprain from his fall into the clay dump had finally cleared up.

He caught sight of his uncle's reflection in the mirror. Eric was leaning on the door jamb, watching Henry's gyrations with amusement.

Eric grinned when he realized he had been noticed. "You'll be as pretty as ever before you know it. I expect you'll be able to go back to work in a day or two."

Henry rolled his eyes at Eric's teasing and sat down on the edge of his bed. "I'm thinking that it's time for me to move on, Eric. Oklahoma's too rough for me. As soon as I got here I was beaten up, and since then I nearly got ground up like sausage and had my head bashed in. I wouldn't mind the danger, but

I don't think the work I've been doing here is making all that much difference, anyway."

Eric looked disappointed, but he didn't try to argue. "I'm sorry to hear it. I've enjoyed your company. I'll miss you."

"I can't thank you enough for taking me in on such short notice, Uncle. I'll miss you, and my friends, too. That's why I should leave now. I've gotten too close to these people. Besides, I nearly killed myself when that clay dump lever gave way too early."

"You did some fine work," Eric insisted. "Undermining the rail trestle was very effective."

Henry gestured to a stool in the corner and Eric took a seat. "That was a tough one. I had to work on it for several nights, sawing and digging, but I only had a couple hours to get the supports pulled out before I was supposed to meet Charlie."

"Why'd you go along with that boy's insane idea, anyway? That really did almost get you killed."

"Well, I knew the saboteur wasn't going to show up. I didn't know about the killer, though. It's just as well. Getting knocked in the head turned out to be a hell of an alibi."

"Do you have an idea where you will go now?"

Henry shrugged. "I can't go back to Brownsville since they're after me for that incident at the Port Isabel shipyards. Maybe I'll head on to Mexico and join up with von Wegner in Vera Cruz. Perhaps he'll send me to Prussia from there."

Eric stood up and retrieved a bottle from the top of the Hoosier cabinet. "Let's have a drink to your success, Jungen." He poured two shot glasses full of a schnapps, then handed one to his nephew before raising his own high. *"Das Vaterland, Heinrich."*

"Das Vaterland über alles, Erich."

Chapter Seventy-one

*"The Minstrel Boy to the war is gone
In the ranks of death you will find him;
His father's sword he hath girded on,
And his wild harp slung behind him."*
                                                    —Thomas Moore, 1798

Alafair had considered letting Shaw go to the train station without her to see the boys off. She didn't want to do anything to cause Gee Dub the slightest distress, and she wasn't sure she could trust herself not to cry. But in the end, she had to go. She had to keep him in sight for as long as possible.

The train had already pulled in by the time they arrived, and one or two Boynton-bound passengers were disembarking. Johnny Turner, son of the owner of the Boynton livery stable, was waiting on the platform surrounded by his parents and two of his sisters. And Laura Ross, Alafair noted. She smiled at the sight. Johnny had been in love with Laura Ross for years. Laura had never seemed to notice, but here she was, seeing Johnny off to war.

Johnny nodded at them as they walked up the platform steps. "Howdy, Mr. and Miz Tucker. Gee Dub. Looks like we're going to walk the red road after all."

Shaw and Gee Dub smiled at this appropriately descriptive Creek phrase for war. Alafair and Laura Ross did not.

Scott and Hattie Tucker were there, as well, along with three of their four sons. The older two, Slim and Stretch, were married and thus draft exempt, for now, at least. The fourth son, Spike, was too young. It was the third boy, twenty-three-year-old Butch, who had come to do his duty. Hattie didn't have Alafair's scruples about weeping in front of her departing son. Scott had his arm around Hattie's shoulders, murmuring comforts to her, when Alafair and her men walked up the platform steps. Butch walked over to greet them, leaving his distraught mother to his father and brothers, grateful for the distraction.

He winked a blue eye at Gee Dub. "Well, here we are."

Gee Dub winked back. "Here we are."

Alafair hugged Butch around the middle. "Your ma's having a hard time, I see."

"She was fine when we left the house. A minute ago I said that maybe I'd get a medal, and she started bawling." He shrugged, baffled by female behavior.

"I'm glad you fellows decided to travel together," Shaw said. "I hear Fort Riley is a mighty big and confusing place. Be nice to have somebody to get lost with."

"I expect, Cousin Shaw. Looking at Gee's goofy mug makes me feel better already."

Gee Dub's mouth quirked. "Pleased to be of service, I'm sure."

As the boys bantered, Alafair could hardly take her eyes off of Gee Dub. He seemed happy, eager, even, but his eyes were unnaturally bright, as though he had a fever. Every plane, shadow, and angle of his face was as familiar to her as her own reflection in the mirror—her dark, silent, witty, gallant, big-hearted boy. Her own heart started to thud painfully and she looked down at the boards beneath her feet. Her shoes were dusty, and the hem of her skirt. She took a shuddering breath.

Scott and Hattie had joined them when she looked up again. She locked eyes with Hattie, and their gazes fiercely held each other up.

"You got everything you need, son?" Shaw was saying. "You got your orders?"

Gee Dub and Butch both withdrew their enlistment papers from their inside coat pockets and held them up for inspection.

"According to the United States Army," Gee Dub said to his cousin, "I reckon I'm 'George' from here on out."

"Ain't that strange!" Butch exclaimed. "They've decided to call me 'Charles'!"

Gee Dub extended his hand. "Glad to meet you, Charles."

Butch took it and they shook. "Likewise, George."

The conductor called an "all aboard," and everyone made a quick inventory of the travelers' possessions. Johnny Turner and his family joined the crowd, and they all began to move toward the train.

Alafair felt like she was moving through molasses. She knew that her outsides were smiling and laughing, but her insides were so numb that she was barely conscious of her actions. She could hear Hattie sobbing. A porter took the boys' little cardboard suitcases. The group drew together, everyone standing so close that Alafair could hardly breathe. The press of bodies was oddly comforting.

Butch stepped up onto the landing, gently disengaged Hattie's hand from his coat, and disappeared into the train car. Johnny Turner turned back with a wave before following Butch.

Gee Dub was hugging his father. Alafair reached out for him, and he embraced her. He leaned down and pressed his cheek against hers. She could feel his breath against her neck.

"Don't forget me, Ma," he whispered into her ear.

If he hadn't been holding her so tightly, she would have fallen flat.

Don't worry I'll be fine I know you will son you be sure and write as soon as you get there I expect this will all be over before I finish basic training don't worry Ma don't worry.

She stood there pressed into Shaw's side until the train had disappeared into the distance and everyone else had drifted away back home.

Don't forget me? Ever since the moment she had known he was growing under her heart, she had nurtured and cared for him with a fierce and terrible love. He had thrived and grown from her laughing dark-eyed baby into a good man. He was perfect. He was beautiful. He was at the height of his youth and health and power. The next time she would see him, if ever she did, he would not be the same. This was going to change him, and there was nothing she could do about it.

She stood next to Shaw, rock solid through sheer will, and did not cry, or scream in anguish, or run after him like she longed to do. She suddenly became aware of Shaw's eyes on her, and she looked up at him. He was gazing at her with an expression of awe.

"By damn, Alafair," he said, too moved not to swear. "You're the one deserves a medal."

She didn't answer because she couldn't. They moved together down the platform steps, to where Martha was standing with the three youngest girls. Martha was dabbing her eyes with a handkerchief, and Blanche and Grace looked solemn. Sophronia was holding the reins of the white-maned roan and murmuring sweet nothings into his ear. The train began to pull away.

Alafair's brow wrinkled. "Where's Charlie?"

Author's Note

The War, the Wobblies, and the Green Corn Rebellion

Though inspired by true events, this is a work of fiction. It's hard to overstate the public hysteria in the United States, and in Oklahoma in particular, during the First World War. I can only try to show how America's entry into the war would have affected someone like Alafair. She lived in the exact middle of an enormous country and, to her, Europe could have been another planet for the effect it had on her daily life. It would have been difficult for her to comprehend the reasons the country was at war. I played with time a bit in this story by adding a week between the Bisbee deportation on July 12, and the first draft lottery, which actually occurred on July 20. The anti-draft uprising, later known as the Green Corn Rebellion, took place on August 4, 1917.

World War I

Most Americans had no desire to get involved in the European war when it began in 1914. There were as many Americans with German ties as there were with English and French ties, and the reasons the Europeans were trying to kill one another was poorly understood by most. When Germany broke its pledge to limit submarine warfare and began sinking American ships in an effort to break the British naval blockade, the U.S. severed diplomatic relations. Then, in January 1917, the British deciphered a telegram from German Foreign Minister Arthur Zimmermann to the German Minister to Mexico, offering United States territory to Mexico if it would join the German cause and attack the U.S. border. The interception of the Zimmermann Note effectively changed American public opinion overnight. Congress declared war on Germany on April 6, 1917.

But not everyone in the country was behind the war, to say the least.

The Unions

The Industrial Workers of the World (I.W.W.) is a socialist labor union formed in Chicago in 1905. The union advocated strikes and work slowdowns in order to achieve their goals of improved working conditions, a living wage, pensions, and child-labor regulation. The I.W.W., along with the U.S. Socialist Party, opposed both the U.S. entry into World War I and involuntary conscription, for which members were violently persecuted. I.W.W. members are known as Wobblies, though nobody knows exactly why.

The Working Class Union (W.C.U.) was a radical union which was formed when the national leadership of the I.W.W. rejected membership for farmers and other self-employed people because they were not true wageworkers. Unlike the I.W.W. and the Socialist Party, the W.C.U. did not object to the idea of violence to gain its ends.

The Green Corn Rebellion

In August of 1917, shortly after Congress passed the Selective Service Act, an armed rebellion led by tenant farmers took place in east-central Oklahoma. On August 2, the Seminole County sheriff and three deputies set out to investigate a reported gathering of radical activists in an area known for its W.C.U. sympathies, but were ambushed and fled for their lives. That evening, the W.C.U. called a secret meeting on a hill outside of Sasakwa, where they made plans to march on Washington D.C., arrest President Wilson, reform the economy, and put an end to the war. They expected to link up with thousands of other farmers and workers on the way, creating a massive army. However, their plans were betrayed to the law by an informer in their ranks, and a large posse of men mobilized in Wewoka and headed for the rebel camp. When the armed citizens burst into the camp, the rebels dispersed, guerrilla-style. For the next week, hundreds of suspected insurgents were rounded up and arrested. Posses engaged in several bloody battles with hold-outs, and the organized rebellion was completely put down within a week. Nearly five hundred men were arrested, but fewer than two hundred were indicted, and one hundred fifty convicted of sedition.

The anti-draft rebellion caused a brutal backlash. On November 9, vigilantes calling themselves the Knights of Liberty "liberated" seventeen Wobblies from jail in Tulsa, whipped them, covered them with hot tar and feathers, and drove them out of the city. Many socialist leaders all over the United States were sent to prison, and some were not released until they were pardoned by President Harding in 1921. The American Socialist Party denied any involvement in the Green Corn Rebellion, but was blamed for the uprising anyway. The rebellion damaged the American socialist movement and contributed to the decline of the Working Class Union and the I.W.W., as well as contributing to the rise of the Ku Klux Klan in Oklahoma and the first national Red Scare in the 1920s.

There are several stories about why the uprising came to be called the Green Corn Rebellion. One of the more likely is that it took place shortly after the Creek Nation's annual Green Corn Ceremony of late July or early August.

The Bisbee Deportation

In the spring of 1917, the I.W.W. sent organizers to unionize miners in Bisbee, Arizona. The mining companies rejected all union demands for better wages and working conditions, so in early July a strike was called and over three thousand men walked out. The county sheriff, in conjunction with the mining companies, formed a posse of over twenty-two hundred men, and at dawn on the morning of July 12, rousted two thousand purported strikers from their beds at gunpoint. Twelve hundred miners who would not renounce unionization were loaded onto twenty-three cattle cars and deported, without water and in ninety-degree heat, two hundred miles to Hermanas, New Mexico, and dumped. An I.W.W. lawyer met the train in Hermanas and secured the release of several men. The local officials in Hermanas didn't quite know what to do with the rest. Many destitute strikers were taken back to Columbus, New Mexico, and housed by the Army in a tent camp for months.

Alafair's Homefront Recipes

When the U.S. entered World War I in April 1917, Europe had already been tearing itself apart for three years, its people starving and their farms destroyed. The U.S. Food Administration, headed by Herbert Hoover, was formed to provide food for American troops as well as to help feed the Allied population. In the U.S., the reduction of consumption was voluntary, but Americans were urged to stop wasting food, and to cut down on the use of wheat, sugar, meat, and fats.

Housewives were urged to sign a food conservation pledge card and many cookbooks were issued by the Food Administration and patriotic publishers. Families like the Tuckers who raised much of their own food were not as affected as those who lived in the cities. Still, every time a housewife purchased wheat flour, she also had to buy an equal amount of other cereals like rye flour or cornmeal and mix them with wheat flour when she baked, or use them exclusively on wheatless days. Citizens embraced the restrictions enthusiastically. It is interesting to note that the prescribed diet improved the nation's health.

Calendar of Patriotic Service
United States Food Administration

Sunday— One wheatless meal, one meatless meal.

Monday—Wheatless day, one meatless meal.

Tuesday—Meatless day, porkless day, one wheatless meal.

Wednesday—Wheatless day, one meatless meal.

Thursday—One meatless meal, one wheatless meal.

Friday—One meatless meal, one wheatless meal.

Saturday—Porkless day, one wheatless meal, one meatless meal.

Every Day— Save wheat, meat, fats, sugar to create provision for our armies and the allies.

Alafair's Hot Water Cornbread

2 cups cornmeal	½ teaspoon salt
1 tablespoon baking powder	1 cup boiling water

Mix dry ingredients together in a large bowl. Stir in boiling water. The batter should be smooth and very thick. Heat about a quarter inch of fat in a large skillet over medium high heat. Drop rounded spoonfuls of batter into the hot fat and flatten each fritter with the back of the spoon. Fry until brown on one side, then flip and brown the other. Drain on a towel-lined plate and serve hot. These are delicious as a savory side with butter, or as a dessert with jam or syrup.

An old family recipe.

War Cake

1 cup molasses	1 teaspoon cinnamon
1 cup corn syrup	½ teaspoon cloves
1 ½ cups water	½ teaspoon nutmeg
1 package raisins	3 cups rye flour
2 tablespoons fat	½ teaspoon soda
1 teaspoon salt	2 teaspoon baking powder

Boil together for five minutes the first nine ingredients. Cool, add the sifted dry ingredients and bake in two loaves for 45 minutes in moderate oven. Makes a dense, surprisingly moist cake; great as a holiday treat.

Recipe from *War Economy in Food*, Washington, Government Printing Office, 1918.

Potato Bread

1 pound potatoes (boiled or mashed)	1 ounce salt
1 quart liquid	1 ounce fat
1 ounce sugar	½ ounce yeast
	3 pounds flour

Boil liquid. Add yeast to ¼ cup of liquid cooked to lukewarm temperature. Dissolve sugar, salt, and fat in remainder of liquid. When lukewarm add yeast and mashed potatoes. Beat well. Add flour and knead thoroughly. Let rise until it has doubled in bulk. Mold into loaves. Let rise again and bake.

Recipe from *Win the War in the Kitchen: Official Recipe Book Containing All Demonstrations Given During Patriotic Food Show*, Chicago, January 5-13, 1918, Illinois State Council of Defense, 1918.

Meatless Sausage

1 cup soaked and cooked dried peas, beans, lentils or lima beans	¼ cup fat
	1 egg
	½ teaspoon salt
½ cup dried breadcrumbs	1 teaspoon sage

Mix and shape as sausage. Roll in flour and fry in drippings.

Recipe from *Foods That Will Win the War and How to Cook Them*, C. Houston Goudiss and Alberta M. Goudiss, Forecast Publishing Co., New York, 1918

Soy Bean Loaf

2 cups cooked soy beans	1 beaten egg
1 tablespoon chopped pickle	1 chopped onion
2 tablespoons oleo	Salt
1 cup cooked rice	Pepper

Put soy beans through a meat chopper, combine with other ingredients and form in a loaf. Brown in the oven. Serve with tomato or brown sauce.

Recipe from *Win the War Cookbook*, St. Louis County Unit, Woman's Committee' Council of National Defense, Missouri Division, 1917.

To receive a free catalog of Poisoned Pen Press titles, please provide your name and address in one of the following ways:

Phone: 1-800-421-3976
Facsimile: 1-480-949-1707
Email: info@poisonedpenpress.com
Website: www.poisonedpenpress.com

Poisoned Pen Press
6962 E. First Ave. Ste 103
Scottsdale, AZ 85251